F. R Johnson

**Stresses in Girder and Roof Trusses**

F. R Johnson

**Stresses in Girder and Roof Trusses**

ISBN/EAN: 9783337337780

Printed in Europe, USA, Canada, Australia, Japan

Cover: Foto ©Andreas Hilbeck / pixelio.de

More available books at **www.hansebooks.com**

# STRESSES

IN

# GIRDER AND ROOF TRUSSES

FOR BOTH DEAD AND LIVE LOADS BY

SIMPLE MULTIPLICATION

## WITH STRESS CONSTANTS FOR 100 CASES

*FOR THE USE OF CIVIL AND MECHANICAL ENGINEERS, ARCHITECTS
AND DRAFTSMEN*

BY

## F. R. JOHNSON, Assoc. M. Inst. C.E.

CIVIL ENGINEER

PART I.—GIRDERS

PART II.—ROOFS

# PREFACE.

To MOST practical engineers and draftsmen who have to design girders and roofs, with little time to spare for mathematical investigation and calculation, the majority of the text-books on this subject are too abstruse.

In this work an attempt has been made to simplify the matter by giving-stress constants for both dead and live loads, which only require to be multiplied by the panel load to give the maximum stress in any member of a truss, under the conditions which will be found in the text.

The Author does not wish to claim originality for the idea of calculating the stresses due to dead and live loads in the terms of a unit panel load, but he trusts it has been put into a practical shape, suitable alike to the wants of Civil and Mechanical Engineers, Architects and Draftsmen. No attempt has been made in any way to go beyond the subject, and the one hundred cases for which stress constants are given, will, it is hoped, be found suitable for every-day practice.

F. R. J.

BOMBAY: 1894.

# NOTE.

As in a work of this kind accuracy is the first consideration, no effort has been spared to avoid errors.

The stress constants have been, as far as possible, determined in two or three different ways, and the results compared.

The signs $+$ and $-$ have also been very carefully checked, and the Author believes that those who do him the honour to use this little book will not find their confidence misplaced.

It need hardly be remarked that, both in the case of the girder and roof trusses, the loads are supposed to rest only at the joints, through the agency of cross girders, purlins, &c., and that if any portion of the load is otherwise laid on, the transverse stress caused thereby must be allowed for.

In conclusion, the Author hopes that these stress constants will lighten the labours of many who, like himself, are identified with the profession of engineering.

# CONTENTS.

## PART I.—GIRDERS.

## PART II.—ROOFS.

# STRESSES
# IN GIRDER AND ROOF TRUSSES
## BY SIMPLE MULTIPLICATION.

---

## PART I.—GIRDERS.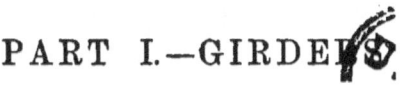

### *INTRODUCTORY*

### 1. ABBREVIATIONS.

S = Stress in.     + = Compression.     − = Tension.

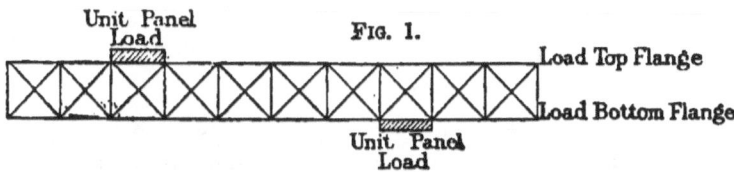

FIG. 1.

Unit Panel Load

Load Top Flange

Load Bottom Flange

Unit Panel Load

For Unit Panel Load see Fig. 1.

### 2. STRESS CONSTANTS FOR DEAD LOAD.

These are the stresses in each member of the girder when each panel is covered with a unit load. Taking Truss Diagram No. 1 as an example with a load of 1 ton, 1 kilogramme, or any other unit distributed over each of the twelve panels on the bottom flange, the stress constants are the resulting stresses in terms of the load.

### 3. MAXIMUM STRESS CONSTANTS FOR LIVE LOAD.

These are the maximum stresses in each member of the girder which could be caused by a unit load per panel advancing from the left abutment, and crossing the girder to the right abutment, or *vice versâ*.

Taking Truss Diagram No. 1 as an example with a load of 1 ton, 1 kilogramme, or any other unit per panel advancing from either abutment, and crossing the girder on the bottom flange, the stress constants are the resulting maximum stresses in terms of the load.

### 4. REFERENCE NUMBERS.

The numbers on the Truss Diagrams serve to indicate each member of a girder for which the stress constant is given. Taking Truss Diagram No. 1 as an example, under the head "Evenly distributed Dead Load, Stress Constants, Top Flange," will be found S. 1·3, and opposite, the stress constant + 5·50.

This means that the stress in the member 1·3 of Truss Diagram No. 1, due to a dead load of unit panel intensity, is compression 5·50.

### 5. POSITION OF LOAD.

It will be noticed that for each diagram the dead load is supposed to be concentrated wholly on one flange.

As regards the parallel girders; in cases where this would not be considered sufficiently accurate half the stresses can be calculated from the stress constants belonging to the truss diagram where the load is on the top flange, and the other half from the constants for the diagram where the load is on the bottom flange.

### 6. THE DYNAMIC METHOD FOR AUGMENTED STRESSES.

The stress constants are equally applicable for calculating the augmented stresses resulting from the dynamic method for proportioning the members of a girder to resist suddenly applied loads.

### 7. Theoretically Imperfect Girders.

It is hardly necessary to observe that in the case of theoretically imperfect girders, i. e. those having a redundance of parts (Truss Diagram No. 14 for instance), certain assumptions have been made as to the way the stresses will go, which of course it is practically difficult to make certain of, and in these cases the only thing to do is to see that the sectional area is sufficient for the worst combination.

### 8. Difference between Parabolic Bowstring Girder and Braced Arch.

It is well to state that an essential difference exists between a parabolic bowstring girder and a parabolic braced arch.

In the former case the maximum stress in the bow results when the whole bridge is covered with the live load, but in the latter case it is not so.

### 9. Concentrated Axle Loads and Effective Live Load.

In English practice it is generally considered sufficient to use the "effective live load" when calculating the stresses in the flanges and bracing.

By "effective live load" is meant the corresponding evenly distributed load, which causes an equivalent stress in the flanges at the centre, to that which results from the worst possible combination of concentrated axle loads.

In cases where this is not considered sufficiently accurate, the method proposed by Mr. Claxton Fidler might be adopted, viz. to calculate the stresses for the ordinary train load (using the stress constants in the following pages), and then work out the stresses caused by the excess engine load per foot, for one or two engine lengths, as may be decided on, and add the results to the former calculation. The excess load can also be taken as a uniform weight per foot, i. e. weight of engine divided by length over buffers minus train load per foot first taken.

To calculate the exact stresses due to the separate axle loads would, except in the case of very small spans, be an unnecessary refinement, particularly when, as is usual now, some allowance is made for impact, which must necessarily be more or less approximate.

It will therefore generally be quite sufficient for all practical purposes to use the "effective live load" in calculating the stresses, and as proposed by Mr. Claxton Fidler, to add the difference between the maximum and minimum stresses to the maximum stresses in the bracing, and half the difference in the case of the flanges, afterwards using a factor of safety of 3 to 4.

Vertical suspenders which carry the roadway, and other verticals which are supposed to distribute the load between the top and bottom flanges, must be made strong enough to bear any concentrated axle load which may come on them, and where the cross girders are spaced further apart than the engine wheels, this would be exceeded by a proportional part of one or more adjacent axle loads.

End posts, when the load is on the top flange, would have this concentrated load to bear, in addition to any possible stress caused by the bracing, and, referring to paragraph 7, it is in all cases necessary to look practically into these matters, when the quantity of metal in the various parts of the truss comes to be apportioned.

## 10. Fully worked out Example.

As an example, the stresses will be calculated in detail for a single line through bridge consisting of two girders of the type shown in Truss Diagram No. 20. Span 60 feet. Dead load 0·5 ton per lineal foot, and effective live load 1·5 tons per lineal foot.

The panels loads for one girder will therefore be 6 feet × 0·5 ton ÷ 2 = 1½ tons for dead load, and 6 feet × 1·5 tons ÷ 2 = 4½ tons for live load.

The stresses are as follows : .

### For Dead Load.

**Top flange :**                                                   Tons

| | | |
|---|---|---|
| S. 1·3 = stress constant 2·00 × 1½ tons panel load = | | + 3·00 |
| 3·5 | 6·00 × 1½ | + 9·00 |
| 5·7 | 9·00 × 1½ | +13·50 |
| 7·9 | 11·00 × 1½ | +16·50 |
| 9·11 | 12·00 × 1½ | +18·00 |

**Bottom flange :**

| | | |
|---|---|---|
| S. 2·4 = stress constant 2·50 × 1½ tons panel load = | | − 3·75 |
| 4·6 | 6·50 × 1½ | − 9·75 |
| 6·8 | 9·50 × 1½ | −14·25 |
| 8·10 | 11·50 × 1½ | −17·25 |
| 10·12 | 12·50 × 1½ | −18·75 |

**Diagonal bracing :**

| | | |
|---|---|---|
| S. 2·3 = stress constant 3·53 × 1½ tons panel load = | | + 5·30 |
| 4·5 | 2·83 × 1½ | + 4·25 |
| 6·7 | 2·12 × 1½ | + 3·18 |
| 8·9 | 1·41 × 1½ | + 2·12 |
| 10·11 | 0·70 × 1½ | + 1·05 |
| 1·4 | 2·83 × 1½ | − 4·25 |
| 3·6 | 2·12 × 1½ | − 3·18 |
| 5·8 | 1·41 × 1½ | − 2·12 |
| 7·10 | 0·70 × 1½ | − 1·05 |
| 9·12 | 0·00 × 1½ | − 0·00 |

**End verticals :**

S. 1·2 = stress constant 2·50 × 1½ tons panel load = + 3·75

## GIRDERS.

*For Live Load.*

Top flange:                                                          Tons

S. 1·3 = stress constant 2·00 × 4½ tons panel load = + 9·00
 3·5                      6·00 × 4½                   +27·00
 5·7                      9·00 × 4½                   +40·50
 7·9                     11·00 × 4½                   +49·50
 9·11                    12·00 × 4½                   +54·00

Bottom flange:

S. 2·4 = stress constant 2·50 × 4½ tons panel load = −11·25
 4·6                      6·50 × 4½                   −29·25
 6·8                      9·50 × 4½                   −42·75
 8·10                    11·50 × 4½                   −51·75
 10·12                   12·50 × 4½                   −56·25

Diagonal bracing:

S. 2·3 = stress constant 3·53 × 4½ tons panel load = +15·89
 2·3                      0·00 × 4½                   − 0·00
 4·5                      2·83 × 4½                   +12·74
 4·5                      0·00 × 4½                   − 0·00
 6·7                      2·26 × 4½                   +10·17
 6·7                      0·14 × 4½                   − 0·63
 8·9                      1·69 × 4½                   + 7·60
 8·9                      0·28 × 4½                   − 1·26
 10·11                    1·27 × 4½                   + 5·72
 10·11                    0·57 × 4½                   − 2·57
 1·4                      0·00 × 4½                   + 0·00
 1·4                      2·83 × 4½                   −12·74
 3·6                      0·14 × 4½                   + 0·63
 3·6                      2·26 × 4½                   −.10·17
 5·8                      0·28 × 4½                   + 1·26
 5·8                      1·69 × 4½                   − 7·60
 7·10                     0·57 × 4½                   + 2·57
 7·10                     1·27 × 4½                   − 5·72
 9·12                     0·85 × 4½                   + 3·83
 9·12                     0·85 × 4½                   − 3·83

End verticals:

S. 1·2 = stress constant 2·50 × 4½ tons panel load = +11·25
 1·2                      0·00 × 4½                   − 0·00

*Maximum Stresses for Combined Dead and Live Loads.*

| Top flange: | | | Tons | | | Tons | | Total tons |
|---|---|---|---|---|---|---|---|---|
| S. 1·3 | = | + | 3·00 | and | + | 9·00 | = | + 12·00 |
| 3·5 | | + | 9·00 | | + | 27·00 | | + 36·00 |
| 5·7 | | + | 13·50 | | + | 40·50 | | + 54·00 |
| 7·9 | | + | 16·50 | | + | 49·50 | | + 66·00 |
| 9·11 | | + | 18·00 | | + | 54·00 | | + 72·00 |

| Bottom flange: | | | | | | | | |
|---|---|---|---|---|---|---|---|---|
| S. 2·4 | = | − | 3·75 | and | − | 11·25 | | − 15·00 |
| 4·6 | | − | 9·75 | | − | 29·25 | | − 39·00 |
| 6·8 | | − | 14·25 | | − | 42·75 | | − 57·00 |
| 8·10 | | − | 17·25 | | − | 51·75 | | − 69·00 |
| 10·12 | | − | 18·75 | | − | 56·25 | | − 75·00 |

| Diagonal bracing: | | | | | | | | |
|---|---|---|---|---|---|---|---|---|
| S. 2·3 | = | + | 5·30 | and | + | 15·89 | | + 21·19 |
| 2·3 | | + | 5·30 | | − | 0·00 | | − 0·00 |
| 4·5 | | + | 4·25 | | + | 12·74 | | + 16·99 |
| 4·5 | | + | 4·25 | | − | 0·00 | | − 0·00 |
| 6·7 | | + | 3·18 | | + | 10·17 | | + 13·35 |
| 6·7 | | + | 3·18 | | − | 0·63 | | − 0·00 |
| 8·9 | | + | 2·12 | | + | 7·60 | | + 9·72 |
| 8·9 | | + | 2·12 | | − | 1·26 | | − 0·00 |
| 10·11 | | + | 1·05 | | + | 5·72 | | + 6·77 |
| 10·11 | | + | 1·05 | | − | 2·57 | | − 1·52 |
| 1·4 | | − | 4·25 | | + | 0·00 | | + 0·00 |
| 1·4 | | − | 4·25 | | − | 12·74 | | − 16·99 |
| 3·6 | | − | 3·18 | | + | 0·63 | | + 0·00 |
| 3·6 | | − | 3·18 | | − | 10·17 | | − 13·35 |
| 5·8 | | − | 2·12 | | + | 1·26 | | + 0·00 |
| 5·8 | | − | 2·12 | | − | 7·60 | | − 9·72 |
| 7·10 | | − | 1·05 | | + | 2·57 | | + 1·52 |
| 7·10 | | − | 1·05 | | − | 5·72 | | − 6·77 |
| 9·12 | | − | 0·00 | | + | 3·83 | | + 3·83 |
| 9·12 | | − | 0·00 | | − | 3·83 | | − 3·83 |
| 1·2 | | + | 3·75 | | + | 11·25 | | + 15·00 |
| 1·2 | | + | 3·75 | | − | 0·00 | | − 0·00 |

It will be noticed that the only web members which suffer counter strains in this case are 10·11 − 7·10 and 9·12.

## STRESS CONSTANTS FOR DEAD AND LIVE LOADS OF UNIT PANEL INTENSITY.

### TRUSS DIAGRAM No. 1.

#### LINVILLE.

##### CONDITIONS.

1. Depth  .. .. .. ..  $\frac{1}{12}$ of the span.
2. Number of panels  .. ..  12.
3. Method of loading  .. ..  On bottom flange.
4. Description of bracing  ..  Vertical, and inclined angle 45°.

#### EVENLY DISTRIBUTED DEAD LOAD.

*Stress Constants.*

Top flange:

| | | | |
|---|---|---|---|
| S. 1·3 | + 5·50 | S. 7·9 | + 16·00 |
| 3·5 | + 10·00 | 9·11 | + 17·50 |
| 5·7 | + 13·50 | 11·13 | + 18·00 |

Bottom flange:

| | | | |
|---|---|---|---|
| S. 2·4 | − 0·00 | S. 8·10 | − 13·50 |
| 4·6 | − 5·50 | 10·12 | − 16·00 |
| 6·8 | − 10·00 | 12·14 | − 17·50 |

Vertical bracing all struts under dead load:

| | | | |
|---|---|---|---|
| S. 1·2 | + 5·50 | S. 9·10 | + 1·50 |
| 3·4 | + 4·50 | 11·12 | + 0·50 |
| 5·6 | + 3·50 | 13·14 | + 0·00 |
| 7·8 | + 2·50 | | |

Diagonal bracing all ties under dead load:

| | | | | | | |
|---|---|---|---|---|---|---|
| S. 1·4 | — | 7·75 | | S. 7·10 | — | 3·52 |
| 3·6 | — | 6·34 | | 9·12 | — | 2·11 |
| 5·8 | — | 4·93 | | 11·14 | — | 0·70 |

## EVENLY DISTRIBUTED LIVE LOAD ADVANCING FROM EITHER ABUTMENT.

### *Maximum Stress Constants.*

Top flange:

| | | | | | | |
|---|---|---|---|---|---|---|
| S. 1·3 | + | 5·50 | | S. 7·9 | + | 16·00 |
| 3·5 | + | 10·00 | | 9·11 | + | 17·50 |
| 5·7 | + | 13·50 | | 11·13 | + | 18·00 · |

Bottom flange:

| | | | | | | |
|---|---|---|---|---|---|---|
| S. 2·4 | — | 0·00 | | S. 8·10 | — | 13·50 |
| 4·6 | — | 5·50 | | 10·12 | — | 16·00 |
| 6·8 | — | 10·00 | | 12·14 | — | 17·50 |

Vertical bracing:

| | | | | | | |
|---|---|---|---|---|---|---|
| S. 1·2 | + | 5·500 | | S. 7·8 | — | 0·500 |
| 1·2 | — | 0·000 | | 9·10 | + | 2·333 |
| 3·4 | + | 4·583 | | 9·10 | — | 0·833 |
| 3·4 | — | 0·083 | | 11·12 | + | 1·750 |
| 5·6 | + | 3·750 | | 11·12 | — | 1·250 |
| 5·6 | — | 0·250 | | 13·14 | + | 0·000 |
| 7·8 | + | 3·000 | | 13·14 | — | 0·000 |

Diagonal bracing:

| | | | | | | |
|---|---|---|---|---|---|---|
| S. 1·4 | + | 0·000 | | S. 7·10 | + | 0·705 |
| 1·4 | — | 7·755 | | 7·10 | — | 4·230 · |
| 3·6 | + | 0·117 . | | 9·12 | + | 1·174 |
| 3·6 | — | 6·462 | | 9·12 | — | 3·289 |
| 5·8 | + | 0·352 | | 11·14 | + | 1·762 |
| 5·8 | — | 5·287 | | 11·14 | — | 2·467 |

*Note.*—The parts 2·4 would practically be made of the same strength as 4·6, and 13·14 the same as 11·12.

## TRUSS DIAGRAM No. 2.

### LINVILLE.

#### CONDITIONS.

1. Depth    ..   ..   ..   ..   $\frac{1}{13}$ of the span.
2. Number of panels   ..   ..   12.
3. Method of loading   ..   ..   On top flange.
4. Description of bracing   ..   Vertical, and inclined angle 45°.

### EVENLY DISTRIBUTED DEAD LOAD.

#### *Stress Constants.*

Top flange:

| | |
|---|---|
| S. 1·3   +   5·50 | S. 7·9   +   16·00 |
| 3·5   +   10·00 | 9·11   +   17·50 |
| 5·7   +   13·50 | 11·13   +   18·00 |

Bottom flange :

| | |
|---|---|
| S. 2·4   —   0·00 | S. 8·10   —   13·50 |
| 4·6   —   5·50 | 10·12   —   16·00 |
| 6·8   —   10·00 | 12·14   —   17·50 |

Vertical bracing all struts under dead load:

| | |
|---|---|
| S. 1·2   +   6·00 | S. 9·10   +   2·50 |
| 3·4   +   5·50 | 11·12   +   1·50 |
| 5·6   +   4·50 | 13·14   +   1·00 |
| 7·8   +   3·50 | |

Diagonal bracing all ties under dead load:

| | |
|---|---|
| S. 1·4   —   7·75 | S. 7·10   —   3·52 |
| 3·6   —   6·34 | 9·12   —   2·11 |
| 5·8   —   4·93 | 11·14   —   0·70 |

EVENLY DISTRIBUTED LIVE LOAD ADVANCING FROM
EITHER ABUTMENT.

*Maximum Stress Constants.*

Top flange :

| S. 1·3 | + | 5·50 | S. 7·9 | + | 16·00 |
|---|---|---|---|---|---|
| 3·5 | + | 10·00 | 9·11 | + | 17·50 |
| 5·7 | + | 13·50 | 11·13 | + | 18·00 |

Bottom flange :

| S. 2·4 | − | 0·00 | S. 8·10 | − | 13·50 |
|---|---|---|---|---|---|
| 4·6 | − | 5·50 | 10·12 | − | 16·00 |
| 6·8 | − | 10·00 | 12·14 | − | 17·50 |

Vertical bracing :

| S. 1·2 | + | 6·000 | S. 7·8 | − | 0·250 |
|---|---|---|---|---|---|
| 1·2 | − | 0·000 | 9·10 | + | 3·000 |
| 3·4 | + | 5·500 | 9·10 | − | 0·500 |
| 3·4 | − | 0·000 | 11·12 | + | 2·333 |
| 5·6 | + | 4·583 | 11·12 | − | 0·833 |
| 5·6 | − | 0·083 | 13·14 | + | 1·000 |
| 7·8 | + | 3·750 | 13·14 | − | 0·000 |

Diagonal bracing :

| S. 1·4 | + | 0·000 | S. 7·10 | + | 0·705 |
|---|---|---|---|---|---|
| 1·4 | − | 7·755 | 7·10 | − | 4·230 |
| 3·6 | + | 0·117 | 9·12 | + | 1·174 |
| 3·6 | − | 6·462 | 9·12 | − | 3·289 |
| 5·8 | + | 0·352 | 11·14 | + | 1·762 |
| 5·8 | − | 5·287 | 11·14 | − | 2·467 |

*Note.*—If this truss is supported at the points 2·2,
the parts 2·4 would practically be made of the same
strength as 4·6, but if supported at the points 1·1, the
parts 1·2 and 2·4 are not necessary.

# TRUSS DIAGRAM No. 3.

### LINVILLE.

#### CONDITIONS.

1. Depth   ..   ..   ..   ..   $\frac{1}{15}$ of the span.
2. Number of panels   ..   ..   12.
3. Method of loading   ..   ..   On bottom flange.
4. Description of bracing   ..   Vertical, and inclined angle 45°.

### EVENLY DISTRIBUTED DEAD LOAD.

#### *Stress Constants.*

Top flange:

| | | | | | |
|---|---|---|---|---|---|
| S. 1·3 | + | 0·00 | S. 7·9 | + | 13·50 |
| 3·5 | + | 5·50 | 9·11 | + | 16·00 |
| 5·7 | + | 10·00 | 11·13 | + | 17·50 |

Bottom flange:

| | | | | | |
|---|---|---|---|---|---|
| S. 2·4 | − | 5·50 | S. 8·10 | − | 16·00 |
| 4·6 | − | 10·00 | 10·12 | − | 17·50 |
| 6·8 | − | 13·50 | 12·14 | − | 18·00 |

Vertical bracing all ties under dead load:

| | | | | | |
|---|---|---|---|---|---|
| S. 1·2 | − | 0·00 | S. 9·10 | − | 2·50 |
| 3·4 | − | 5·50 | 11·12 | − | 1·50 |
| 5·6 | − | 4·50 | 13·14 | − | 1·00 |
| 7·8 | − | 3·50 | | | |

Diagonal bracing all struts under dead load:

| | | | | | |
|---|---|---|---|---|---|
| S. 2·3 | + | 7·75 | S. 8·9 | + | 3·52 |
| 4·5 | + | 6·34 | 10·11 | + | 2·11 |
| 6·7 | + | 4·93 | 12·13 | + | 0·70 |

EVENLY DISTRIBUTED LIVE LOAD ADVANCING FROM
EITHER ABUTMENT.

*Maximum Stress Constants.*

Top flange:

| | | |
|---|---|---|
| S. 1·3 | + | 0·00 |
| 3·5 | + | 5·50 |
| 5·7 | + | 10·00 |

| | | |
|---|---|---|
| S. 7·9 | + | 13·50 |
| 9·11 | + | 16·00 |
| 11·13 | + | 17·50 |

Bottom flange:

| | | |
|---|---|---|
| S. 2·4 | − | 5·50 |
| 4·6 | − | 10·00 |
| 6·8 | − | 13·50 |

| | | |
|---|---|---|
| S. 8·10 | − | 16·00 |
| 10·12 | − | 17·50 |
| 12·14 | − | 18·00 |

Vertical bracing:

| | | |
|---|---|---|
| S. 1·2 | + | 0·000 |
| 1·2 | − | 0·000 |
| 3·4 | + | 0·000 |
| 3·4 | − | 5·500 |
| 5·6 | + | 0·083 |
| 5·6 | − | 4·583 |
| 7·8 | + | 0·250 |

| | | |
|---|---|---|
| S. 7·8 | − | 3·750 |
| 9·10 | + | 0·500 |
| 9·10 | − | 3·000 |
| 11·12 | + | 0·833 |
| 11·12 | − | 2·333 |
| 13·14 | + | 0·000 |
| 13·14 | − | 1·000 |

Diagonal bracing:

| | | |
|---|---|---|
| S. 2·3 | + | 7·755 |
| 2·3 | − | 0·000 |
| 4·5 | + | 6·462 |
| 4·5 | − | 0·117 |
| 6·7 | + | 5·287 |
| 6·7 | − | 0·352 |

| | | |
|---|---|---|
| S. 8·9 | + | 4·230 |
| 8·9 | − | 0·705 |
| 10·11 | + | 3·289 |
| 10·11 | − | 1·174 |
| 12·13 | + | 2·467 |
| 12·13 | − | 1·762 |

*Note.*—The parts 1·2 and 1·3 are not necessary to stability.

## TRUSS DIAGRAM No. 4.

### LINVILLE.

#### CONDITIONS.

1. Depth .. .. .. .. .. $\frac{1}{13}$ of the span.
2. Number of panels .. .. 12.
3. Method of loading .. .. On top flange.
4. Description of bracing .. Vertical, and inclined angle 45°.

### EVENLY DISTRIBUTED DEAD LOAD.

#### *Stress Constants.*

Top flange :

| S. 1·3 | + | 0·00 | S. 7·9 | + | 13·50 |
| 3·5 | + | 5·50 | 9·11 | + | 16·00 |
| 5·7 | + | 10·00 | 11·13 | + | 17·50 |

Bottom flange :

| S. 2·4 | − | 5·50 | S. 8·10 | − | 16·00 |
| 4·6 | − | 10·00 | 10·12 | − | 17·50 |
| 6·8 | − | 13·50 | 12·14 | − | 18·00 |

Vertical bracing all ties under dead load except 1·2 :

| S. 1·2 | + | 0·50 | S. 9·10 | − | 1·50 |
| 3·4 | − | 4·50 | 11·12 | − | 0·50 |
| 5·6 | − | 3·50 | 13·14 | − | 0·00 |
| 7·8 | − | 2·50 | | | |

Diagonal bracing all struts under dead load :

| S. 2·3 | + | 7·75 | S. 8·9 | + | 3·52 |
| 4·5 | + | 6·34 | 10·11 | + | 2·11 |
| 6·7 | + | 4·93 | 12·13 | + | 0·70 |

EVENLY DISTRIBUTED LIVE LOAD ADVANCING FROM
EITHER ABUTMENT.

*Maximum Stress Constants.*

Top flange:

| | | |
|---|---|---|
| S. 1·3 | + | 0·00 |
| 3·5 | + | 5·50 |
| 5·7 | + | 10·00 |

| | | |
|---|---|---|
| S. 7·9 | + | 13·50 |
| 9·11 | + | 16·00 |
| 11·13 | + | 17·50 |

Bottom flange:

| | | |
|---|---|---|
| S. 2·4 | − | 5·50 |
| 4·6 | − | 10·00 |
| 6·8 | − | 13·50 |

| | | |
|---|---|---|
| S. 8·10 | − | 16·00 |
| 10·12 | − | 17·50 |
| 12·14 | − | 18·00 |

Vertical bracing:

| | | |
|---|---|---|
| S. 1·2 | + | 0·500 |
| 1·2 | − | 0·000 |
| 3·4 | + | 0·083 |
| 3·4 | − | 4·583 |
| 5·6 | + | 0·250 |
| 5·6 | − | 3·750 |
| 7·8 | + | 0·500 |

| | | |
|---|---|---|
| S. 7·8 | − | 3·000 |
| 9·10 | + | 0·833 |
| 9·10 | − | 2·333 |
| 11·12 | + | 1·250 |
| 11·12 | − | 1·750 |
| 13·14 | + | 0·000 |
| 13·14 | − | 0·000 |

Diagonal bracing:

| | | |
|---|---|---|
| S. 2·3 | + | 7·755 |
| 2·3 | − | 0·000 |
| 4·5 | + | 6·462 |
| 4·5 | − | 0·117 |
| 6·7 | + | 5·287 |
| 6·7 | − | 0·352 |

| | | |
|---|---|---|
| S. 8·9 | + | 4·230 |
| 8·9 | − | 0·705 |
| 10·11 | + | 3·289 |
| 10·11 | − | 1·174 |
| 12·13 | + | 2·467 |
| 12·13 | − | 1·762 |

*Note.*—The parts 1·3 would practically be made of
the same strength as 3·5, and 13·14 the same as 11·12.
The parts 1·2 require particularly to be considered for
axle loads.

## TRUSS DIAGRAM No. 5.

### LATTICE.

### CONDITIONS.

1. Depth    ..   ..   ..   ..   $\frac{1}{12}$ of the span.
2. Number of panels   ..   ..   12.
3. Method of loading ..   ..   On bottom flange.
4. Description of bracing   ..   Crossed diagonals, angle 45°.

### EVENLY DISTRIBUTED DEAD LOAD.

*Stress Constants.*

Top flange:

| | |
|---|---|
| S. 1·3   +   3·00 | S. 7·9   +   15·00 |
| 3·5   +   8·00 | 9·11   +   17·00 |
| 5·7   +   12·00 | 11·13   +   18·00 |

Bottom flange:

| | |
|---|---|
| S. 2·4   −   2·50 | S. 8·10   −   14·50 |
| 4·6   −   7·50 | 10·12   −   16·50 |
| 6·8   −   11·50 | 12·14   −   17·50 |

Diagonal bracing struts under dead load:

| | |
|---|---|
| S. 2·3   +   3·53 | S. 8·9   +   1·41 |
| 4·5   +   2·83 | 10·11   +   0·70 |
| 6·7   +   2·12 | 12·13   +   0·00 |

End verticals:

S. 1·2    ..    ..    ..   +   3·00

Diagonal bracing ties under dead load:

| | |
|---|---|
| S. 1·4   −   4·24 | S. 7·10   −   2·12 |
| 3·6   −   3·53 | 9·12   −   1·41 |
| 5·8   −   2·83 | 11·14   −   0·70 |

PLATE 1

To face Page 16 .

# TRUSS DIAGRAMS

E & F N Spon, London & New York

Tho⁹ Kell & Son L⁻ᵗʰ

EVENLY DISTRIBUTED LIVE LOAD ADVANCING FROM
EITHER ABUTMENT.

*Maximum Stress Constants.*

Top flange:

| | | |
|---|---|---|
| S. 1·3 | + | 3·00 |
| 3·5 | + | 8·00 |
| 5·7 | + | 12·00 |

| | | |
|---|---|---|
| S. 7·9 | + | 15·00 |
| 9·11 | + | 17·00 |
| 11·13 | + | 18·00 |

Bottom flange:

| | | |
|---|---|---|
| S. 2·4 | − | 2·50 |
| 4·6 | − | 7·50 |
| 6·8 | − | 11·50 |

| | | |
|---|---|---|
| S. 8·10 | − | 14·50 |
| 10·12 | − | 16·50 |
| 12·14 | − | 17·50 |

Diagonal bracing:

| | | |
|---|---|---|
| S. 2·3 | + | 3·525 |
| 2·3 | − | 0·000 |
| 4·5 | + | 2·945 |
| 4·5 | − | 0·115 |
| 6·7 | + | 2·349 |
| 6·7 | − | 0·234 |
| 8·9 | + | 1·879 |
| 8·9 | − | 0·469 |
| 10·11 | + | 1·414 |
| 10·11 | − | 0·707 |
| 12·13 | + | 1·057 |
| 12·13 | − | 1·057 |

| | | |
|---|---|---|
| S. 1·4 | + | 0·000 |
| 1·4 | − | 4·242 |
| 3·6 | + | 0·000 |
| 3·6 | − | 3·525 |
| 5·8 | + | 0·115 |
| 5·8 | − | 2·945 |
| 7·10 | + | 0·234 |
| 7·10 | − | 2·349 |
| 9·12 | + | 0·469 |
| 9·12 | − | 1·879 |
| 11·14 | + | 0·707 |
| 11·14 | − | 1·414 |

End verticals:

| | | | | | |
|---|---|---|---|---|---|
| S. 1·2 | .. | .. | .. | + | 3·00 |
| 1·2 | .. | .. | .. | − | 0·00 |

C

## TRUSS DIAGRAM No. 6.

### LATTICE.

#### CONDITIONS.

1. Depth .. .. .. .. .. .. $\frac{1}{12}$ of the span.
2. Number of panels .. .. 12.
3. Method of loading .. .. On top flange.
4. Description of bracing .. Crossed diagonals, angle 45°.

#### EVENLY DISTRIBUTED DEAD LOAD.

*Stress Constants.*

Top flange :

| S. 1·3 | + | 2·50 | | S. 7·9 | + | 14·50 |
|---|---|---|---|---|---|---|
| 3·5 | + | 7.50 | | 9·11 | + | 16·50 |
| 5·7 | + | 11·50 | | 11·13 | + | 17·50 |

Bottom flange :

| S. 2·4 | − | 3·00 | | S. 8·10 | − | 15·00 |
|---|---|---|---|---|---|---|
| 4·6 | − | 8·00 | | 10·12 | − | 17·00 |
| 6·8 | − | 12·00 | | 12·14 | − | 18·00 |

Diagonal bracing struts under dead load :

| S. 2·3 | + | 4·24 | | S. 8·9 | + | 2·12 |
|---|---|---|---|---|---|---|
| 4·5 | + | 3·53 | | 10·11 | + | 1·41 |
| 6·7 | + | 2·83 | | 12·13 | + | 0·70 |

End verticals :

| S. 1·2 | .. | .. | .. | + | 3·00 |
|---|---|---|---|---|---|

Diagonal bracing ties under dead load :

| S. 1·4 | − | 3·53 | | S. 7·10 | − | 1·41 |
|---|---|---|---|---|---|---|
| 3·6 | − | 2·83 | | 9·12 | − | 0·70 |
| 5·8 | − | 2·12 | | 11·14 | − | 0·00 |

EVENLY DISTRIBUTED LIVE LOAD ADVANCING FROM
EITHER ABUTMENT.

*Maximum Stress Constants.*

Top flange:

| | | | | |
|---|---|---|---|---|
| S. 1·3 | + | 2·50 | S. 7·9 | + 14·50 |
| 3·5 | + | 7·50 | 9·11 | + 16·50 |
| 5·7 | + | 11·50 | 11·13 | + 17·50 |

Bottom flange:

| | | | | |
|---|---|---|---|---|
| S. 2·4 | − | 3·00 | S. 8·10 | − 15·00 |
| 4·6 | − | 8·00 | 10·12 | − 17·00 |
| 6·8 | − | 12·00 | 12·14 | − 18·00 |

Diagonal bracing:

| | | | | |
|---|---|---|---|---|
| S. 2·3 | + | 4·242 | S. 1·4 | + 0·000 |
| 2·3 | − | 0·000 | 1·4 | − 3·525 |
| 4·5 | + | 3·525 | 3·6 | + 0·115 |
| 4·5 | − | 0·000 | 3·6 | − 2·945 |
| 6·7 | + | 2·945 | 5·8 | + 0·234 |
| 6·7 | − | 0·115 | 5·8 | − 2·349 |
| 8·9 | + | 2·349 | 7·10 | + 0·469 |
| 8·9 | − | 0·234 | 7·10 | − 1·879 |
| 10·11 | + | 1·879 | 9·12 | + 0·707 |
| 10·11 | − | 0·469 | 9·12 | − 1·414 |
| 12·13 | + | 1·414 | 11·14 | + 1·057 |
| 12·13 | − | 0·707 | 11·14 | − 1·057 |

End verticals:

| | | | | | |
|---|---|---|---|---|---|
| S. 1·2 | .. | .. | .. | + | 3·000 |
| 1·2 | .. | .. | .. | − | 0·000 |

## TRUSS DIAGRAM No. 7.

### LATTICE.

### CONDITIONS.

1. Depth.. .. .. .. .. $\frac{1}{13}$ of the span.
2. Number of panels .. .. 12.
3. Method of loading .. .. On bottom flange.
4. Description of bracing .. Verticals and crossed diagonals, angle 45°.

### EVENLY DISTRIBUTED DEAD LOAD.

#### Stress Constants.

Top flange :

| | |
|---|---|
| S. 1·3   +   2·75 | S. 7·9   +   14·75 |
| 3·5   +   7·75 | 9·11   +   16·75 |
| 5·7   +   11·75 | 11·13   +   17·75 |

Bottom flange :

| | |
|---|---|
| S. 2·4   −   2·75 | S. 8·10   −   14·75 |
| 4·6   −   7·75 | 10·12   −   16·75 |
| 6·8   −   11·75 | 12·14   −   17·75 |

Diagonal bracing struts under dead load :

| | |
|---|---|
| S. 2·3   +   3·88 | S. 8·9   +   1·76 |
| 4·5   +   3·17 | 10·11   +   1·06 |
| 6·7   +   2·47 | 12·13   +   0·35 |

Diagonal bracing ties under dead load :

| | |
|---|---|
| S. 1·4   −   3·88 | S. 7·10   −   1·76 |
| 3·6   −   3·17 | 9·12   −   1·06 |
| 5·8   −   2·47 | 11·14   −   0·35 |

Vertical bracing :

S. on all the verticals except 1·2   −   0·50
S. 1·2   ..   ..   ..   +   2·75

*Note.*—With load top flange all stresses the same except vertical bracing.

Vertical bracing load on top flange:

    S. on all the verticals except 1·2   +   0·50
    S. 1·2      ..     ..     ..    +   3·00

EVENLY DISTRIBUTED LIVE LOAD ADVANCING FROM EITHER ABUTMENT.

*Maximum Stress Constants.*

Top flange:

    S. 1·3   +   2·75      S. 7·9   +   14·75
        3·5   +   7·75        9·11   +   16·75
        5·7   +   11·75     11·13   +   17·75

Bottom flange:

    S. 2·4   −   2·75      S. 8·10   −   14·75
        4·6   −   7·75      10·12   −   16·75
        6·8   −   11·75    12·14   −   17·75

Diagonal bracing:

    S. 2·3   +   3·877      S. 1·4   +   0·000
        2·3   −   0·000        1·4   −   3·877
        4·5   +   3·231        3·6   +   0·059
        4·5   −   0·059        3·6   −   3·231
        6·7   +   2·643        5·8   +   0·176
        6·7   −   0·176        5·8   −   2·643
        8·9   +   2·115        7·10   +   0·352
        8·9   −   0·352        7·10   −   2·115
      10·11   +   1·644      9·12   +   0·586
      10·11   −   0·586      9·12   −   1·644
      12·13   +   1·233     11·14   +   0·881
      12·13   −   0·881     11·14   −   1·233

Vertical bracing :

    S. on all the verticals except 1·2  −   0·50

    S. 1·2      ..      ..      ..     +   2·75

*Note.*—With load top flange all stresses the same except vertical bracing.

Vertical bracing load on top flange :

    S. on all the verticals except 1·2  +   0·50

    S. 1·2 ..    ..    ..    ..    +   3·00

*Note.*—The verticals are only supposed to distribute the load between the flanges.

---

## TRUSS DIAGRAM No. 8.

### LINVILLE.

#### CONDITIONS.

1. Depth   ...  ..  ..  $\frac{1}{7}$ of the span.
2. Number of panels  ..  ..  11.
3. Method of loading  ..  ..  On bottom flange.
4. Description of bracing  ..  Vertical, and inclined angle 45°.

#### EVENLY DISTRIBUTED DEAD LOAD.

*Stress Constants.*

Top flange :

| | | | | |
|---|---|---|---|---|
| S. 1·3 | + | 5·00 | S. 7·9 | + 14·00 |
| 3·5 | + | 9·00 | 9·11 | + 15·00 |
| 5·7 | + | 12·00 | 11·11 | + 15·00 |

Bottom flange :

| | | | | |
|---|---|---|---|---|
| S. 2·4 | − | 0·00 | S. 8·10 | − 12·00 |
| 4·6 | − | 5·00 | 10·12 | − 14·00 |
| 6·8 | − | 9·00 | 12·12 | − 15·00 |

Vertical bracing all struts under dead load :

| | | |
|---|---|---|
| S. 1·2 | .. .. .. | + 5·00 |
| 3·4 | .. .. .. | + 4·00 |
| 5·6 | .. .. .. | + 3·00 |
| 7·8 | .. .. .. | + 2·00 |
| 9·10 | .. .. .. | + 1·00 |
| 11·12 (vertical) | .. .. | + 0·00 |

Diagonal bracing all ties under dead load :

| | | | | | |
|---|---|---|---|---|---|
| S. 1·4 | .. | .. | .. | — | 7·07 |
| 3·6 | .. | .. | .. | — | 5·65 |
| 5·8 | .. | .. | .. | — | 4·24 |
| 7·10 | .. | .. | .. | — | 2·83 |
| 9·12 | .. | .. | .. | — | 1·41 |
| 11·12 (diagonal) | .. | .. | — | 0·00 | |

### EVENLY DISTRIBUTED LIVE LOAD ADVANCING FROM EITHER ABUTMENT.

*Maximum Stress Constants.*

Top flange :

| | | | | |
|---|---|---|---|---|
| S. 1·3 | + | 5·00 | S. 7·9 | + 14·00 |
| 3·5 | + | 9·00 | 9·11 | + 15·00 |
| 5·7 | + | 12·00 | 11·11 | + 15·00 |

Bottom flange :

| | | | | |
|---|---|---|---|---|
| S. 2·4 | — | 0·00 | S. 8·10 | — 12·00 |
| 4·6 | — | 5·00 | 10·12 | — 14·00 |
| 6·8 | — | 9·00 | 12·12 | — 15·00 |

Vertical bracing :

| | | | | | |
|---|---|---|---|---|---|
| S. 1·2 | .. | .. | .. | + | 5·000 |
| 1·2 | .. | .. | .. | — | 0·000 |
| 3·4 | .. | .. | .. | + | 4·091 |
| 3·4 | .. | .. | .. | — | 0·091 |
| 5·6 | .. | .. | .. | + | 3·273 |
| 5·6 | .. | .. | .. | — | 0·273 |
| 7·8 | .. | .. | .. | + | 2·545 |
| 7·8 | .. | .. | .. | — | 0·545 |
| 9·10 | .. | .. | .. | + | 1·910 |
| 9·10 | .. | .. | .. | — | 0·910 |
| 11·12 (vertical) | .. | .. | + | 1·364 | |
| 11·12 (vertical) | .. | .. | — | 1·364 | |

Diagonal bracing:

| | | | | | |
|---|---|---|---|---|---|
| S. 1·4 | .. | .. | .. | + | 0·000 |
| 1·4 | .. | .. | .. | − | 7·070 |
| 3·6 | .. | .. | .. | + | 0·128 |
| 3·6 | .. | .. | .. | − | 5·768 |
| 5·8 | .. | .. | .. | + | 0·384 |
| 5·8 | .. | .. | .. | − | 4·614 |
| 7·10 | .. | .. | .. | + | 0·762 |
| 7·10 | .. | .. | .. | − | 3·588 |
| 9·12 | .. | .. | .. | + | 1·283 |
| 9·12 | .. | .. | .. | − | 2·693 |
| 11·12 (diagonal) | .. | .. | | + | 1·923 |
| 11·12 (diagonal) | .. | .. | | − | 1·923 |

*Note.*—The parts 2·4 would practically be made of the same strength as 4·6.

---

## TRUSS DIAGRAM No. 9.

### LINVILLE.

#### CONDITIONS.

1. Depth   ..   ..   ..   ..   $\frac{1}{11}$ of the span.
2. Number of panels   ..   ..   11.
3. Method of loading   ..   ..   On top flange.
4. Description of bracing   ..   Vertical, and inclined angle 45°.

EVENLY DISTRIBUTED DEAD LOAD.

*Stress Constants.*

Top flange:

| | | | | |
|---|---|---|---|---|
| S. 1·3 | + 5·00 | | S. 7·9 | + 14·00 |
| 3·5 | + 9·00 | | 9·11 | + 15·00 |
| 5·7 | + 12·00 | | 11·11 | + 15·00 |

PLATE 2.

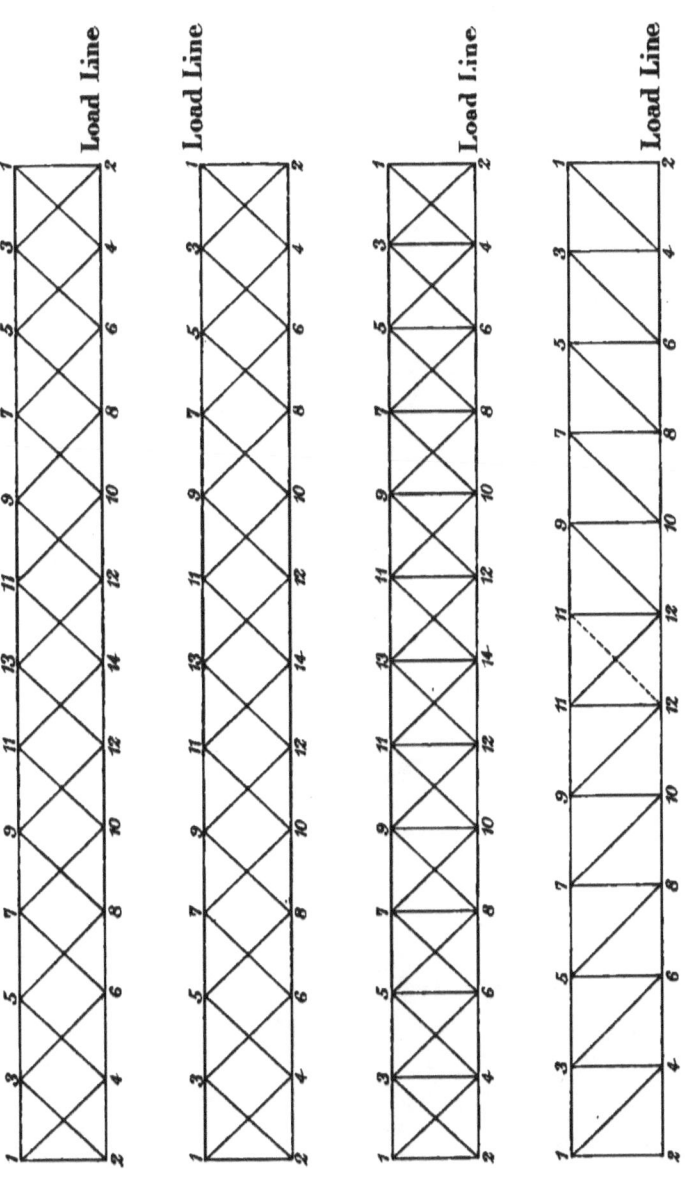

E & F N Spon, London & New York

Bottom flange:

| | | | | | | |
|---|---|---|---|---|---|---|
| S. 2·4 | — | 0·00 | | S. 8·10 | — | 12·00 |
| 4·6 | — | 5·00 | | 10·12 | — | 14·00 |
| 6·8 | — | 9·00 | | 12·12 | — | 15·00 |

Vertical bracing all struts under dead load:

| | | | | | |
|---|---|---|---|---|---|
| S. 1·2 | .. | .. | .. | + | 5·50 |
| 3·4 | .. | .. | .. | + | 5·00 |
| 5·6 | .. | .. | .. | + | 4·00 |
| 7·8 | .. | .. | .. | + | 3·00 |
| 9·10 | .. | .. | .. | + | 2·00 |
| 11·12 (vertical) | .. | .. | | + | 1·00 |

Diagonal bracing all ties under dead load:

| | | | | | |
|---|---|---|---|---|---|
| S. 1·4 | .. | .. | .. | — | 7·07 |
| 3·6 | .. | .. | .. | — | 5·65 |
| 5·8 | .. | .. | .. | — | 4·24 |
| 7·10 | .. | .. | .. | — | 2·83 |
| 9·12 | .. | .. | .. | — | 1·41 |
| 11·12 (diagonal) | .. | | .. | — | 0·00 |

EVENLY DISTRIBUTED LIVE LOAD ADVANCING FROM
EITHER ABUTMENT.

*Maximum Stress Constants.*

Top flange:

| | | | | | |
|---|---|---|---|---|---|
| S. 1·3 | + | 5·00 | | S. 7·9 | + 14·00 |
| 3·5 | + | 9·00 | | 9·11 | + 15·00 |
| 5·7 | + | 12·00 | | 11·11 | + 15·00 |

Bottom flange:

| | | | | | |
|---|---|---|---|---|---|
| S. 2·4 | — | 0·00· | | S. 8·10 | — 12·00 |
| 4·6 | — | 5·00 | | 10·12 | — 14·00 |
| 6·8 | — | 9·00 | | 12·12 | — 15·00 |

Vertical bracing :

| | | | | |
|---|---|---|---|---|
| S. 1·2 | .. .. .. | + | 5·500 |
| 1·2 | .. .. .. | − | 0·000 |
| 3·4 | .. .. .. | + | 5·000 |
| 3·4 | .. .. .. | − | 0·000 |
| 5·6 | .. .. .. | + | 4·091 |
| 5·6 | .. .. .. | − | 0·091 |
| 7·8 | .. .. .. | + | 3·273 |
| 7·8 | .. .. .. | − | 0·273 |
| 9·10 | .. .. .. | + | 2·545 |
| 9·10 | .. .. .. | − | 0·545 |
| 11·12 (vertical) | .. .. | + | 1·910 |
| 11·12 (vertical) | .. .. | − | 0·910 |

Diagonal bracing :

| | | | | |
|---|---|---|---|---|
| S. 1·4 | .. .. .. | + | 0·000 |
| 1·4 | .. .. .. | − | 7·070 |
| 3·6 | .. .. .. | + | 0·128 |
| 3·6 | .. .. .. | − | 5·768 |
| 5·8 | .. .. .. | + | 0·384 |
| 5·8 | .. .. .. | − | 4·614 |
| 7·10 | .. .. .. | + | 0·762 |
| 7·10 | .. .. .. | − | 3·588 |
| 9·12 | .. .. .. | + | 1·283 |
| 9·12 | .. .. .. | − | 2·693 |
| 11·12 (diagonal) | .. .. | + | 1·923 |
| 11·12 (diagonal) | .. .. | − | 1·923 |

*Note.*—If the truss is supported at the points 2·2 the parts 2·4 would practically be made of the same strength as 4·6; but if supported at the points 1·1 the parts 1·2 and 2·4 are not necessary.

# TRUSS DIAGRAM No. 10.

## LINVILLE.

### CONDITIONS. '

1. Depth  .. .. .. ..  $\frac{1}{11}$ of the span.
2. Number of panels .. .. 11.
3. Method of loading .. .. On bottom flange.
4. Description of bracing .. Vertical, and inclined angle 45°.

## EVENLY DISTRIBUTED DEAD LOAD.

### Stress Constants.

Top flange:

| | | | | | |
|---|---|---|---|---|---|
| S. 1·3 | + | 0·00 | S. 7·9 | + | 12·00 |
| 3·5 | + | 5·00 | 9·11 | + | 14·00 |
| 5·7 | + | 9·00 | 11·11 | + | 15·00 |

Bottom flange:

| | | | | | |
|---|---|---|---|---|---|
| S. 2·4 | − | 5·00 | S. 8·10 | − | 14·00 |
| 4·6 | − | 9·00 | 10·12 | − | 15·00 |
| 6·8 | − | 12·00 | 12·12 | − | 15·00 |

Vertical bracing all ties under dead load :

| | | | | | |
|---|---|---|---|---|---|
| S. 1·2 | .. | .. | .. | − | 0·00 |
| 3·4 | .. | .. | .. | − | 5·00 |
| 5·6 | .. | .. | .. | − | 4·00 |
| 7·8 | .. | .. | .. | − | 3·00 |
| 9·10 | .. | .. | .. | − | 2·00 |
| 11·12 (vertical) | .. | .. | − | 1·00 |

Diagonal bracing all struts under dead load :

| | | | | | |
|---|---|---|---|---|---|
| S. 2·3 | .. | .. | .. | + | 7·07 |
| 4·5 | .. | .. | .. | + | 5·65 |
| 6·7 | .. | .. | .. | + | 4·24 |
| 8·9 | .. | .. | .. | + | 2·83 |
| 10·11 | .. | .. | .. | + | 1·41 |
| 12·11 (diagonal) | .. | .. | + | 0·00 |

### Evenly distributed Live Load advancing from either Abutment.

*Maximum Stress Constants.*

Top flange:

| | | |
|---|---|---|
| S. 1·3 | + | 0·00 |
| 3·5 | + | 5·00 |
| 5·7 | + | 9·00 |

| | | |
|---|---|---|
| S. 7·9 | + | 12·00 |
| 9·11 | + | 14·00 |
| 11·11 | + | 15·00 |

Bottom flange:

| | | |
|---|---|---|
| S. 2·4 | − | 5·00 |
| 4·6 | − | 9·00 |
| 6·8 | − | 12·00 |

| | | |
|---|---|---|
| S. 8·10 | − | 14·00 |
| 10·12 | − | 15·00 |
| 12·12 | − | 15·00 |

Vertical bracing:

| | | |
|---|---|---|
| S. 1·2 | + | 0·000 |
| 1·2 | − | 0·000 |
| 3·4 | + | 0·000 |
| 3·4 | − | 5·000 |
| 5·6 | + | 0·091 |
| 5·6 | − | 4·091 |
| 7·8 | + | 0·273 |
| 7·8 | − | 3·273 |
| 9·10 | + | 0·545 |
| 9·10 | − | 2·545 |
| 11·12 (vertical) | + | 0·910 |
| 11·12 (vertical) | − | 1·910 |

Diagonal bracing:

| | | |
|---|---|---|
| S. 2·3 | + | 7·070 |
| 2·3 | − | 0·000 |
| 4·5 | + | 5·768 |
| 4·5 | − | 0·128 |
| 6·7 | + | 4·614 |
| 6·7 | − | 0·384 |
| 8·9 | + | 3·588 |
| 8·9 | − | 0·762 |

Diagonal bracing—*continued*.

| | | | | |
|---|---|---|---|---|
| 10·11 | .. | .. | .. | + 2·693 |
| 10·11 | .. | .. | .. | − 1·283 |
| 12·11 (diagonal) | .. | .. | + 1·921 | |
| 12·11 (diagonal) | .. | .. | − 1·921 | |

*Note.*—The parts 1·2 and 1·3 are not necessary to stability.

## TRUSS DIAGRAM No. 11.

### LINVILLE.

#### CONDITIONS.

1. Depth .. .. .. .. $\frac{1}{11}$ of the span.
2. Number of panels .. .. 11.
3. Method of loading .. .. On top flange.
4. Description of bracing .. Vertical, and inclined angle 45°.

#### EVENLY DISTRIBUTED DEAD LOAD.

##### *Stress Constants.*

Top flange:

| | | | | |
|---|---|---|---|---|
| S. 1·3 | + 0·00 | S. 7·9 | + 12·00 |
| 3·5 | + 5·00 | 9·11 | + 14·00 |
| 5·7 | + 9·00 | 11·11 | + 15·00 |

Bottom flange:

| | | | |
|---|---|---|---|
| S. 2·4 | − 5·00 | S. 8·10 | − 14·00 |
| 4·6 | − 9·00 | 10·12 | − 15·00 |
| 6·8 | − 12·00 | 12·12 | − 15·00 |

Vertical bracing all ties under dead load except 1·2:

| | | | | |
|---|---|---|---|---|
| S. 1·2 | .. | .. | .. | + 0·50 |
| 3·4 | .. | .. | .. | − 4·00 |
| 5·6 | .. | .. | .. | − 3·00 |
| 7·8 | .. | .. | .. | − 2·00 |
| 9·10 | .. | .. | .. | − 1·00 |
| 11·12 (vertical) | .. | . | | − 0·00 |

Diagonal bracing all struts under dead load :

| | | | | |
|---|---|---|---|---|
| S. 2·3 | .. | .. | .. | + 7·07 |
| 4·5 | .. | .. | .. | + 5·65 |
| 6·7 | .. | .. | .. | + 4·24 |
| 8·9 | .. | .. | .. | + 2·83 |
| 10·11 | . | .. | .. | + 1·41 |
| 12·11 (diagonal) | .. | | .. | + 0·00 |

## EVENLY DISTRIBUTED LIVE LOAD ADVANCING FROM EITHER ABUTMENT.

### *Maximum Stress Constants.*

Top flange :

| | | | | | |
|---|---|---|---|---|---|
| S. 1·3 | + | 0·00 | S. 7·9 | + | 12·00 |
| 3·5 | + | 5·00 | 9·11 | + | 14·00 |
| 5·7 | + | 9·00 | 11·11 | + | 15·00 |

Bottom flange :

| | | | | | |
|---|---|---|---|---|---|
| S. 2·4 | − | 5·00 | S. 8·10 | − | 14·00 |
| 4·6 | − | 9·00 | 10·12 | − | 15·00 |
| 6·8 | − | 12·00 | 12·12 | − | 15·00 |

Vertical bracing :

| | | | | | |
|---|---|---|---|---|---|
| S. 1·2 | .. | .. | .. | + | 0·500 |
| 1·2 | .. | .. | .. | − | 0·000 |
| 3·4 | .. | .. | .. | + | 0·091 |
| 3·4 | .. | .. | .. | − | 4·091 |
| 5·6 | .. | .. | .. | + | 0·273 |
| 5·6 | .. | .. | .. | − | 3·273 |
| 7·8 | .. | .. | .. | + | 0·545 |
| 7·8 | .. | .. | .. | − | 2·545 |
| 9·10 | .. | .. | .. | + | 0·910 |
| 9·10 | .. | .. | .. | − | 1·910 |
| 11·12 (vertical) | .. | .. | | + | 1·364 |
| 11·12 (vertical) | .. | .. | | − | 1·364 |

Diagonal bracing :

| | | | | | |
|---|---|---|---|---|---|
| S. 2·3 | .. | .. | .. | + | 7·070 |
| 2·3 | .. | .. | .. | − | 0·000 |
| 4·5 | .. | .. | .. | + | 5·768 |
| 4·5 | .. | .. | .. | − | 0·128 |
| 6·7 | .. | .. | .. | + | 4·614 |
| 6·7 | .. | .. | .. | − | 0·384 |
| 8·9 | .. | .. | .. | + | 3·588 |
| 8·9 | .. | .. | .. | − | 0·762 |
| 10·11 | .. | .. | .. | + | 2·693 |
| 10·11 | .. | .. | .. | − | 1·283 |
| 12·11 (diagonal) | .. | .. | | + | 1·921 |
| 12·11 (diagonal) | .. | .. | | − | 1·921 |

*Note.*—The parts 1·3 would practically be made of the same strength as 3·5, and the parts 1·2 require particularly to be considered for axle loads.

---

# TRUSS DIAGRAM No. 12.

### LATTICE.

### CONDITIONS.

1. Depth  .. .. .. .. .. $\frac{1}{11}$ of the span.
2. Number of panels  .. .. 11.
3. Method of loading  .. .. On bottom flange.
4. Description of bracing  .. Crossed diagonals, angle 45°.

### EVENLY DISTRIBUTED DEAD LOAD.

*Stress Constants.*

Top flange :

| | | | | |
|---|---|---|---|---|
| S. 1·3 | + | 2·75 | S. 7·9 + | 13·25 |
| 3·5 | + | 7·25 | 9·11 + | 14·75 |
| 5·7 | + | 10·75 | 11·11 + | 15·25 |

Bottom flange :

| | | | | |
|---|---|---|---|---|
| S. 2·4 | − | 2·25 | S. 8·10 − | 12·75 |
| 4·6 | − | 6·75 | 10·12 − | 14·25 |
| 6·8 | − | 10·25 | 12·12 − | 14·75 |

Diagonal bracing struts under dead load except 12·11:

| | | | | | | |
|---|---|---|---|---|---|---|
| S. 2·3 | + | 3·20 | | S. 8·9 | + | 1·02 |
| 4·5 | + | 2·43 | | 10·11 | + | 0·38 |
| 6·7 | + | 1·79 | | 12·11 | − | 0·38 |

Diagonal bracing ties under dead load:

| | | | | | | |
|---|---|---|---|---|---|---|
| S. 1·4 | − | 3·84 | | S. 7·10 | − | 1·79 |
| 3·6 | − | 3·20 | | 9·12 | − | 1·02 |
| 5·8 | − | 2·43 | | 11·12 | − | 0·38 |

End verticals:

| | | | | | |
|---|---|---|---|---|---|
| S. 1·2 | .. | .. | .. | + | 2·75 |

## EVENLY DISTRIBUTED LIVE LOAD ADVANCING FROM EITHER ABUTMENT.

### *Maximum Stress Constants.*

Top flange:

| | | | | | | |
|---|---|---|---|---|---|---|
| S. 1·3 | + | 2·75 | | S. 7·9 | + | 13·25 |
| 3·5 | + | 7·25 | | 9·11 | + | 14·75 |
| 5·7 | + | 10·75 | | 11·11 | + | 15·25 |

Bottom flange:

| | | | | | | |
|---|---|---|---|---|---|---|
| S. 2·4 | − | 2·25 | | S. 8·10 | − | 12·75 |
| 4·6 | − | 6·75 | | 10·12 | − | 14·25 |
| 6·8 | − | 10·25 | | 12·12 | − | 14·75 |

Diagonal bracing:

| | | | | | | |
|---|---|---|---|---|---|---|
| S. 2·3 | + | 3·204 | | S. 1·4 | + | 0·000 |
| 2·3 | − | 0·000 | | 1·4 | − | 3·845 |
| 4·5 | + | 2·563 | | 3·6 | + | 0·000 |
| 4·5 | − | 0·128 | | 3·6 | − | 3·204 |
| 6·7 | + | 2·051 | | 5·8 | + | 0·128 |
| 6·7 | − | 0·255 | | 5·8 | − | 2·563 |
| 8·9 | + | 1·538 | | 7·10 | + | 0·255 |
| 8·9 | − | 0·512 | | 7·10 | − | 2·051 |

Diagonal bracing—*continued.*

| | | | | | |
|---|---|---|---|---|---|
| 10·11 | + | 1·153 | 9·12 | + | 0·512 |
| 10·11 | − | 0·768 | 9·12 | − | 1·538 |
| 12·11 | + | 0·768 | 11·12 | + | 0·768 |
| 12·11 | − | 1·153 | 11·12 | − | 1·153 |

End verticals :

S. 1·2     ..     ..     ..     + 2·75

---

## TRUSS DIAGRAM No. 13.

### LATTICE.

#### CONDITIONS.

1. Depth.. .. .. .. .. $\frac{1}{11}$ of the span.
2. Number of panels .. .. 11.
3. Method of loading .. .. On top flange.
4. Description of bracing .. Crossed diagonals, angle 45°.

#### EVENLY DISTRIBUTED DEAD LOAD.

*Stress Constants.*

Top flange :

| | | | | | |
|---|---|---|---|---|---|
| S. 1·3 | + | 2·25 | S. 7·9 | + | 12·75 |
| 3·5 | + | 6·75 | 9·11 | + | 14·25 |
| 5·7 | + | 10·25 | 11·11 | + | 14·75 |

Bottom flange :

| | | | | | |
|---|---|---|---|---|---|
| S. 2·4 | − | 2·75 | S. 8·10 | − | 13·25 |
| 4·6 | − | 7·25 | 10·12 | − | 14·75 |
| 6·8 | − | 10·75 | 12·12 | − | 15·25 |

Diagonal bracing struts under dead load :

| | | | | | |
|---|---|---|---|---|---|
| S. 2·3 | + | 3·84 | S. 8·9 | + | 1·79 |
| 4·5 | + | 3·20 | 10·11 | + | 1·02 |
| 6·7 | + | 2·43 | 12·11 | + | 0·38 |

End verticals :

S. 1·2     ..     ..     ..     + 2·75

D

Diagonal bracing ties under dead load, except 11·12:

| | | | | | | |
|---|---|---|---|---|---|---|
| S. | 1·4 | − | 3·20 | S. 7·10 | − | 1·02 |
| | 3·6 | − | 2·43 | 9·12 | − | 0·38 |
| | 5·8 | − | 1·79 | 11·12 | + | 0·38 |

EVENLY DISTRIBUTED LIVE LOAD ADVANCING FROM
EITHER ABUTMENT.

*Maximum Stress Constants.*

Top flange:

| | | | | | | |
|---|---|---|---|---|---|---|
| S. | 1·3 | + | 2·25 | S. 7·9 | + | 12·75 |
| | 3·5 | + | 6·75 | 9·11 | + | 14·25 |
| | 5·7 | + | 10·25 | 11·11 | + | 14·75 |

Bottom flange:

| | | | | | | |
|---|---|---|---|---|---|---|
| S. | 2·4 | − | 2·75 | 8·10 | − | 13·25 |
| | 4·6 | − | 7·25 | 10·12 | − | 14·75 |
| | 6·8 | − | 10·75 | 12·12 | − | 15·25 |

Diagonal bracing:

| | | | | | | |
|---|---|---|---|---|---|---|
| S. | 2·3 | + | 3·845 | S. 1·4 | + | 0·000 |
| | 2·3 | − | 0·000 | 1·4 | − | 3·204 |
| | 4·5 | + | 3·204 | 3·6 | + | 0·128 |
| | 4·5 | − | 0·000 | 3·6 | − | 2·563 |
| | 6·7 | + | 2·563 | 5·8 | + | 0·255 |
| | 6·7 | − | 0·128 | 5·8 | − | 2·051 |
| | 8·9 | + | 2·051 | 7·10 | + | 0·512 |
| | 8·9 | − | 0·255 | 7·10 | − | 1·538 |
| | 10·11 | + | 1·538 | 9·12 | + | 0·768 |
| | 10·11 | − | 0·512 | 9·12 | − | 1·153 |
| | 12·11 | + | 1·153 | 11·12 | + | 1·153 |
| | 12·11 | − | 0·768 | 11·12 | − | 0·768 |

End verticals:

| | | | | | |
|---|---|---|---|---|---|
| S. | 1·2 | .. | .. | .. | +   2·75 |

PLATE 3.

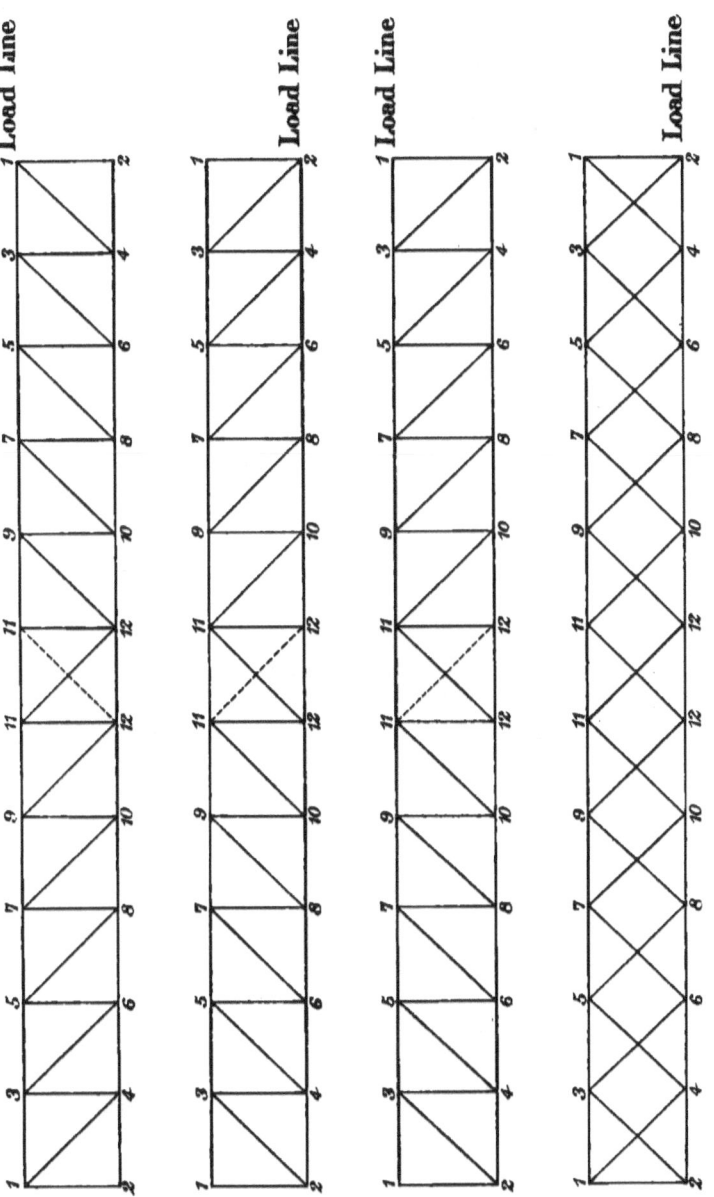

Tho⁸ Kell & Son Lith

E & F N Spon,London & NewYork

# TRUSS DIAGRAM No. 14.

### LATTICE.

### CONDITIONS.

1. Depth .. .. .. .. $\frac{1}{11}$ of the span.
2. Number of panels .. .. 11.
3. Method of loading .. .. On bottom flange.
4. Description of bracing .. Verticals and crossed diagonals, angle 45°.

### EVENLY DISTRIBUTED DEAD LOAD.

#### *Stress Constants.*

Top flange:

| | | | | | |
|---|---|---|---|---|---|
| S. 1·3 | + | 2·50 | S. 7·9 | + | 13·00 |
| 3·5 | + | 7·00 | 9·11 | + | 14·50 |
| 5·7 | + | 10·50 | 11·11 | + | 15·00 |

Bottom flange:

| | | | | | |
|---|---|---|---|---|---|
| S. 2·4 | − | 2·50 | 8·10 | − | 13·00 |
| 4·6 | − | 7·00 | 10·12 | − | 14·50 |
| 6·8 | − | 10·50 | 12·12 | − | 15·00 |

Diagonal bracing struts under dead load:

| | | | | | |
|---|---|---|---|---|---|
| S. 2·3 | + | 3·52 | S. 8·9 | + | 1·41 |
| 4·5 | + | 2·82 | 10·11 | + | 0·70 |
| 6·7 | + | 2·11 | 12·11 | + | 0·00 |

Diagonal bracing ties under dead load:

| | | | | | |
|---|---|---|---|---|---|
| S. 1·4 | − | 3·52 | S. 7·10 | − | 1·41 |
| 3·6 | − | 2·82 | 9·12 | − | 0·70 |
| 5·8 | − | 2·11 | 11·12 | − | 0·00 |

Vertical bracing :

    S. on all the verticals except 1·2  —  0·50

    S. 1·2      ..      ..      ..  +  2·50

*Note.*—With load top flange all stresses the same except vertical bracing.

Vertical bracing load on top flange :

    S. on all the verticals except 1·2  +  0·50

    S. 1·2      ..      ..      ..  +  2·75

### EVENLY DISTRIBUTED LIVE LOAD ADVANCING FROM EITHER ABUTMENT.

Top flange :      *Maximum Stress Constants.*

| | | | | | |
|---|---|---|---|---|---|
| S. 1·3 | + | 2·50 | S. 7·9 | + | 13·00 |
| 3·5 | + | 7·00 | 9·11 | + | 14·50 |
| 5·7 | + | 10·50 | 11·11 | + | 15·00 |

Bottom flange :

| | | | | | |
|---|---|---|---|---|---|
| S. 2·4 | — | 2·50 | S. 8·10 | — | 13·00 |
| 4·6 | — | 7·00 | 10·12 | — | 14·50 |
| 6·8 | — | 10·50 | 12·12 | — | 15·00 |

Diagonal bracing :

| | | | | | |
|---|---|---|---|---|---|
| S. 2·3 | + | 3·525 | S. 1·4 | + | 0·000 |
| 2·3 | — | 0·000 | 1·4 | — | 3·525 |
| 4·5 | + | 2·883 | 3·6 | + | 0·063 |
| 4·5 | — | 0·063 | 3·6 | — | 2·883 |
| 6·7 | + | 2·306 | 5·8 | + | 0·186 |
| 6·7 | .. | 0·186 | 5·8 | — | 2·306 |
| 8·9 | + | 1·793 | 7·10 | + | 0·375 |
| 8·9 | — | 0·375 | 7·10 | — | 1·793 |
| 10·11 | + | 1·346 | 9·12 | + | 0·641 |
| 10·11 | — | 0·641 | 9·12 | — | 1·346 |
| 12·11 | + | 0·961 | 11·12 | + | 0·961 |
| 12·11 | — | 0·961 | 11·12 | — | 0·961 |

Vertical bracing:

S. on all the verticals except 1·2  —   0·50
S. 1·2         ..        ..        ..      +   2·50

*Note.*—With load top flange all stresses the same except vertical bracing.

Vertical bracing load on top flange:

S. on all the verticals except 1·2  +   0·50
S. 1·2         ..        ..        ..      +   2·75

*Note.*—The verticals are only supposed to distribute the load between the flanges.

---

## TRUSS DIAGRAM No. 15.

### LINVILLE.

#### CONDITIONS.

1. Depth      ..   ..   ..   ..   $\frac{1}{10}$ of the span.
2. Number of panels   ..   ..   10.
3. Method of loading   ..   ..   On bottom flange.
4. Description of bracing   ..   Verticals and diagonals, angle 45°.

#### EVENLY DISTRIBUTED DEAD LOAD.

##### *Stress Constants.*

Top flange:

| S. 1·3 | + 4·50 | S. 7·9 | + 12·00 |
| 3·5 | + 8·00 | 9·11 | + 12·50 |
| 5·7 | + 10·50 | | |

Bottom flange:

| S. 2·4 | — 0·00 | S. 8·10 | — 10·50 |
| 4·6 | — 4·50. | 10·12 | — 12·00 |
| 6·8 | — 8·00 | | |

Vertical bracing all struts under dead load:

| S. 1·2 | + 4·50 | S. 7·8 | + 1·50 |
| 3·4 | + 3·50 | 9·10 | + 0·50 |
| 5·6 | + 2·50 | 11·12 | + 0·00 |

Diagonal bracing all ties under dead load:

| | | | | | |
|---|---|---|---|---|---|
| S. 1·4 | — | 6·34 | S. 7·10 | — | 2·11 |
| 3·6 | — | 4·93 | 9·12 | — | 0·70 |
| 5·8 | — | 3·52 | | | |

## EVENLY DISTRIBUTED LIVE LOAD ADVANCING FROM EITHER ABUTMENT.

### *Maximum Stress Constants.*

Top flange:

| | | | | | |
|---|---|---|---|---|---|
| S. 1·3 | + | 4·50 | S. 7·9 | + | 12·00 |
| 3·5 | + | 8·00 | 9·11 | + | 12·50 |
| 5·7 | + | 10·50 | | | |

Bottom flange:

| | | | | | |
|---|---|---|---|---|---|
| S. 2·4 | — | 0·00 | S. 8·10 | — | 10·50 |
| 4·6 | — | 4·50 | 10·12 | — | 12·00 |
| 6·8 | — | 8·00 | | | |

Vertical bracing:

| | | | | | |
|---|---|---|---|---|---|
| S. 1·2 | + | 4·50 | S. 7·8 | + | 2·10 |
| 1·2 | — | 0·00 | 7·8 | — | 0·60 |
| 3·4 | + | 3·60 | 9·10 | + | 1·50 |
| 3·4 | — | 0·10 | 9·10 | — | 1·00 |
| 5·6 | + | 2·80 | 11·12 | + | 0·00 |
| 5·6 | — | 0·30 | 11·12 | — | 0·00 |

Diagonal bracing:

| | | | | | |
|---|---|---|---|---|---|
| S. 1·4 | + | 0·00 | S. 5·8 | — | 3·94 |
| 1·4 | — | 6·34 | 7·10 | + | 0·84 |
| 3·6 | + | 0·14 | 7·10 | — | 2·95 |
| 3·6 | — | 5·07 | 9·12 | + | 1·41 |
| 5·8 | + | 0·42 | 9·12 | — | 2·11 |

*Note.*—The parts 2·4 would practically be made of the same strength as 4·6 and 11·12 the same as 9·10.

# TRUSS DIAGRAM No. 16.

### LINVILLE.

#### CONDITIONS.

1. Depth .. .. .. .. $\frac{1}{10}$ of the span.
2. Number of panels .. .. 10.
3. Method of loading .. .. On top flange.
4. Description of bracing .. Verticals and diagonals, angle 45°.

### EVENLY DISTRIBUTED DEAD LOAD.

#### *Stress Constants.*

Top flange:

| | | |
|---|---|---|
| S. 1·3 | + 4·50 | S. 7·9 + 12·00 |
| 3·5 | + 8·00 | 9·11 + 12·50 |
| 5·7 | + 10·50 | |

Bottom flange:

| | | |
|---|---|---|
| S. 2·4 | − 0·00 | S. 8·10 − 10·50 |
| 4·6 | − 4·50 | 10·12 − 12·00 |
| 6·8 | − 8·00 | |

Vertical bracing all struts under dead load:

| | | |
|---|---|---|
| S. 1·2 | + 5·00 | S. 7·8 + 2·50 |
| 3·4 | + 4·50 | 9·10 + 1·50 |
| 5·6 | + 3·50 | 11·12 + 1·00 |

Diagonal bracing all ties under dead load:

| | | |
|---|---|---|
| S. 1·4 | − 6·34 | S. 7·10 − 2·11 |
| 3·6 | − 4·93 | 9·12 − 0·70 |
| 5·8 | − 3·52 | |

EVENLY DISTRIBUTED LIVE LOAD ADVANCING FROM EITHER ABUTMENT.

*Maximum Stress Constants.*

Top flange:

| | | | | | |
|---|---|---|---|---|---|
| S. 1·3 | + | 4·50 | S. 7·9 | + | 12·00 |
| 3·5 | + | 8·00 | 9·11 | + | 12·50 |
| 5·7 | + | 10·50 | | | |

Bottom flange:

| | | | | | |
|---|---|---|---|---|---|
| S. 2·4 | − | 0·00 | S. 8·10 | − | 10·50 |
| 4·6 | − | 4·50 | 10·12 | − | 12·00 |
| 6·8 | − | 8·00 | | | |

Vertical bracing:

| | | | | | |
|---|---|---|---|---|---|
| S. 1·2 | + | 5·00 | 7·8 | + | 2·80 |
| 1·2 | − | 0·00 | 7·8 | − | 0·30 |
| 3·4 | + | 4·50 | 9·10 | + | 2·10 |
| 3·4 | − | 0·00 | 9·10 | − | 0·60 |
| 5·6 | + | 3·60 | 11·12 | + | 1·00 |
| 5·6 | − | 0·10 | 11·12 | − | 0·00 |

Diagonal bracing:

| | | | | | |
|---|---|---|---|---|---|
| S. 1·4 | + | 0·00 | S. 5·8 | − | 3·94 |
| 1·4 | − | 6·34 | 7·10 | + | 0·85 |
| 3·6 | + | 0·14 | 7·10 | − | 2·96 |
| 3·6 | − | 5·07 | 9·12 | + | 1·41 |
| 5·8 | + | 0·42 | 9·12 | − | 2·11 |

*Note.*—If the truss is supported at the points 2·2 the parts 2·4 would practically be made of the same strength as 4·6, but if supported at the points 1·1 the parts 1·2 and 2·4 are not necessary.

PLATE 4

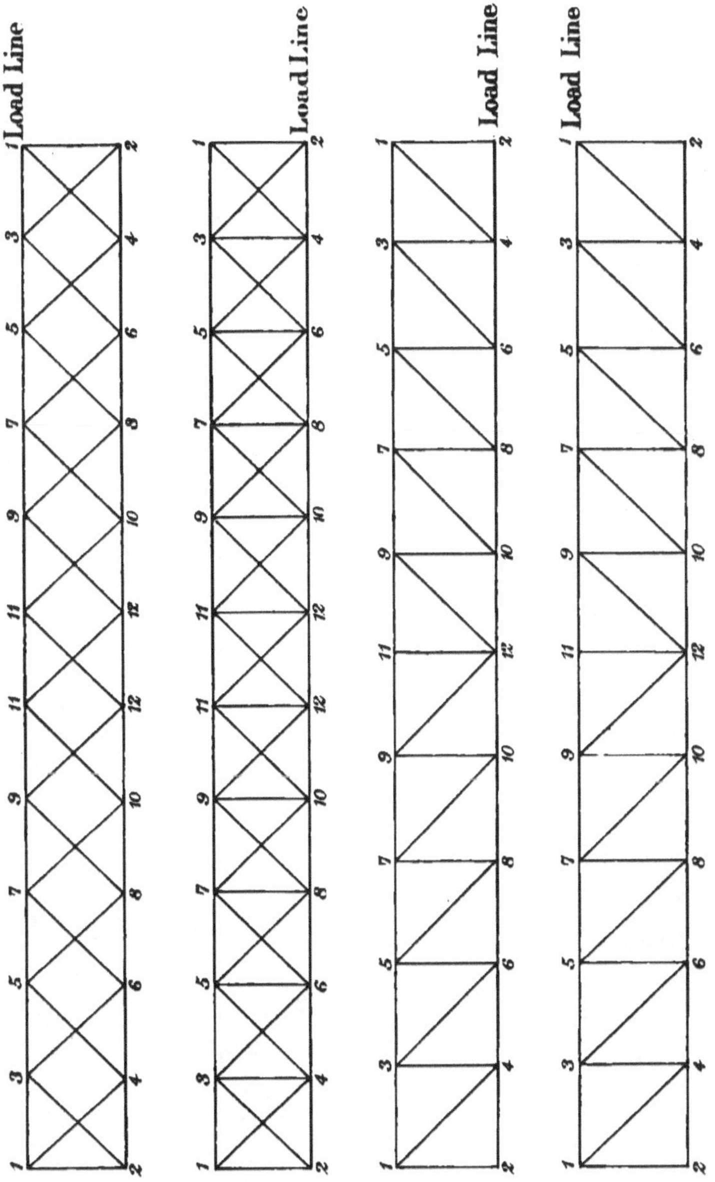


Thos Kell & Son Lith

E & F N Spon, London & New York

## TRUSS DIAGRAM No. 17.

### LINVILLE.

### CONDITIONS.

1. Depth      ..   ..   ..   ..   $\frac{1}{10}$ of the span.
2. Number of panels  ..   ..   10.
3. Method of loading ..   ..   On bottom flange.
4. Description of bracing  ..   Verticals and diagonals, angle 45°.

### EVENLY DISTRIBUTED DEAD LOAD.

#### Stress Constants.

Top flange:

| | | | | |
|---|---|---|---|---|
| S. 1·3 | + | 0·00 | S. 7·9 | + 10·50 |
| 3·5 | + | 4·50 | 9·11 | + 12·00 |
| 5·7 | + | 8·00 | | |

Bottom flange:

| | | | | |
|---|---|---|---|---|
| S. 2·4 | − | 4·50 | S. 8·10 | − 12·00 |
| 4·6 | − | 8·00 | 10·12 | − 12·50 |
| 6·8 | − | 10·50 | | |

Vertical bracing all ties under dead load:

| | | | | |
|---|---|---|---|---|
| S. 1·2 | − | 0·00 | S. 7·8 | − 2·50 |
| 3·4 | − | 4·50 | 9·10 | − 1·50 |
| 5·6 | − | 3·50 | 11·12 | − 1·00 |

Diagonal bracing all struts under dead load:

| | | | | |
|---|---|---|---|---|
| S. 2·3 | + | 6·34 | S. 8·9 | + 2·11 |
| 4·5 | + | 4·93 | 10·11 | + 0·70 |
| 6·7 | + | 3·52 | | |

EVENLY DISTRIBUTED LIVE LOAD ADVANCING FROM
EITHER ABUTMENT.

*Maximum Stress Constants.*

Top flange:

| | | |
|---|---|---|
| S. 1·3 | + | 0·00 |
| 3·5 | + | 4·50 |
| 5·7 | + | 8·00 |

| | | |
|---|---|---|
| S. 7·9 | + | 10·50 |
| 9·11 | + | 12·00 |

Bottom flange:

| | | |
|---|---|---|
| S. 2·4 | — | 4·50 |
| 4·6 | — | 8·00 |
| 6·8 | — | 10·50 |

| | | |
|---|---|---|
| S. 8·10 | — | 12·00 |
| 10·12 | — | 12·50 |

Vertical bracing:

| | | |
|---|---|---|
| S. 1·2 | + | 0·00 |
| 1·2 | — | 0·00 |
| 3·4 | + | 0·00 |
| 3·4 | — | 4·50 |
| 5·6 | + | 0·10 |
| 5·6 | — | 3·60 |

| | | |
|---|---|---|
| S. 7·8 | + | 0·30 |
| 7·8 | — | 2·80 |
| 9·10 | + | 0·60 |
| 9·10 | — | 2·10 |
| 11·12 | + | 0·00 |
| 11·12 | — | 1·00 |

Diagonal bracing:

| | | |
|---|---|---|
| S. 2·3 | + | 6·34 |
| 2·3 | — | 0·00 |
| 4·5 | + | 5·07 |
| 4·5 | — | 0·14 |
| 6·7 | + | 3·94 |

| | | |
|---|---|---|
| S. 6·7 | — | 0·42 |
| 8·9 | + | 2·95 |
| 8·9 | — | 0·84 |
| 10·11 | + | 2·11 |
| 10·11 | — | 1·41 |

*Note.*—The parts 1·2 and 1·3 are not necessary to stability.

## TRUSS DIAGRAM No. 18.

### LINVILLE.

#### CONDITIONS.

1. Depth     .. .. .. ..   $\frac{1}{10}$ of the span.
2. Number of panels ..  .. 10.
3. Method of loading ..  .. On top flange.
4. Description of bracing .. Verticals and diagonals, angle 45°.

### EVENLY DISTRIBUTED DEAD LOAD.

#### *Stress Constants.*

Top flange:

| | | |
|---|---|---|
| S. 1·3 | + | 0·00 |
| 3·5 | + | 4·50 |
| 5·7 | + | 8·00 |

| | | |
|---|---|---|
| S. 7·9 | + | 10·50 |
| 9·11 | + | 12·00 |

Bottom flange:

| | | |
|---|---|---|
| S. 2·4 | − | 4·50 |
| 4·6 | − | 8·00 |
| 6·8 | − | 10·50 |

| | | |
|---|---|---|
| S. 8·10 | − | 12·00 |
| 10·12 | − | 12·50 |

Vertical bracing all ties under dead load except 1·2:

| | | |
|---|---|---|
| S. 1·2 | + | 0·50 |
| 3·4 | − | 3·50 |
| 5·6 | − | 2·50 |

| | | |
|---|---|---|
| S. 7·8 | − | 1·50 |
| 9·10 | − | 0·50 |
| 11·12 | − | 0·00 |

Diagonal bracing all struts under dead load:

| | | |
|---|---|---|
| S. 2·3 | + | 6·34 |
| 4·5 | + | 4·93 |
| 6·7 | + | 3·52 |

| | | |
|---|---|---|
| S. 8·9 | + | 2·11 |
| 10·11 | + | 0·70 |

## Evenly distributed Live Load advancing from either Abutment.

### *Maximum Stress Constants.*

Top flange:

| | | |
|---|---|---|
| S. 1·3 | + | 0·00 |
| 3·5 | + | 4·50 |
| 5·7 | + | 8·00 |

| | | |
|---|---|---|
| S. 7·9 | + | 10·50 |
| 9·11 | + | 12·00 |

Bottom flange:

| | | |
|---|---|---|
| S. 2·4 | — | 4·50 |
| 4·6 | — | 8·00 |
| 6·8 | — | 10·50 |

| | | |
|---|---|---|
| S. 8·10 | — | 12·00 |
| 10·12 | — | 12·50 |

Vertical bracing:

| | | |
|---|---|---|
| S. 1·2 | + | 0·500 |
| 1·2 | — | 0·000 |
| 3·4 | + | 0·100 |
| 3·4 | — | 3·600 |
| 5·6 | + | 0·300 |
| 5·6 | — | 2·800 |

| | | |
|---|---|---|
| S. 7·8 | + | 0·600 |
| 7·8 | — | 2·100 |
| 9·10 | + | 1·000 |
| 9·10 | — | 1·500 |
| 11·12 | + | 0·000 |
| 11·12 | — | 0·000 |

Diagonal bracing:

| | | |
|---|---|---|
| S. 2·3 | + | 6·340 |
| 2·3 | — | 0·000 |
| 4·5 | + | 5·070 |
| 4·5 | — | 0·140 |
| 6·7 | + | 3·940 |

| | | |
|---|---|---|
| S. 6·7 | — | 0·420 |
| 8·9 | + | 2·950 |
| 8·9 | — | 0·840 |
| 10·11 | + | 2·110 |
| 10·11 | — | 1·410 |

*Note.*—The parts 1·3 would practically be made of the same strength as 3·5, and 11·12 the same as 9·10. The parts 1·2 require particularly to be considered for axle loads.

## TRUSS DIAGRAM No. 19.

### LATTICE.

#### CONDITIONS.

1. Depth .. .. .. .. .. $\frac{1}{10}$ of the span.
2. Number of panels .. .. 10.
3. Method of loading .. .. On bottom flange.
4. Description of bracing .. Crossed diagonals, angle 45°.

### EVENLY DISTRIBUTED DEAD LOAD.

*Stress Constants.*

Top flange:

| S. 1·3 | + | 2·50 | | S. 7·9 | + | 11·50 |
| 3·5 | + | 6·50 | | 9·11 | + | 12·50 |
| 5·7 | + | 9·50 | | | | |

Bottom flange:

| S. 2·4 | − | 2·00 | | S. 8·10 | − | 11·00 |
| 4·6 | − | 6·00 | | 10·12 | − | 12·00 |
| 6·8 | − | 9·00 | | | | |

Diagonal bracing all struts under dead load:

| S. 2·3 | + | 2·83 | | S. 8·9 | + | 0·70 |
| 4·5 | + | 2·12 | | 10·11 | + | 0·00 |
| 6·7 | + | 1·41 | | | | |

Diagonal bracing all ties under dead load:

| S. 1·4 | − | 3·53 | | S. 7·10 | − | 1·41 |
| 3·6 | − | 2·83 | | 9·12 | − | 0·70 |
| 5·8 | − | 2·12 | | | | |

End verticals:

| S. 1·2 | .. | .. | .. | + | 2·50 |

EVENLY DISTRIBUTED LIVE LOAD ADVANCING FROM
EITHER ABUTMENT.

*Maximum Stress Constants.*

Top flange:

| | | |
|---|---|---|
| S. 1·3 | + | 2·50 |
| 3·5 | + | 6·50 |
| 5·7 | + | 9·50 |

| | | |
|---|---|---|
| S. 7·9 | + | 11·50 |
| 9·11 | + | 12·50 |

Bottom flange:

| | | |
|---|---|---|
| S. 2·4 | − | 2·00 |
| 4·6 | − | 6·00 |
| 6·8 | − | 9·00 |

| | | |
|---|---|---|
| S. 8·10 | − | 11·00 |
| 10·12 | − | 12·00 |

Diagonal bracing:

| | | |
|---|---|---|
| S. 2·3 | + | 2·830 |
| 2·3 | − | 0·000 |
| 4·5 | + | 2·260 |
| 4·5 | − | 0·140 |
| 6·7 | + | 1·690 |
| 6·7 | − | 0·280 |
| 8·9 | + | 1·270 |
| 8·9 | − | 0·570 |
| 10·11 | + | 0·840 |
| 10·11 | − | 0·840 |

| | | |
|---|---|---|
| S. 1·4 | + | 0·000 |
| 1·4 | − | 3·530 |
| 3·6 | + | 0·000 |
| 3·6 | − | 2·830 |
| 5·8 | + | 0·140 |
| 5·8 | − | 2·260 |
| 7·10 | + | 0·280 |
| 7·10 | − | 1·690 |
| 9·12 | + | 0·570 |
| 9·12 | − | 1·270 |

End verticals:

| | | | | | |
|---|---|---|---|---|---|
| S. 1·2 | .. | .. | .. | + | 2·500 |
| 1·2 | .. | .. | .. | − | 0·000 |

# TRUSS DIAGRAM No. 20.

### LATTICE.

#### CONDITIONS.

1. Depth   ..   ..   ..   ..   $\frac{1}{10}$ of the span.
2. Number of panels   ..   ..   10.
3. Method of loading   ..   ..   On top flange.
4. Description of bracing   ..   Crossed diagonals, angle 45°.

### EVENLY DISTRIBUTED DEAD LOAD.

Top flange :     *Stress Constants.*

   S. 1·3   +   2·00    S. 7·9   +   11·00
    3·5   +   6·00     9·11   +   12·00
    5·7   +   9·00

Bottom flange :

   S. 2·4   −   2·50    S. 8·10   −   11·50
    4·6   −   6·50     10·12   −   12·50
    6·8   −   9·50

Diagonal bracing all struts under dead load :

   S. 2·3   +   3·53 ·    S. 8·9   +   1·41
    4·5   +   2·83     10·11   +   0·70
    6·7   +   2·12

Diagonal bracing all ties under dead load :

   S. 1·4   −   2·83    S. 7·10   −   0·70
    3·6   −   2·12     9·12   −   0·00
    5·8   −   1·41

End verticals :

   S. 1·2    ..    ..    ..   +   2·50

EVENLY DISTRIBUTED LIVE LOAD ADVANCING FROM
EITHER ABUTMENT.

*Maximum Stress Constants.*

Top flange:

|  |  |  |  |  |  |
|---|---|---|---|---|---|
| S. 1·3 | + | 2·00 | S. 7·9 | + | 11·00 |
| 3·5 | + | 6·00 | 9·11 | + | 12·00 |
| 5·7 | + | 9·00 |  |  |  |

Bottom flange:

|  |  |  |  |  |  |
|---|---|---|---|---|---|
| S. 2·4 | − | 2·50 | S. 8·10 | − | 11·50 |
| 4·6 | − | 6·50 | 10·12 | − | 12·50 |
| 6·8 | − | 9·50 |  |  |  |

Diagonal bracing:

|  |  |  |  |  |  |
|---|---|---|---|---|---|
| S. 2·3 | + | 3·53 | S. 1·4 | + | 0·00 |
| 2·3 | − | 0·00 | 1·4 | − | 2·83 |
| 4·5 | + | 2·83 | 3·6 | + | 0·14 |
| 4·5 | − | 0·00 | 3·6 | − | 2·26 |
| 6·7 | + | 2·26. | 5·8 | + | 0·28 |
| 6·7 | − | 0·14 | 5·8 | − | 1·69 |
| 8·9 | + | 1·69 | 7·10 | + | 0·57 |
| 8·9 | − | 0·28 | 7·10 | − | 1·27 |
| 10·11 | + | 1·27 | 9·12 | + | 0·85 |
| 10·11 | − | 0·57 | 9·12 | − | 0·85 |

End verticals:

|  |  |  |  |  |  |
|---|---|---|---|---|---|
| S. 1·2 | .. | .. | .. | + | 2·50 |
| 1·2 | .. | .. | .. | − | 0·00 |

PLATE 5

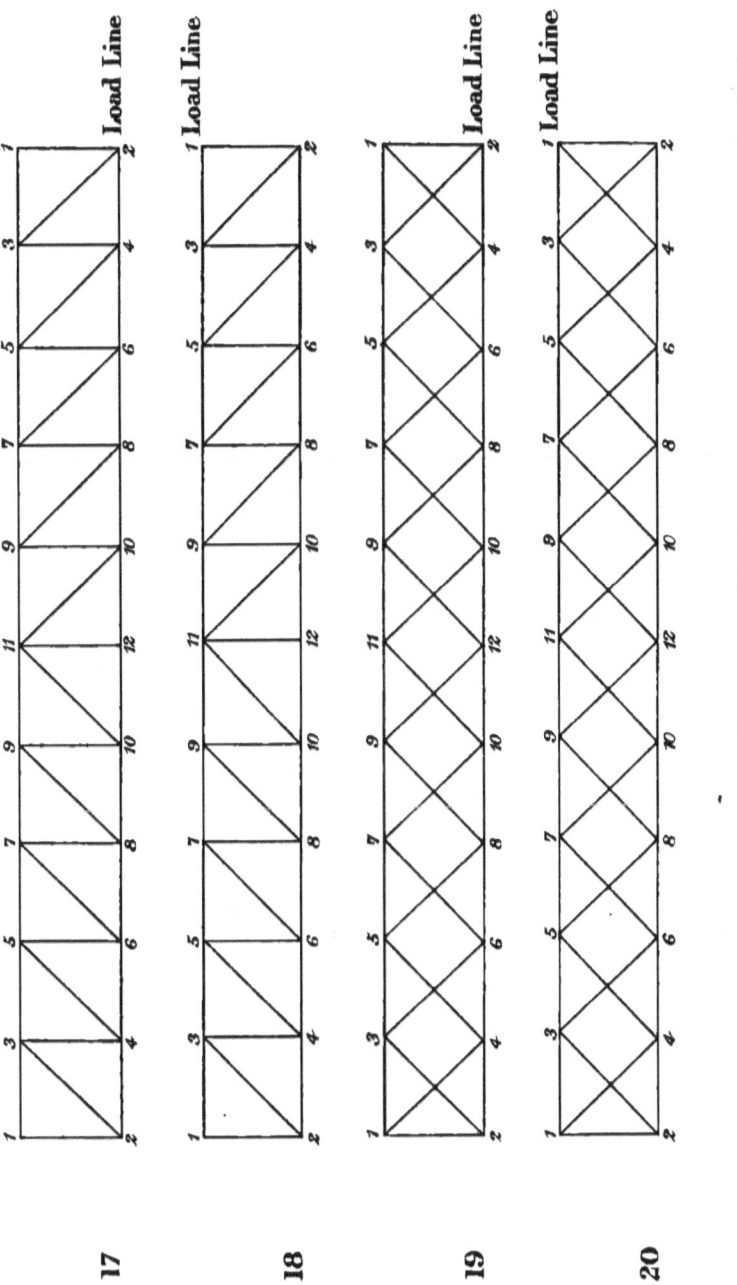

Tho.ª Kell & Son Lith

E & F N Spon, London & New York

# TRUSS DIAGRAM No. 21.

## LATTICE.

### CONDITIONS.

1. Depth .. .. .. .. $\frac{1}{10}$ of the span.
2. Number of panels .. .. 10.
3. Method of loading .. On bottom flange.
4. Description of bracing .. Verticals and crossed diagonals. angle 45°.

### EVENLY DISTRIBUTED DEAD LOAD.

#### *Stress Constants.*

Top flange:

    S. 1·3  +  2·25          S. 7·9  +  11·25

    3·5  +  6·25            9·11  +  12·25

    5·7  +  9·25

Bottom flange:

    S. 2·4  −  2·25          S. 8·10 − 11·25

    4·6  −  6·25           10·12 − 12·25

    6·8  −  9·25

Diagonal bracing struts under dead load:

    S. 2·3  +  3·17          S. 8·9  +  1·06

    4·5  +  2·47           10·11  +  0·35

    6·7  +,  1·76

Diagonal bracing ties under dead load:

    S. 1·4  −  3·17          S. 7·10 − 1·06

    3·6  −  2·47           9·12 − 0·35

    5·8  −  1·76

E

Vertical bracing:

S. on all the verticals except 1·2  &minus;   0·50
S. 1·2      ..      ..      ..      +    2·25

*Note.*—With load top flange all stresses the same except vertical bracing.

Vertical bracing load on top flange:

S. on all the verticals except 1·2  +   0·50
S. 1·2      ..      ..      ..      +    2·50

### EVENLY DISTRIBUTED LIVE LOAD ADVANCING FROM EITHER ABUTMENT.

*Maximum Stress Constants.*

Top flange:

| | | | | | |
|---|---|---|---|---|---|
| S. 1·3 | + | 2·25 | S. 7·9 | + | 11·25 |
| 3·5 | + | 6·25 | 9·11 | + | 12·25 |
| 5·7 | + | 9·25 | | | |

Bottom flange:

| | | | | | |
|---|---|---|---|---|---|
| S. 2·4 | − | 2·25 | S. 8·10 | − | 11·25 |
| 4·6 | − | 6·25 | 10·12 | − | 12·25 |
| 6·8 | − | 9·25 | | | |

Diagonal bracing:

| | | | | | |
|---|---|---|---|---|---|
| S. 2·3 | + | 3·17 | S. 1·4 | + | 0·00 |
| 2·3 | − | 0·00 | 1·4 | − | 3·17 |
| 4·5 | + | 2·54 | 3·6 | + | 0·07 |
| 4·5 | − | 0·07 | 3·6 | − | 2·54 |
| 6·7 | + | 1·97 | 5·8 | + | 0·21 |
| 6·7 | − | 0·21 | 5·8 | − | 1·97 |
| 8·9 | + | 1·48 | 7·10 | + | 0·42 |
| 8·9 | − | 0·42 | 7·10 | − | 1·48 |
| 10·11 | + | 1·06 | 9·12 | + | 0·71 |
| 10·11 | − | 0·71 | 9·12 | − | 1·06 |

Vertical bracing:

S. on all the verticals except 1·2    —    0·50
S. 1·2        ..        ..        ..        +    2·25

*Note.*—With load top flange all stresses the same except vertical bracing.

Vertical bracing load on top flange:

S. on all the verticals except 1·2    +    0·50
S. 1·2        ..        ..        ..        +    2·50

*Note.*—The verticals are only supposed to distribute the load between the flanges.

---

## TRUSS DIAGRAM No. 22.

### MULTIPLE LATTICE.

#### CONDITIONS.

1. Depth.. .. .. .. .. $\frac{1}{10}$ of the span.
2. Number of panels .. .. 20.
3. Method of loading .. .. On bottom flange.
4. Description of bracing .. Multiple lattice, 45°.

#### EVENLY DISTRIBUTED DEAD LOAD.

*Stress Constants.*

Top flange:

| | | | | |
|---|---|---|---|---|
| S. 1·3 | + 2·50 | S. 11·13 | + 20·00 |
| 3·5 | + 7·00 | 13·15 | + 22·00 |
| 5·7 | + 11·00 | 15·17 | + 23·50 |
| 7·9 | + 14·50 | 17·19 | + 24·50 |
| 9·11 | + 17·50 | 19·21 | + 25·00 |

Bottom flange:

| | | | | |
|---|---|---|---|---|
| S. 2·4 | — 2·00 | S. 12·14 | — 19·50 |
| 4·6 | — 6·50 | 14·16 | — 21·50 |
| 6·8 | — 10·50 | 16·18 | — 23·00 |
| 8·10 | — 14·00 | 18·20 | — 24·00 |
| 10·12 | — 17·00 | 20·22 | — 24·50 |

Diagonal bracing struts under dead load except 20·19 :

| | | | | | |
|---|---|---|---|---|---|
| S. A·3 | + | 3·18 | S. 12·15 | + | 1·07 |
| 2·5 | + | 2·83 | 14·17 | + | 0·71 |
| 4·7 | + | 2·48 | 16·19 | + | 0·35 |
| 6·9 | + | 2·12 | 18·21 | + | 0·00 |
| 8·11 | + | 1·77 | 20·19 | − | 0·35 |
| 10·13 | + | 1·41 | | | |

Diagonal bracing ties under dead load :

| | | | | | |
|---|---|---|---|---|---|
| S. A·4 | − | 3·89 | S. 11·16 | − | 1·77 |
| 1·6 | − | 3·53 | 13·18 | − | 1·41 |
| 3·8 | − | 3·18 | 15·20 | − | 1·07 |
| 5·10 | − | 2·83 | 17·22 | − | 0·71 |
| 7·12 | − | 2·48 | 19·20 | − | 0·35 |
| 9·14 | − | 2·12 | | | |

End verticals :

| | | | | | |
|---|---|---|---|---|---|
| S. 1·A | .. | .. | .. | + | 2·50 |
| A·2 | .. | .. | .. | + | 7·50 |

Transverse stress at A inwards ..　　..　0·50

Remaining verticals :

These are merely stiffeners.

### Evenly distributed Live Load advancing from either Abutment.

*Maximum Stress Constants.*

Top flange :

| | | | | | |
|---|---|---|---|---|---|
| S. 1·3 | + | 2·50 | S. 11·13 | + | 20·00 |
| 3·5 | + | 7·00 | 13·15 | + | 22·00 |
| 5·7 | + | 11·00 | 15·17 | + | 23·50 |
| 7·9 | + | 14·50 | 17·19 | + | 24·50 |
| 9·11 | + | 17·50 | 19·21 | + | 25·00 |

Bottom flange:

| | | | | | |
|---|---|---|---|---|---|
| S. 2·4 | − | 2·00 | S. 12·14 | − | 19·50 |
| 4·6 | − | 6·50 | 14·16 | − | 21·50 |
| 6·8 | − | 10·50 | 16·18 | − | 23·00 |
| 8·10 | − | 14·00 | 18·20 | − | 24·00 |
| 10·12 | − | 17·00 | 20·22 | − | 24·50 |

Diagonal bracing:

| | | | | | |
|---|---|---|---|---|---|
| S. A·3 | + | 3·18 | A·4 | + | 0·00 |
| A·3 | − | 0·00 | A·4 | − | 3·89 |
| 2·5 | + | 2·83 | 1·6 | + | 0·00 |
| 2·5 | − | 0·00 | 1·6 | − | 3·53 |
| 4·7 | + | 2·54 | 3·8 | + | 0·00 |
| 4·7 | − | 0·06 | 3·8 | − | 3·18 |
| 6·9 | + | 2·26 | 5·10 | + | 0·00 |
| 6·9 | − | 0·14 | 5·10 | − | 2·83 |
| 8·11 | + | 1·98 | 7·12 | + | 0·06 |
| 8·11 | − | 0·21 | 7·12 | − | 2·54 |
| 10·13 | + | 1·69 | 9·14 | + | 0·14 |
| 10·13 | − | 0·28 | 9·14 | − | 2·26 |
| 12·15 | + | 1·48 | 11·16 | + | 0·21 |
| 12·15 | − | 0·41 | 11·16 | − | 1·98 |
| 14·17 | + | 1·27 | 13·18 | + | 0·28 |
| 14·17 | − | 0·56 | 13·18 | − | 1·69 |
| 16·19 | + | 1·05 | 15·20 | + | 0·41 |
| 16·19 | − | 0·70 | 15·20 | − | 1·48 |
| 18·21 | + | 0·85 | 17·22 | + | 0·56 |
| 18·21 | − | 0·85 | 17·22 | − | 1·27 |
| 20·19 | + | 0·71 | 19·20 | + | 0·70 |
| 20·19 | − | 1·06 | 19·20 | − | 1·05 |

End verticals:

| | | | | | |
|---|---|---|---|---|---|
| S. 1·A | + | 2·50 | S. A·2 | + | 7·50 |
| 1·A | − | 0·00 | A·2 | − | 0·00 |

Transverse stress at A inwards ..     ..     0·50

Remaining verticals:

These are merely stiffeners.

# TRUSS DIAGRAM No. 23.

### MULTIPLE LATTICE.

### CONDITIONS.

1. Depth .. .. .. .. $\frac{1}{10}$ of the span.
2. Number of panels .. .. 20.
3. Method of loading .. .. On top flange.
4. Description of bracing .. Multiple lattice, angle 45°.

### EVENLY DISTRIBUTED DEAD LOAD.

*Stress Constants.*

Top flange :

| | | |
|---|---|---|
| S. 1·3 + 2·00 | S. 11·13 + 19·50 |
| 3·5 + 6·50 | 13·15 + 21·50 |
| 5·7 + 10·50 | 15·17 + 23·00 |
| 7·9 + 14·00 | 17·19 + 24·00 |
| 9·11 + 17·00 | 19·21 + 24·50 |

Bottom flange :

| | |
|---|---|
| S. 2·4 − 2·50 | S. 12·14 − 20·00 |
| 4·6 − 7·00 | 14·16 − 22·00 |
| 6·8 − 11·00 | 16·18 − 23·50 |
| 8·10 − 14·50 | 18·20 − 24·50 |
| 10·12 − 17·50 | 20·22 − 25·00 |

Diagonal bracing struts under dead load :

| | |
|---|---|
| S. A·3 + 3·89 | S. 12·15 + 1·77 |
| 2·5 + 3·53 | 14·17 + 1·41 |
| 4·7 + 3·18 | 16·19 + 1·07 |
| 6·9 + 2·83 | 18·21 + 0·71 |
| 8·11 + 2·48 | 20·19 + 0·35 |
| 10·13 + 2·12 | |

Diagonal bracing ties under dead load except 19·20:

| S. A·4 | − | 3·18 | S. 11·16 | − | 1·07 |
|---|---|---|---|---|---|
| 1·6 | − | 2·83 | 13·18 | − | 0·71 |
| 3·8 | − | 2·48 | 15·20 | − | 0·35 |
| 5·10 | − | 2·12 | 17·22 | − | 0·00 |
| 7·12 | − | 1·77 | 19·20 | + | 0·35 |
| 9·14 | − | 1·41 | | | |

End verticals:

| S. 1·A | .. | .. | .. | + | 2·50 |
|---|---|---|---|---|---|
| A·2 | .. | .. | .. | + | 7·50 |

Transverse stress at A outwards    ..   0·50

Remaining verticals:

These are merely stiffeners.

EVENLY DISTRIBUTED LIVE LOAD ADVANCING FROM EITHER ABUTMENT.

*Maximum Stress Constants.*

Top flange:

| S. 1·3 | + | 2·00 | S. 11·13 | + | 19·50 |
|---|---|---|---|---|---|
| 3·5 | + | 6·50 | 13·15 | + | 21·50 |
| 5·7 | + | 10·50 | 15·17 | + | 23·00 |
| 7·9 | + | 14·00 | 17·19 | + | 24·00 |
| 9·11 | + | 17·00 | 19·21 | + | 24·50 |

Bottom flange:

| S. 2·4 | − | 2·50 | S. 12·14 | − | 20·00 |
|---|---|---|---|---|---|
| 4·6 | − | 7·00 | 14·16 | − | 22·00 |
| 6·8 | − | 11·00 | 16·18 | − | 23·50 |
| 8·10 | − | 14·50 | 18·20 | − | 24·50 |
| 10·12 | − | 17·50 | 20·22 | − | 25·00 |

Diagonal bracing:

| | | | | | | |
|---|---|---|---|---|---|---|
| S. A·3 | + | 3·89 | S. A·4 | + | 0·00 |
| A·3 | − | 0·00 | A·4 | − | 3·18 |
| 2·5 | + | 3·53 | 1·6 | + | 0·00 |
| 2·5 | − | 0·00 | 1·6 | − | 2·83 |
| 4·7 | + | 3·18 | 3·8 | + | 0·06 |
| 4·7 | − | 0·00 | 3·8 | − | 2·54 |
| 6·9 | + | 2·83 | 5·10 | + | 0·14 |
| 6·9 | − | 0·00 | 5·10 | − | 2·26 |
| 8·11 | + | 2·54 | 7·12 | + | 0·21 |
| 8·11 | − | 0·06 | 7·12 | − | 1·98 |
| 10·13 | + | 2·26 | 9·14 | + | 0·28 |
| 10·13 | − | 0·14 | 9·14 | − | 1·69 |
| 12·15 | + | 1·98 | 11·16 | + | 0·41 |
| 12·15 | − | 0·21 | 11·16 | − | 1·48 |
| 14·17 | + | 1·69 | 13·18 | + | 0·56 |
| 14·17 | − | 0·28 | 13·18 | − | 1·27 |
| 16·19 | + | 1·48 | 15·20 | + | 0·71 |
| 16·19 | − | 0·41 | 15·20 | − | 1·06 |
| 18·21 | + | 1·27 | 17·22 | + | 0·85 |
| 18·21 | − | 0·56 | 17·22 | − | 0·85 |
| 20·19 | + | 1·06 | 19·20 | + | 1·05 |
| 20·19 | − | 0·71 | 19·20 | − | 0·70 |

End verticals:

| | | | | | | |
|---|---|---|---|---|---|---|
| S. 1·A | + | 2·50 | S. A·2 | + | 7·50 |
| 1·A | − | 0·50 | A·2 | − | 0·00 |

Transverse stress at A outwards　　..　0·50

Remaining verticals:

These are merely stiffeners.

# TRUSS DIAGRAM No. 24.

## INVERTED LINVILLE.

### CONDITIONS.

1. Depth .. .. .. .. $\frac{1}{10}$ of the span.
2. Number of panels .. .. 5.
3. Method of loading .. .. On top flange.
4. Description of bracing .. Vertical and inclined, angle 63° 26'.

## EVENLY DISTRIBUTED DEAD LOAD.

### *Stress Constants.*

Top flange:

| | | | | |
|---|---|---|---|---|
| S. 1·3 | .. | .. | .. | + 4·000 |
| 3·5 | .. | .. | .. | + 6·000 |
| 5·5 | .. | .. | .. | + 6·000 |

Bottom flange:

| | | | | |
|---|---|---|---|---|
| S. 1·2 | .. | .. | .. | − 4·472 |
| 2·4 | .. | .. | .. | − 4·000 |
| 4·4 | .. | .. | .. | − 6·000 |

Vertical bracing:

| | | | | |
|---|---|---|---|---|
| S. 2·3 | .. | .. | .. | + 2·000 |
| 4·5 | .. | .. | ... | + 1·000 |

Inclined bracing:

| | | | | |
|---|---|---|---|---|
| S. 3·4 | .. | .. | .. | − 2·236 |
| 5·4 | .. | .. | .. | − 0·000 |

## EVENLY DISTRIBUTED LIVE LOAD ADVANCING FROM EITHER ABUTMENT.

### *Maximum Stress Constants.*

Top flange:

| | | | | |
|---|---|---|---|---|
| S. 1·3 | .. | .. | .. | + 4·000 |
| 3·5 | .. | .. | .. | + 6·000 |
| 5·5 | .. | .. | .. | + 6·000 |

Bottom flange:

| | | | | |
|---|---|---|---|---|
| S. 1·2 | .. | .. | .. | − 4·472 |
| 2·4 | .. | .. | .. | − 4·000 |
| 4·4 | .. | .. | .. | − 6·000 |

Vertical bracing:

| | | | | |
|---|---|---|---|---|
| S. 2·3 | + 2·000 | S. 4·5 | + 1·200 |
| 2·3 | − 0·000 | 4·5 | − 0·200 |

Inclined bracing:

| | | | | |
|---|---|---|---|---|
| S. 3·4 | + 0·447 | S. 5·4 | + 1·341 |
| 3·4 | − 2·683 | 5·4 | − 1·341 |

*Note.*—In this type of truss it is usual to make the diagonals capable of sustaining tension only, and in that case, with a moving load, another diagonal would be required in the centre panel to relieve 5·4 of compression and possibly other diagonals in the side panels; but this would depend upon the relative values of the dead and live loads.

If this truss is turned upside down the stresses remain the same, but the signs + and − are reversed.

PLATE 6

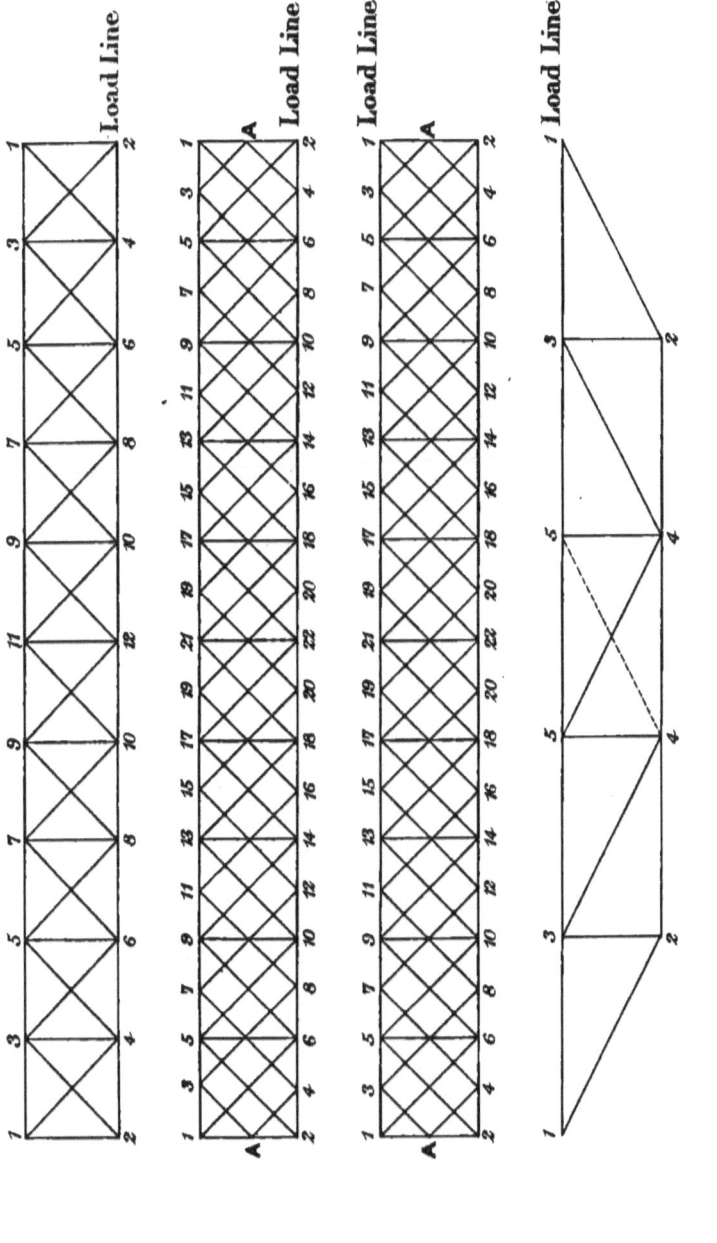

Tho⁵ Kell & Son Lich

E & F N Spon, London: & New York

## TRUSS DIAGRAM No. 25.

### INVERTED LINVILLE.

#### CONDITIONS.

1. Depth  .. .. .. ..  $\frac{1}{10}$ of the span.
2. Number of panels .. ..  6.
3. Method of loading .. ..  On top flange.
4. Description of bracing ..  Vertical, and inclined angle 59° 2′.

### EVENLY DISTRIBUTED DEAD LOAD.

#### *Stress Constants.*

Top flange:

|  |  |  |  |  |  |
|---|---|---|---|---|---|
| S. 1·3 | .. | .. | .. | + | 4·165 |
| 3·5 | .. | .. | .. | + | 6·664 |
| 5·7 | .. | .. | .. | + | 7·500 |

Bottom flange:

|  |  |  |  |  |  |
|---|---|---|---|---|---|
| S. 1·2 | .. | .. | .. | − | 4·857 |
| 2·4 | .. | .. | .. | − | 4·165 |
| 4·6 | .. | .. | .. | − | 6·664 |

Vertical bracing:

|  |  |  |  |  |  |
|---|---|---|---|---|---|
| S. 2·3 | .. | .. | .. | + | 2·500 |
| 4·5 | .. | .. | .. | + | 1·500 |
| 6·7 | .. | .. | .. | + | 1·000 |

Inclined bracing:

|  |  |  |  |  |  |
|---|---|---|---|---|---|
| S. 3·4 | .. | .. | .. | − | 2·914 |
| 5·6 | .. | .. | .. | − | 0·971 |

## EVENLY DISTRIBUTED LIVE LOAD ADVANCING FROM EITHER ABUTMENT.

### Maximum Stress Constants.

Top flange :

| | | | | | |
|---|---|---|---|---|---|
| S. 1·3 | .. | .. | .. | + | 4·165 |
| 3·5 | .. | .. | .. | + | 6·664 |
| 5·7 | .. | .. | .. | + | 7·500 |

Bottom flange :

| | | | | | |
|---|---|---|---|---|---|
| S. 1·2 | .. | .. | .. | − | 4·857 |
| 2·4 | .. | .. | .. | − | 4·165 |
| 4·6 | .. | .. | .. | − | 6·664 |

Vertical bracing :

| | | | | | |
|---|---|---|---|---|---|
| S. 2·3 | + | 2·500 | S. 4·5 | − | 0·166 |
| 2·3 | − | 0·000 | 6·7 | + | 1·000 |
| 4·5 | + | 1·666 | 6·7 | − | 0·000 |

Inclined bracing :

| | | | | | |
|---|---|---|---|---|---|
| S. 3·4 | + | 0·322 | S. 5·6 | + | 0·971 |
| 3·4 | − | 3·237 | 5·6 | − | 1·943 |

*Note.*—In this type of truss it is usual to make the diagonals capable of sustaining tension only, and in that case with a moving load cross diagonals would be required in some of the panels, depending upon the relative values of the dead and live loads.

If this truss is turned upside down the stresses remain the same, but the signs + and − are reversed.

## TRUSS DIAGRAM No. 26.

### WARREN.

### CONDITIONS.

1. Depth.. .. .. .. .. Span × 0·0866.
2. Number of panels .. .. 10.
3. Method of loading .. .. On bottom flange.
4. Description of bracing .. Inclined, angle 30°.

### EVENLY DISTRIBUTED DEAD LOAD.

*Stress Constants.*

Top flange:

| S. 1·3 | + | 5·19 | S. 7·9 | + | 13·85 |
|---|---|---|---|---|---|
| 3·5 | + | 9·24 | 9·9 | + | 14·43 |
| 5·7 | + | 12·12 | | | |

Bottom flange:

| S. 2·4 | − | 2·60 | S. 8·10 | − | 12·99 |
|---|---|---|---|---|---|
| 4·6 | − | 7·22 | 10·12 | − | 14·14 |
| 6·8 | − | 10·68 | | | |

Inclined bracing struts under dead load:

| S. 1·2 | + | 5·19 | S. 7·8 | + | 1·73 |
|---|---|---|---|---|---|
| 3·4 | + | 4·04 | 9·10 | + | 0·57 |
| 5·6 | + | 2·88 | | | |

Inclined bracing ties under dead load:

| S. 1·4 | − | 5·19 | S. 7·10 | − | 1·73 |
|---|---|---|---|---|---|
| 3·6 | − | 4·04 | 9·12 | − | 0·57 |
| 5·8 | − | 2·88 | | | |

EVENLY DISTRIBUTED LIVE LOAD ADVANCING FROM
EITHER ABUTMENT.

*Maximum Stress Constants.*

Top flange:

| | | | | |
|---|---|---|---|---|
| S. 1·3. | + 5·19 | | S. 7·9 | + 13·85 |
| 3·5 | + 9·24 | | 9·9 | + 14·43 |
| 5·7 | + 12·12 | | | |

Bottom flange:

| | | | | |
|---|---|---|---|---|
| S. 2·4 | − 2·60 | | S. 8·10 | − 12·99 |
| 4·6 | − 7·22 | | 10·12 | − 14·14 |
| 6·8 | − 10·68 | | | |

Inclined bracing:

| | | | | |
|---|---|---|---|---|
| S. 1·2 | + 5·197 | | S. 1·4 | + 0·000 |
| 1·2 | − 0·000 | | 1·4 | − 5·197 |
| 3·4 | + 4·158 | | 3·6 | + 0·115 |
| 3·4 | − 0·115 | | 3·6 | − 4·158 |
| 5·6 | + 3·234 | | 5·8 | + 0·346 |
| 5·6 | − 0·346 | | 5·8 | − 3·234 |
| 7·8 | + 2·425 | | 7·10 | + 0·693 |
| 7·8 | − 0·693 | | 7·10 | − 2·425 |
| 9·10 | + 1·732 | | 9·12 | + 1·155 |
| 9·10 | − 1·155 | | 9·12 | − 1·732 |

## TRUSS DIAGRAM No. 27.

### WARREN.

#### CONDITIONS.

1. Depth.. .. .. .. .. Span × 0·0866.
2. Number of panels .. .. 10.
3. Method of loading .. .. On top flange.
4. Description of bracing .. Inclined angle, 30°.

### EVENLY DISTRIBUTED DEAD LOAD.

Top flange:          *Stress Constants.*

| | | | | | |
|---|---|---|---|---|---|
| S. 1·3 | + | 0·00 | S. 7·9 | + | 11·98 |
| 3·5 | + | 5·05 | 9·11 | + | 13·71 |
| 5·7 | + | 9·09 | 11·11 | + | 14·29 |

Bottom flange:

| | | | | | |
|---|---|---|---|---|---|
| S. 2·4 | − | 2·74 | S. 8·10 | − | 13·13 |
| 4·6 | − | 7·35 | 10·12 | − | 14·29 |
| 6·8 | − | 10·82 | | | |

Inclined bracing struts under dead load:

| | | | | | |
|---|---|---|---|---|---|
| S. 2·3 | + | 5·46 | S. 8·9 | + | 2·31 |
| 4·5 | + | 4·62 | 10·11 | + | 1·15 |
| 6·7 | + | 3·46 | | | |

Inclined bracing ties under dead load:

| | | | | | |
|---|---|---|---|---|---|
| S. 3·4 | − | 4·62 | S. 9·10 | − | 1·15 |
| 5·6 | − | 3·46 | 11·12 | − | 0·00 |
| 7·8 | − | 2·31 | | | |

End verticals:

| | | | | | |
|---|---|---|---|---|---|
| S. 1·2 | .. | .. | .. | + | 0·25 |

## Evenly distributed Live Load Advancing from either Abutment.

### Maximum Stress Constants.

Top flange :

| | | | | | |
|---|---|---|---|---|---|
| S. 1·3 | + | 0·00 | S. 7·9 | + | 11·98 |
| 3·5 | + | 5·05 | 9·11 | + | 13·71 |
| 5·7 | + | 9·09 | 11·11 | + | 14·29 |

Bottom flange :

| | | | | | |
|---|---|---|---|---|---|
| S. 2·4 | − | 2·74 | S. 8·10 | − | 13·13 |
| 4·6 | − | 7·35 | 10·12 | − | 14·29 |
| 6·8 | − | 10·82 | | | |

Inclined bracing :

| | | | | | |
|---|---|---|---|---|---|
| S. 2·3 | + | 5·460 | 3·4 | + | 0·046 |
| 2·3 | − | 0·000 | 3·4 | − | 4·666 |
| 4·5 | + | 4·666 | 5·6 | + | 0·219 |
| 4·5 | − | 0·046 | 5·6 | − | 3·682 |
| 6·7 | + | 3·682 | 7·8 | + | 0·508 |
| 6·7 | − | 0·219 | 7·8 | − | 2·818 |
| 8·9 | + | 2·818 | 9·10 | + | 0·912 |
| 8·9 | − | 0·508 | 9·10 | − | 2·067 |
| 10·11 | + | 2·067 | 11·12 | + | 1·432 |
| 10·11 | − | 0·912 | 11·12 | − | 1·432 |

End verticals :

| | | | | | |
|---|---|---|---|---|---|
| S. 1·2 | .. | .. | .. | + | 0·25 |
| 1·2 | .. | .. | .. | − | 0·00 |

*Note.*—The parts 1·3 would practically be made of the same strength as 3·5, and the parts 1·2 require particularly to be considered for axle loads.

## TRUSS DIAGRAM No. 28.

### WARREN.

#### CONDITIONS.

1. Depth　.. .. .. ..　Span × 0·0866.
2. Number of panels .. ..　10.
3. Method of loading .. ..　On bottom flange.
4. Description of bracing ..　Inclined angle 30°, and verticals.

#### EVENLY DISTRIBUTED DEAD LOAD.

##### *Stress Constants.*

Top flange:

| | | |
|---|---|---|
| S. 1·3 | + | 0·00 |
| 3·5 | + | 5·12 |
| 5·7 | + | 9·16 |

| | | |
|---|---|---|
| S. 7·9 | + | 12·04 |
| 9·11 | + | 13·77 |
| 11·11 | + | 14·35 |

Bottom flange:

| | | |
|---|---|---|
| S. 2·4 | − | 2·67 |
| 4·6 | − | 7·28 |
| 6·8 | − | 10·74 |

| | | |
|---|---|---|
| S. 8·10 | − | 13·05 |
| 10·12 | − | 14·21 |

Inclined bracing struts under dead load:

| | | |
|---|---|---|
| S. 2·3 | + | 5·34 |
| 4·5 | + | 4·33 |
| 6·7 | + | 3·17 |

| | | |
|---|---|---|
| S. 8·9 | + | 2·02 |
| 10·11 | + | 0·87 |

Inclined bracing ties under dead load:

| | | |
|---|---|---|
| S. 3·4 | − | 4·90 |
| 5·6 | − | 3·75 |
| 7·8 | − | 2·60 |

| | | |
|---|---|---|
| S. 9·10 | − | 1·44 |
| 11·12 | − | 0·29 |

F

End verticals :

     S. 1·2     ..     ..     ..     ..     0·000

Remaining verticals :

     S.    ..     ..     ..     ..     −   0·50

## EVENLY DISTRIBUTED LIVE LOAD ADVANCING FROM EITHER ABUTMENT.

### *Maximum Stress Constants.*

Top flange :

| | | | | | |
|---|---|---|---|---|---|
| S. 1·3 | + | 0·00 | S. 7·9 | + | 12·04 |
| 3·5 | + | 5·12 | 9·11 | + | 13·77 |
| 5·7 | + | 9·16 | 11·11 | + | 14·35 |

Bottom flange :

| | | | | | |
|---|---|---|---|---|---|
| S. 2·4 | − | 2·67 | S. 8·10 | − | 13·05 |
| 4·6 | − | 7·28 | 10·12 | − | 14·21 |
| 6·8 | − | 10·74 | | | |

Inclined bracing :

| | | | | | |
|---|---|---|---|---|---|
| S. 2·3 | + | 5·34 | S. 3·4 | + | 0·02 |
| 2·3 | − | 0·00 | 3·4 | − | 4·92 |
| 4·5 | + | 4·40 | 5·6 | + | 0·15 |
| 4·5 | − | 0·07 | 5·6 | − | 3·90 |
| 6·7 | + | 3·42 | 7·8 | + | 0·37 |
| 6·7 | − | 0·25 | 7·8 | − | 2·97 |
| 8·9 | + | 2·54 | 9·10 | + | 0·70 |
| 8·9 | − | 0·52 | 9·10 | − | 2·14 |
| 10·11 | + | 1·77 | 11·12 | + | 1·12 |
| 10·11 | − | 0·90 | 11·12 | − | 1·41 |

End verticals:

| S. 1·2 | .. | .. | .. | | 0·000 |
|---|---|---|---|---|---|
| 1·2 | .. | .. | .. | — | 0·000 |

Remaining verticals:

| S. | .. | .. | .. | .. | + | 0·00 |
|---|---|---|---|---|---|---|
| S. | .. | .. | .. | .. | — | 0·50 |

*Note.*—With load on top flange the verticals would occupy the position of the dotted lines. They are merely supposed to distribute the load between the flanges. With load on top flange the stresses in the verticals would be S. 1·2 = + 0·125 and in remaining verticals S = + 0·50. With load bottom flange the parts 1·2 and 1·3 are not required.

---

## TRUSS DIAGRAM No. 29.

### WARREN.

#### CONDITIONS.

1. Depth.. .. .. .. ..   Span × 0·1082.
2. Number of panels .. ..   8.
3. Method of loading .. ..   On bottom flange.
4. Description of bracing ..   Inclined, angle 30°.

#### EVENLY DISTRIBUTED DEAD LOAD.

*Stress Constants.*

Top flange:

| S. 1·3 | + | 4·04 | S. 5·7 | + | 8·66 |
|---|---|---|---|---|---|
| 3·5 | + | 6·93 | 7·7 | + | 9·24 |

Bottom flange:

| S. 2·4 | — | 2·02 | S. 6·8 | — | 7·80 |
|---|---|---|---|---|---|
| 4·6 | — | 5·48 | 8·10 | — | 8·95 |

F 2

Inclined bracing struts under dead load:

|  |  |  |  |  |  |
|---|---|---|---|---|---|
| S. 1·2 | + | 4·04 | S. 5·6 | + | 1·73 |
| 3·4 | + | 2·88 | 7·8 | + | 0·57 |

Inclined bracing ties under live load:

|  |  |  |  |  |  |
|---|---|---|---|---|---|
| S. 1·4 | − | 4·04 | S. 5·8 | − | 1·73 |
| 3·6 | − | 2·88 | 7·10 | − | 0·57 |

## EVENLY DISTRIBUTED LIVE LOAD ADVANCING FROM EITHER ABUTMENT.

### *Maximum Stress Constants.*

Top flange:

|  |  |  |  |  |  |
|---|---|---|---|---|---|
| S. 1.3 | + | 4·04 | S. 5·7 | + | 8·66 |
| 3·5 | + | 6·93 | 7·7 | + | 9·24 |

Bottom flange:

|  |  |  |  |  |  |
|---|---|---|---|---|---|
| S. 2·4 | − | 2·02 | S. 6·8 | − | 7·80 |
| 4·6 | − | 5·48 | 8·10 | − | 8·95 |

Inclined bracing:

|  |  |  |  |  |  |
|---|---|---|---|---|---|
| S. 1·2 | + | 4·04 | S. 1·4 | + | 0·00 |
| 1·2 | − | 0·00 | 1·4 | − | 4·04 |
| 3·4 | + | 3·02 | 3·6 | + | 0·14 |
| 3·4 | − | 0·14 | 3·6 | − | 3·02 |
| 5·6 | + | 2·16 | 5·8 | + | 0·43 |
| 5·6 | − | 0·43 | 5·8 | − | 2·16 |
| 7·8 | + | 1·44 | 7·10 | + | 0·87 |
| 7·8 | − | 0·87 | 7·10 | − | 1·44 |

PLATE 7

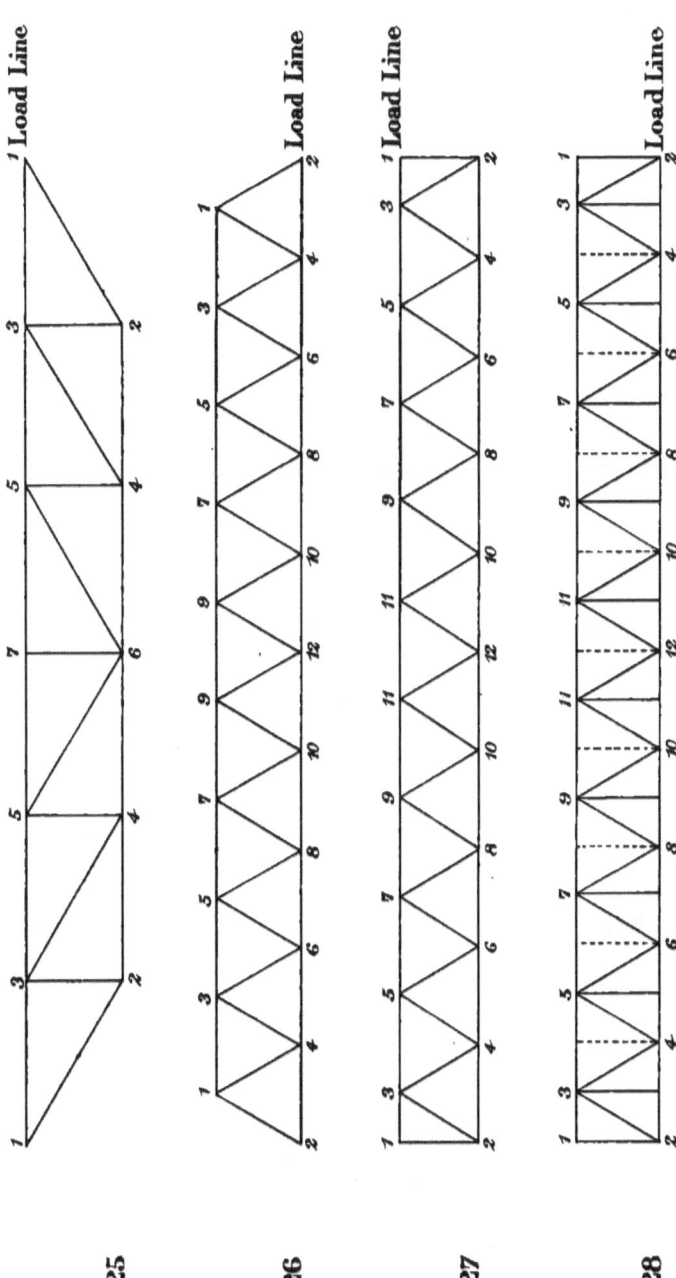

E & F N Spon, London & New York

Tho.ᵈ Kell & Son, Lith

# TRUSS DIAGRAM No. 30.

## WARREN.

### CONDITIONS.

1. Depth.. .. .. .. .. Span × 0·1082.
2. Number of panels .. .. 8.
3. Method of loading .. .. On top flange.
4. Description of bracing .. Inclined angle 30°.

## EVENLY DISTRIBUTED DEAD LOAD.

### *Stress Constants.*

Top flange:

| | | | | | |
|---|---|---|---|---|---|
| S. 1·3 | + | 0·00 | S. 7·9 | + | 8·52 |
| 3·5 | + | 3·89 | 9·9 | + | 9·09 |
| 5·7 | + | 6·78 | | | |

Bottom flange:

| | | | | | |
|---|---|---|---|---|---|
| S. 2·4 | — | 2·16 | S. 6·8 | — | 7·94 |
| 4·6 | — | 5·63 | 8·10 | — | 9·09 |

Inclined bracing struts under dead load:

| | | | | | |
|---|---|---|---|---|---|
| S. 2·3 | + | 4·31 | S. 6·7 | + | 2·31 |
| 4·5 | + | 3·46 | 8·9 | + | 1·15 |

Inclined bracing ties under dead load:

| | | | | | |
|---|---|---|---|---|---|
| S. 3·4 | — | 3·46 | S. 7·8 | — | 1·15 |
| 5·6 | — | 2·31 | 9·10 | — | 0·00 |

End verticals:

S. 1·2 .. .. .. + 0·25

EVENLY DISTRIBUTED LIVE LOAD ADVANCING FROM
EITHER ABUTMENT.

*Maximum Stress Constants.*

Top flange:

| | | |
|---|---|---|
| S. 1·3   +   0·00 | S. 7·9   +   8·52 |
| 3·5   +   3·89 | 9·9   +   9·09 |
| 5·7   +   6·78 | |

Bottom flange:

| | |
|---|---|
| S. 2·4   −   2·16 | S. 6·8   −   7·94 |
| 4·6   −   5·63 | 8·10   −   9·09 |

Inclined bracing:

| | |
|---|---|
| S. 2·3   +   4·31 | S. 3·4   +   0·04 |
| 2·3   −   0·00 | 3·4   −   3·50 |
| 4·5   +   3·50 | 5·6   +   0·27 |
| 4·5   −   0·04 | 5·6   −   2·58 |
| 6·7   +   2·58 | 7·8   +   0·63 |
| 6·7   −   0·27 | 7·8   −   1·78 |
| 8·9   +   1·78 | 9·10   +   1·14 |
| 8·9   −   0·63 | 9·10   −   1·14 |

End verticals:

| | |
|---|---|
| S. 1·2   ..   ..   ..   +   0·25 |
| 1·2   ..   ..   ..   −   0·00 |

*Note.*—The parts 1·3 would practically be made of
the same strength as 3·5 and the parts 1·2 require
particularly to be considered for axle loads.

# TRUSS DIAGRAM No. 31.

### WARREN.

#### CONDITIONS.

1. Depth .. .. .. .. Span × 0·1082.
2. Number of panels .. .. 8.
3. Method of loading .. .. On bottom flange.
4. Description of bracing .. Inclined angle 30°, and verticals.

### EVENLY DISTRIBUTED DEAD LOAD.

#### *Stress Constants.*

Top flange:

| | | | | | |
|---|---|---|---|---|---|
| S. 1·3 | + | 0·00 | S. 7·9 | + | 8·58 |
| 3·5 | + | 3·96 | 9·9 | + | 9·16 |
| 5·7 | + | 6·85 | | | |

Bottom flange:

| | | | | | |
|---|---|---|---|---|---|
| S. 2·4 | − | 2·09 | S. 6·8 | − | 7·86 |
| 4·6 | − | 5·55 | 8·10 | − | 9·01 |

Inclined bracing struts under dead load:

| | | | | | |
|---|---|---|---|---|---|
| S. 2·3 | + | 4·18 | S. 6·7 | + | 2·02 |
| 4·5 | + | 3·17 | 8·9 | + | 0·87 |

Inclined bracing ties under dead load:

| | | | | | |
|---|---|---|---|---|---|
| S. 3·4 | − | 3·75 | S. 7·8 | − | 1·44 |
| 5·6 | − | 2·60 | 9·10 | − | 0·29 |

End verticals:

S. 1·2 .. .. .. 0·00

Remaining verticals:

S.    ..     ..     ..     ..     —    0·50

## EVENLY DISTRIBUTED LIVE LOAD ADVANCING FROM EITHER ABUTMENT.

### *Maximum Stress Constants.*

Top flange:

| | | |
|---|---|---|
| S. 1·3 | + | 0·00 |
| 3·5 | + | 3·96 |
| 5·7 | + | 6·85 |

| | | |
|---|---|---|
| S. 7·9 | + | 8·58 |
| 9·9 | + | 9·16 |

Bottom flange:

| | | |
|---|---|---|
| S. 2·4 | — | 2·09 |
| 4·6 | — | 5·55 |

| | | |
|---|---|---|
| S. 6·8 | — | 7·86 |
| 8·10 | — | 9·01 |

Inclined bracing:

| | | |
|---|---|---|
| S. 2·3 | + | 4·18 |
| 2·3 | — | 0·00 |
| 4·5 | + | 3·27 |
| 4·5 | — | 0·10 |
| 6·7 | + | 2·37 |
| 6·7 | — | 0·35 |
| 8·9 | + | 1·61 |
| 8·9 | — | 0·74 |

| | | |
|---|---|---|
| S. 3·4 | + | 0·02 |
| 3·4 | — | 3·77 |
| 5·6 | + | 0·20 |
| 5·6 | — | 2·80 |
| 7·8 | + | 0·53 |
| 7·8 | — | 1·97 |
| 9·10 | + | 1·00 |
| 9·10 | — | 1·29 |

End verticals:

| | | | | | |
|---|---|---|---|---|---|
| S. 1·2 | .. | .. | .. | + | 0·00 |
| 1·2 | .. | .. | .. | — | 0·00 |

*Note.*—With load on top flange:

Remaining verticals:

S.    ..    ..    ..    ..    +   0·00
S.    ..    ..    ..    ..    −   0·50

*Note.*—With load on top flange the verticals would occupy the position of the dotted lines. They are merely supposed to distribute the load between the flanges. With load on top flange the stresses in the verticals would be S. 1·2 = + 0·125 and in remaining verticals S. + 0·50. With load bottom flange, the parts 1·2 and 1·3 are not required.

## TRUSS DIAGRAM No. 32.

### LINVILLE.

#### CONDITIONS.

1. Depth..   ..   ..   ..   ..   $\frac{1}{8}$ of the span.
2. Number of panels   ..   ..   9.
3. Method of loading   ..   ..   On bottom flange.
4. Description of bracing   ..   Vertical and inclined, angle
                   55° 18′.

### EVENLY DISTRIBUTED DEAD LOAD.

#### *Stress Constants.*

Top flange:

| S. 1·3 | + 5·77 | S. 7·9 | + 14·44 |
|---|---|---|---|
| 3·5 | + 10·11 | 9·9 | + 14·44 |
| 5·7 | + 13·00 | | |

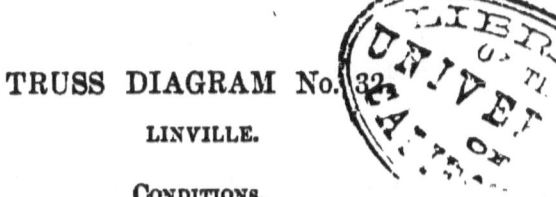

Bottom flange:

| | | | |
|---|---|---|---|
| S. 2·4 | — | 0·00 | S. 8·10 — 13·00 |
| 4·6 | — | 5·77 | 10·10 — 14·44 |
| 6·8 | — | 10·11 | |

Vertical bracing all struts under dead load:

| | | | | |
|---|---|---|---|---|
| S. 1·2 | .. | .. | .. | + 4·00 |
| 3·4 | .. | .. | .. | + 3·00 |
| 5·6 | .. | .. | .. | + 2·00 |
| 7·8 | .. | .. | .. | + 1·00 |
| 9·10 (vertical) | .. | .. | | + 0·00 |

Inclined bracing all ties under dead load:

| | | | | |
|---|---|---|---|---|
| S. 1·4 | .. | .. | .. | — 7·03 |
| 3·6 | .. | .. | .. | — 5·27 |
| 5·8 | .. | .. | .. | — 3·51 |
| 7·10 | .. | .. | .. | — 1·76 |
| 9·10 (diagonal) | .. | .. | | — 0·00 |

· EVENLY DISTRIBUTED LIVE LOAD ADVANCING FROM
EITHER ABUTMENT.

*Maximum Stress Constants.*

Top flange:

| | | | |
|---|---|---|---|
| S. 1·3 | + 5·77 | S. 7·9 | + 14·44 |
| 3·5 | + 10·11 | 9·9 | + 14·44 |
| 5·7 | + 13·00 | | |

Bottom flange:

| | | | |
|---|---|---|---|
| S. 2·4 | — | 0·00 | S. 8·10 — 13·00 |
| 4·6 | — | 5·77 | 10·10 — 14·44 |
| 6·8 | — | 10·11 | |

Vertical bracing :

| | | | | | |
|---|---|---|---|---|---|
| S. 1·2 | .. | .. | .. | + | 4·000 |
| 1·2 | .. | .. | .. | − | 0·000 |
| 3·4 | .. | .. | .. | + | 3·111 |
| 3·4 | .. | .. | .. | − | 0·111 |
| 5·6 | .. | .. | .. | + | 2·333 |
| 5·6 | .. | .. | .. | − | 0·333 |
| 7·8 | .. | .. | .. | + | 1·666 |
| 7·8 | .. | .. | .. | − | 0·666 |
| 9·10 (vertical) | .. | .. | + | 1·111 |
| 9·10 (vertical) | .. | .. | − | 1·111 |

Inclined bracing :

| | | | | | |
|---|---|---|---|---|---|
| S. 1·4 | .. | .. | .. | + | 0·000 |
| 1·4 | .. | .. | .. | − | 7·028 |
| 3·6 | .. | .. | .. | + | 0·195 |
| 3·6 | .. | .. | .. | − | 5·467 |
| 5·8 | .. | .. | .. | + | 0·579 |
| 5·8 | .. | .. | .. | − | 4·093· |
| 7·10 | .. | .. | .. | + | 1·159 |
| 7·10 | .. | .. | .. | − | 2·916 |
| 9·10 (diagonal) | .. | .. | + | 1·950 |
| 9·10 (diagonal) | .. | .. | − | 1·950 |

*Note.*—The parts 2·4 would practically be made of the same strength as 4·6.

## TRUSS DIAGRAM No. 33.

### LINVILLE.

#### CONDITIONS.

1. Depth..   ..   ..   ..   ..    $\frac{1}{8}$ of the span.
2. Number of panels   ..   ..    9.
3. Method of loading   ..   ..    On top flange.
4. Description of bracing   ..    Vertical and inclined, angle
                                      55° 18'.

### EVENLY DISTRIBUTED DEAD LOAD.

Top flange :       *Stress Constants.*

| S. 1·3 | + | 5·77 | S. 7·9 | + | 14·44 |
| 3·5 | + | 10·11 | 9·9 | + | 14·44 |
| 5·7 | + | 13·00 | | | |

Bottom flange :

| S. 2·4 | − | 0·00 | S. 8·10 | − | 13·00 |
| 4·6 | − | 5·77 | 10·10 | − | 14·44 |
| 6·8 | − | 10·11 | | | |

Vertical bracing all struts under dead load :

| S. 1·2 | .. | .. | ... | + | 4·50 |
| 3·4 | .. | .. | .. | + | 4·00 |
| 5·6 | .. | .. | .. | + | 3·00 |
| 7·8 | .. | .. | .. | + | 2·00 |
| 9·10 (vertical) | .. | .. | | + | 1·00 |

Inclined bracing all ties under dead load ·

| S. 1·4 | .. | .. | .. | − | 7·03 |
| 3·6 | .. | .. | .. | − | 5·27 |
| 5·8 | .. | .. | .. | − | 3·51 |
| 7·10 | .. | .. | .. | − | 1·76 |
| 9·10 (diagonal) | .. | .. | | − | 0·00 |

PLATE 8

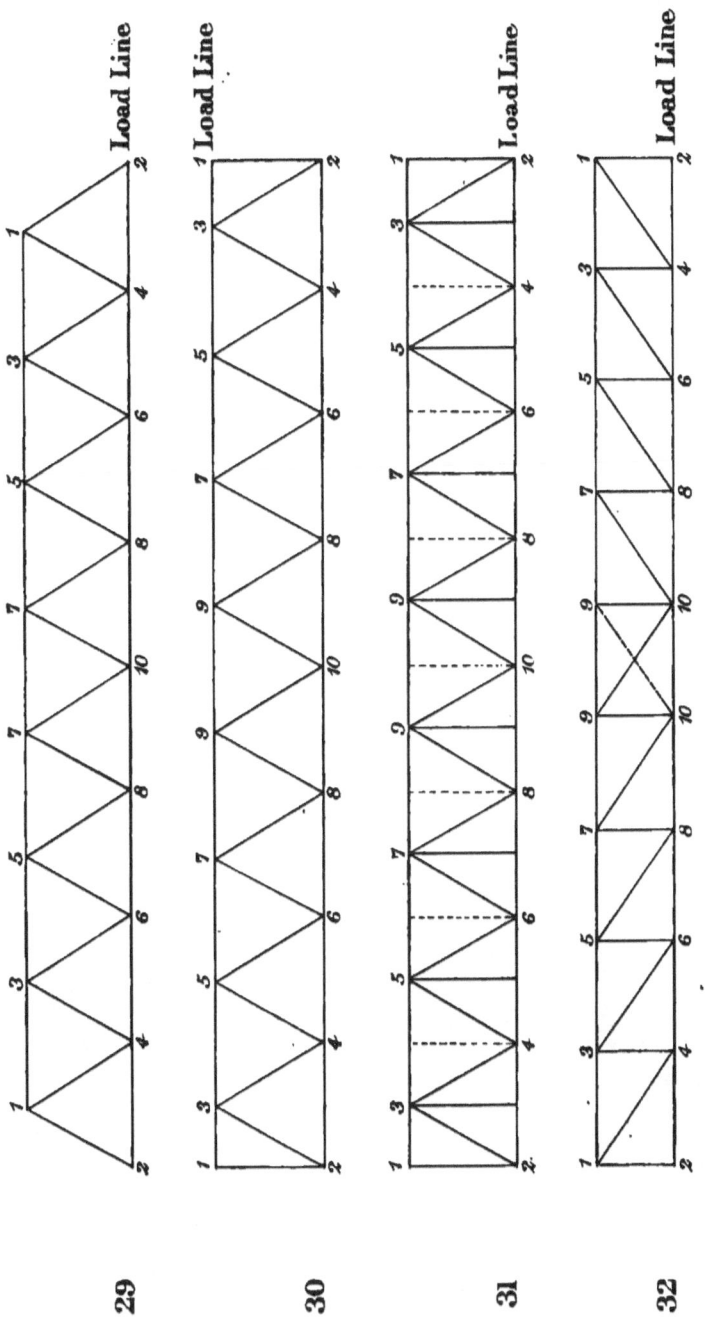

*Maximum Stress Constants.*

Top flange:

| | | | | |
|---|---|---|---|---|
| S. 1·3 | + 5·77 | | S. 7·9 | + 14·44 |
| 3·5 | + 10·11 | | 9·9 | + 14·44 |
| 5·7 | + 13·00 | | | |

Bottom flange:

| | | | | |
|---|---|---|---|---|
| S. 2·4 | − 0·00 | | S. 8·10 | − 13·00 |
| 4·6 | − 5·77 | | 10·10 | − 14·44 |
| 6·8 | − 10·11 | | | |

Vertical bracing:

| | | | | | |
|---|---|---|---|---|---|
| S. 1·2 | .. | .. | .. | + | 4·500 |
| 1·2 | .. | .. | .. | − | 0·000 |
| 3·4 | .. | .. | .. | + | 4·000 |
| 3·4 | .. | .. | .. | − | 0·000 |
| 5·6 | .. | .. | .. | + | 3·111 |
| 5·6 | .. | .. | .. | − | 0·111 |
| 7·8 | .. | .. | .. | + | 2·333 |
| 7·8 | .. | .. | .. | − | 0·333 |
| 9·10 (vertical) | .. | .. | + | 1·666 |
| 9·10 (vertical) | .. | .. | − | 0·666 |

Inclined bracing:

| | | | | | |
|---|---|---|---|---|---|
| S. 1·4 | .. | .. | .. | + | 0·000 |
| 1·4 | .. | .. | .. | − | 7·028 |
| 3·6 | .. | .. | .. | + | 0·195 |
| 3·6 | .. | .. | .. | − | 5·467 |
| 5·8 | .. | .. | .. | + | 0·579 |
| 5·8 | .. | .. | .. | − | 4·093 |
| 7·10 | .. | .. | .. | + | 1·159 |
| 7·10 | .. | .. | .. | − | 2·916 |
| 9·10 (diagonal) | .. | .. | + | 1·950 |
| 9·10 (diagonal) | .. | .. | − | 1·950 |

*Note.*—If this truss is supported at the points 2·2
the parts 2·4 would practically be made of the same
strength as 4·6, but if supported at the points 1·1 the
parts 1·2 and 2·4 are not necessary.

# TRUSS DIAGRAM No. 34.

## GANTRY.

### CONDITIONS.

1. Depth at centre   ..   ..    $\frac{1}{8}$ of the span.
2. Number of panels   ..   ..    3.
3. Method of loading   ..   ..    On top flange.
4. Description of bracing   ..    Vertical and inclined, angle 69° 26'.

### EVENLY DISTRIBUTED DEAD LOAD.

#### *Stress Constants.*

Top flange:
    S. 1·3      ..    ..    ..    + 2·666
       3·3      ..    ..    ..    + 2·666

Bottom flange:
    S. 1·2      ..    ..    ..    − 2·847
       2·2      ..    ..    ..    − 2·666

Vertical bracing:
    S. 2·3      ..    ..    ..    + 1·000

Inclined bracing:
    S. 2·3      ..    ..    ..    0·000

### EVENLY DISTRIBUTED LIVE LOAD ADVANCING FROM EITHER ABUTMENT.

#### *Maximum Stress Constants.*

Top flange:
    S. 1·3      ..    ..    ..    + 2·666
       3·3      ..    ..    ..    + 2·666

Bottom flange:

| | | | | | |
|---|---|---|---|---|---|
| S. 1·2 | .. | .. | .. | − | 2·847 |
| 2·2 | .. | .. | .. | − | 2·666 |

Vertical bracing:

| | | | | | |
|---|---|---|---|---|---|
| S. 2·3 | .. | .. | .. | + | 1·000 |
| 2·3 | .. | .. | .. | − | 0·000 |

Inclined bracing:

| | | | | | |
|---|---|---|---|---|---|
| S. 2·3 | .. | .. | .. | + | 0·949 |
| 2·3 | .. | .. | .. | − | 0·949 |

*Note.*—In this type of truss it is usual to make the diagonals capable of sustaining tension only, and in that case, with a moving load, a cross diagonal would be required. If this truss is turned upside-down the stresses remain the same, but the signs + and − are reversed.

---

## TRUSS DIAGRAM No. 35.

### INVERTED LINVILLE.

#### CONDITIONS.

1. Depth at centre .. .. $\frac{1}{8}$ of the span.
2. Number of panels .. .. 5.
3. Method of loading .. .. On top flange.
4. Description of bracing .. Vertical and inclined, angle 58°.

#### EVENLY DISTRIBUTED DEAD LOAD.

*Stress Constants.*

Top flange:

| | | | | | |
|---|---|---|---|---|---|
| S. 1·3 | .. | .. | .. | + | 3·200 |
| 3·5 | .. | .. | .. | + | 4·800 |
| 5·5 | .. | .. | .. | + | 4·800 |

Bottom flange:

| S. 1·2 | .. | .. | .. | − | 3·774 |
|--------|----|----|----|----|-------|
| 2·4 | .. | .. | .. | − | 3·200 |
| 4·4 | .. | .. | .. | − | 4·800 |

Vertical bracing:

| S. 2·3 | .. | .. | .. | + | 2·000 |
|--------|----|----|----|----|-------|
| 4·5 | .. | .. | .. | + | 1·000 |

Inclined bracing:

| S. 3·4 | .. | .. | .. | − | 1·887 |
|--------|----|----|----|----|-------|
| 5·4 | .. | .. | .. | − | 0·000 |

## EVENLY DISTRIBUTED LIVE LOAD ADVANCING FROM EITHER ABUTMENT.

### *Maximum Stress Constants.*

Top flange:

| S. 1·3 | .. | .. | .. | + | 3·200 |
|--------|----|----|----|----|-------|
| 3·5 | .. | .. | .. | + | 4·800 |
| 5·5 | .. | .. | .. | + | 4·800 |

Bottom flange:

| S. 1·2 | .. | .. | .. | − | 3·774 |
|--------|----|----|----|----|-------|
| 2·4 | .. | .. | .. | − | 3·200 |
| 4·4 | .. | .. | .. | − | 4·800 |

Vertical bracing:

| S. 2·3 | + | 2·000 | S. 4·5 | + | 1·200 |
|--------|----|-------|--------|----|-------|
| 2·3 | − | 0·000 | 4·5 | − | 0·200 |

Inclined bracing:

| | | | | | | |
|---|---|---|---|---|---|---|
| S. 3·4 | + | 0·377 | | S. 5·4 | + | 1·132 |
| 3·4 | − | 2·264 | | 5·4 | − | 1·132 |

*Note.*—In this type of truss it is usual to make the diagonal capable of sustaining tension only, and in that case with a moving load, cross diagonals would be required in some of the panels, depending upon the relative values of the dead and live loads. If this truss is turned upside down the stresses remain the same, but the signs + and − are reversed.

---

## TRUSS DIAGRAM No. 36.

### INVERTED LINVILLE.

#### CONDITIONS.

1. Depth at centre　..　.. ⅛ of the span.
2. Number of panels　.. 6.
3. Method of loading　.. On top flange.
4. Description of bracing.. Vertical and inclined, angle 53° 8′.

#### EVENLY DISTRIBUTED DEAD LOAD.

##### *Stress Constants.*

Top flange:

| | | | | | |
|---|---|---|---|---|---|
| S. 1·3 | .. | .. | .. | + | 3·333 |
| 3·5 | .. | .. | .. | + | 5·333 |
| 5·7 | .. | .. | .. | + | 6·000 |

Bottom flange:

| | | | | | |
|---|---|---|---|---|---|
| S. 1·2 | .. | .. | .. | − | 4·165 |
| 2·4 | .. | .. | .. | − | 3·333 |
| 4·6 | .. | .. | .. | − | 5·333 |

G

Vertical bracing:

| | | | | | | |
|---|---|---|---|---|---|---|
| S. 2·3 | .. | .. | .. | + | 2·500 |
| 4·5 | .. | .. | .. | + | 1·500 |
| 6·7 | .. | .. | .. | + | 1·000 |

Inclined bracing:

| | | | | | | |
|---|---|---|---|---|---|---|
| S. 3·4 | .. | .. | .. | − | 2·500 |
| 5·6 | .. | .. | .. | − | 0·833 |

### EVENLY DISTRIBUTED LIVE LOAD ADVANCING FROM EITHER ABUTMENT.

#### *Maximum Stress Constants.*

Top flange:

| | | | | | | |
|---|---|---|---|---|---|---|
| S. 1·3 | .. | .. | .. | + | 3·333 |
| 3·5 | .. | .. | .. | + | 5·333 |
| 5·7 | .. | .. | .. | + | 6·000 |

Bottom flange:

| | | | | | | |
|---|---|---|---|---|---|---|
| S. 1·2 | .. | .. | .. | − | 4·165 |
| 2·4 | .. | .. | .. | − | 3·333 |
| 4·6 | .. | .. | .. | − | 5·333 |

Vertical bracing:

| | | | | | | |
|---|---|---|---|---|---|---|
| S. 2·3 | + | 2·500 | S. 4·5 | − | 0·166 |
| 2·3 | − | 0·000 | 6·7 | + | 1·000 |
| 4·5 | + | 1·666 | 6·7 | − | 0·000 |

Inclined bracing:

| | | | | | | |
|---|---|---|---|---|---|---|
| S. 3·4 | + | 0·276 | S. 5·6 | + | 0·833 |
| 3·4 | − | 2·775 | 5·6 | − | 1·666 |

*Note.*—In this type of truss it is usual to make the diagonals capable of sustaining tension only, and in that case, with a moving load, cross diagonals would

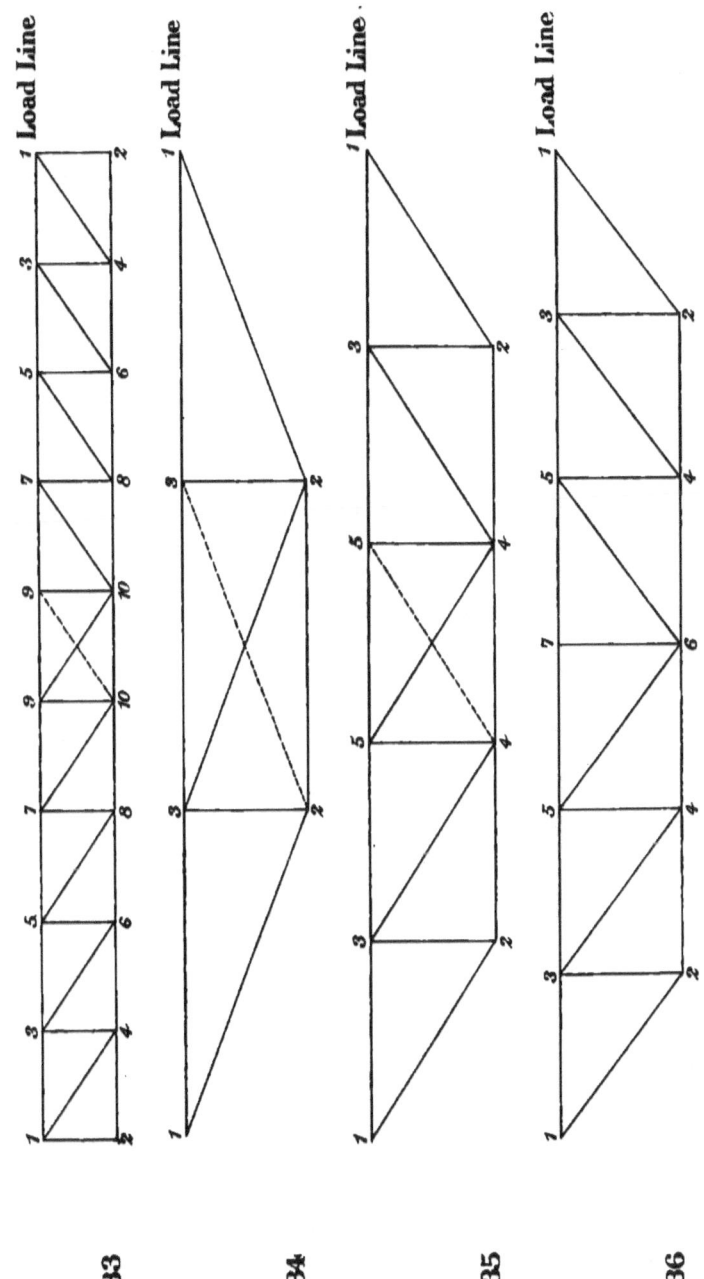

be required in some of·the panels, depending upon the relative values of the dead and live loads. If this truss is turned upside down the stresses remain the same, but the signs + and − are reversed.

---

## TRUSS DIAGRAM No. 37.

### PARABOLIC BOWSTRING.

#### CONDITIONS.

1. Depth at centre    ..    ..    $\frac{1}{8}$ of the span.
2. Number of panels    ..    ..    8.
3. Method of loading    ..    ..    On bottom flange.
4. Description of bracing    ..    Vertical and inclined two ways.

### EVENLY DISTRIBUTED DEAD LOAD.

#### *Stress Constants.*

Top flange:

     S. 2·3   +   8·73      S. 5·7   +   8·14

        3·5   +   8·38         7·9   +   8·02

Bottom flange:

     S. 2·4   −   8·00      S. 6·8   −   8·00

        4·6   −   8·00        8·10   −   8·00

Vertical bracing:

     S. 3·4   −   1·00      S. 7·8   −   1·00

        5·6   −   1·00        9·10   −   1·00

Inclined bracing:

     S. 3.6   ..     ..     ..     ..     0·00

        5·8   ..     ..     ..     ..     0·00

        7·10   ..     ..     ..     ..     0·00

EVENLY DISTRIBUTED LIVE LOAD ADVANCING FROM
EITHER ABUTMENT.

*Maximum Stress Constants.*

Top flange:

| | | | | | |
|---|---|---|---|---|---|
| S. 2·3 | + | 8·73 | S. 5·7 | + | 8·14 |
| 3·5 | + | 8·38 | 7·9 | + | 8·02 |

Bottom flange:

| | | | | | |
|---|---|---|---|---|---|
| S. 2·4 | − | 8·00 | S. 6·8 | − | 8·00 |
| 4·6 | − | 8·00 | 8·10 | − | 8·00 |

Vertical bracing:

| | | | | | |
|---|---|---|---|---|---|
| S. 3·4 | + | 0·000 | S. 7·8 | + | 0·500 |
| 3·4 | − | 1·000 | 7·8 | − | 1·500 |
| 5·6 | + | 0·312 | 9·10 | + | 0·000 |
| 5·6 | − | 1·312 | 9·10 | − | 1·000 |

Inclined bracing:

| | | | | | |
|---|---|---|---|---|---|
| S. 3·6 | + | 1·084 | S. 5·8 | − | 1·250 |
| 3·6 | − | 1·084 | 7·10 | + | 1·368 |
| 5·8 | + | 1·250 | 7·10 | − | 1·368 |

# TRUSS DIAGRAM No. 38.

### PARABOLIC BOWSTRING.

#### CONDITIONS.

1. Depth at centre    ..    ..    $\frac{1}{8}$ of the span.
2. Number of panels    ..    ..    8.
3. Method of loading    ..    ..    On bottom flange.
4. Description of bracing    ..    Vertical and inclined one way.

### EVENLY DISTRIBUTED DEAD LOAD.

#### *Stress Constants.*

Top flange:

| | | |
|---|---|---|
| S. 2·3 | + | 8·73 |
| 3·5 | + | 8·38 |

| | | |
|---|---|---|
| S. 5·7 | + | 8·14 |
| 7·9 | + | 8·02 |

Bottom flange:

| | | |
|---|---|---|
| S. 2·4 | – | 8·00 |
| 4·6 | – | 8·00 |

| | | |
|---|---|---|
| S. 6·8 | – | 8·00 |
| 8·10 | – | 8·00 |

Vertical bracing:

| | | |
|---|---|---|
| S. 3·4 | – | 1·00 |
| 5·6 | – | 1·00 |

| | | |
|---|---|---|
| S. 7·8 | – | 1·00 |
| 9·10 | – | 1·00 |

Inclined bracing:

| | |
|---|---|
| S. 3·6 | 0·00 |
| 5·8 | 0·00 |
| 7·10 | 0·00 |

| | |
|---|---|
| S. 9·8 | 0·00 |
| 7·6 | 0·00 |
| 5·4 | 0·00 |

EVENLY DISTRIBUTED LIVE LOAD ADVANCING FROM
EITHER ABUTMENT.

*Maximum Stress Constants.*

Top flange:

| | | |
|---|---|---|
| S. 2·3 + 8·73 | S. 5·7 + 8·14 |
| 3·5 + 8·38 | 7·9 + 8·02 |

Bottom flange:

| | |
|---|---|
| S. 2·4 − 8·00 | S. 6·8 − 8·00 |
| 4·6 − 8·00 | 8·10 − 8·00 |

Vertical bracing:

| | |
|---|---|
| S. 3·4 + 0·000 | S. 7·8 + 0·500 |
| 3·4 − 1·000 | 7·8 − 1·500 |
| 5·6 + 0·312 | 9·10 + 0·562 |
| 5·6 − 1·312 | 9·10 − 1·562 |

Inclined bracing:

| | |
|---|---|
| S. 3·6 + 1·084 | S. 9·8 + 1·414 |
| 3·6 − 1·084 | 9·8 − 1·414 |
| 5·8 + 1·250 | 7·6 + 1·368 |
| 5·8 − 1·250 | 7·6 − 1·368 |
| 7·10 + 1·368 | 5·4 + 1·250 |
| 7·10 − 1·368 | 5·4 − 1·250 |

## TRUSS DIAGRAM No. 39.

### PARABOLIC BOWSTRING.

### CONDITIONS.

1. Depth at centre  ..  ..  $\frac{1}{8}$ of the span.
2. Number of panels..  ..  8.
3. Method of loading  ..  On bottom flange.
4. Description of bracing..  Vertical and inclined cross bracing.

### EVENLY DISTRIBUTED DEAD LOAD.

#### *Stress Constants.*

Top flange :

    S. 2·3  +  8·73      S. 5·7  +  8·14

        3·5  +  8·38          7·9  +  8·02

Bottom flange :

    S. 2·4  —  8·00      S. 6·8  —  8·00

        4·6  —  8·00       8·10  —  8·00

Vertical bracing :

    S. 3·4  —  1·00      S. 7·8  —  1·00

        5·6  —  1·00       9·10  —  1·00

Inclined bracing :

    S. 3·6    0·00      S. 4·5    0·00

        5·8    0·00        6·7    0·00

        7·10   0·00        8·9    0·00

EVENLY DISTRIBUTED LIVE LOAD ADVANCING FROM
EITHER ABUTMENT.

*Maximum Stress Constants.*

Top flange:

| | | |
|---|---|---|
| S. 2·3 | + | 8·73 |
| 3·5 | + | 8·38 |

| | | |
|---|---|---|
| S. 5·7 | + | 8·14 |
| 7·9 | + | 8·02 |

Bottom flange:

| | | |
|---|---|---|
| S. 2·4 | − | 8·00 |
| · 4·6 | − | 8·00 |

| | | |
|---|---|---|
| S. 6·8 | − | 8·00 |
| 8·10 | − | 8·00 |

Vertical bracing:

| | | |
|---|---|---|
| S. 3·4 | + | 0·000 |
| 3·4 | − | 1·000 |
| 5·6 | + | 0·312 |
| 5·6 | − | 1·000 |

| | | |
|---|---|---|
| S. 7·8 | + | 0·500 |
| 7·8 | − | 1·000 |
| 9·10 | + | 0·562 |
| 9·10 | − | 1·000 |

Inclined bracing all ties with live load:

| | | |
|---|---|---|
| S. 3·6 | − | 1·084 |
| 5·8 | − | 1·250 |
| 7·10 | − | 1·368 |

| | | |
|---|---|---|
| S. 4·5 | − | 1·250 |
| 6·7 | − | 1·368 |
| 8·9 | − | 1·414 |

# TRUSS DIAGRAM No. 40.

### PARABOLIC BOWSTRING.

### CONDITIONS.

1. Depth at centre .. .. $\frac{1}{8}$ of the span.
2. Number of panels .. 8.
3. Method of loading .. On bottom flange.
4. Description of bracing.. Vertical and inclined cross bracing.

### EVENLY DISTRIBUTED DEAD LOAD.

#### *Stress Constants.*

Top flange:

| | | | | | |
|---|---|---|---|---|---|
| S. 2·3 | + | 8·73 | S. 5·7 | + | 8·14 |
| 3·5 | + | 8·38 | 7·9 | + | 8·02 |

Bottom flange:

| | | | | | |
|---|---|---|---|---|---|
| S. 2·4 | − | 8·00 | S. 6·8 | − | 8·00 |
| 4·6 | − | 8·00 | 8·10 | − | 8·00 |

Vertical bracing:

| | | | | | |
|---|---|---|---|---|---|
| S. 3·4 | − | 1·00 | S. 7·8 | − | 1·00 |
| 5·6 | − | 1·00 | 9·10 | − | 1·00 |

Inclined bracing:

| | | | | |
|---|---|---|---|---|
| S. 3·6 | 0·00 | S. 4·5 | 0·00 |
| 5·8 | 0·00 | 6·7 | 0·00 |
| 7·10 | 0·00 | 8·9 | 0·00 |

EVENLY DISTRIBUTED LIVE LOAD ADVANCING FROM
EITHER ABUTMENT.

*Maximum Stress Constants.*

Top flange:

| | |
|---|---|
| S. 2·3   +   8·73 | S. 5·7   +   8·14 |
| 3·5   +   8·38 | 7·9   +   8·02 |

Bottom flange:

| | |
|---|---|
| S. 2·4   −   8·00 | S. 4·8   −   8·00 |
| 4·6   −   8·00 | 8·10   −   8·00 |

Vertical bracing all ties with live load:

| | |
|---|---|
| S. 3·4   −   1·000 | S. 7·8   −   1·500 |
| 5·6   −   1·312 | 9·10   −   1·562 |

Inclined bracing all struts with live load:

| | |
|---|---|
| S. 3·6   +   1·084 | S. 4·5   +   1·250 |
| 5·8   +   1·250 | 6·7   +   1·368 |
| 7·10   +   1·368 | 8·9   +   1·414 |

PLATE 10

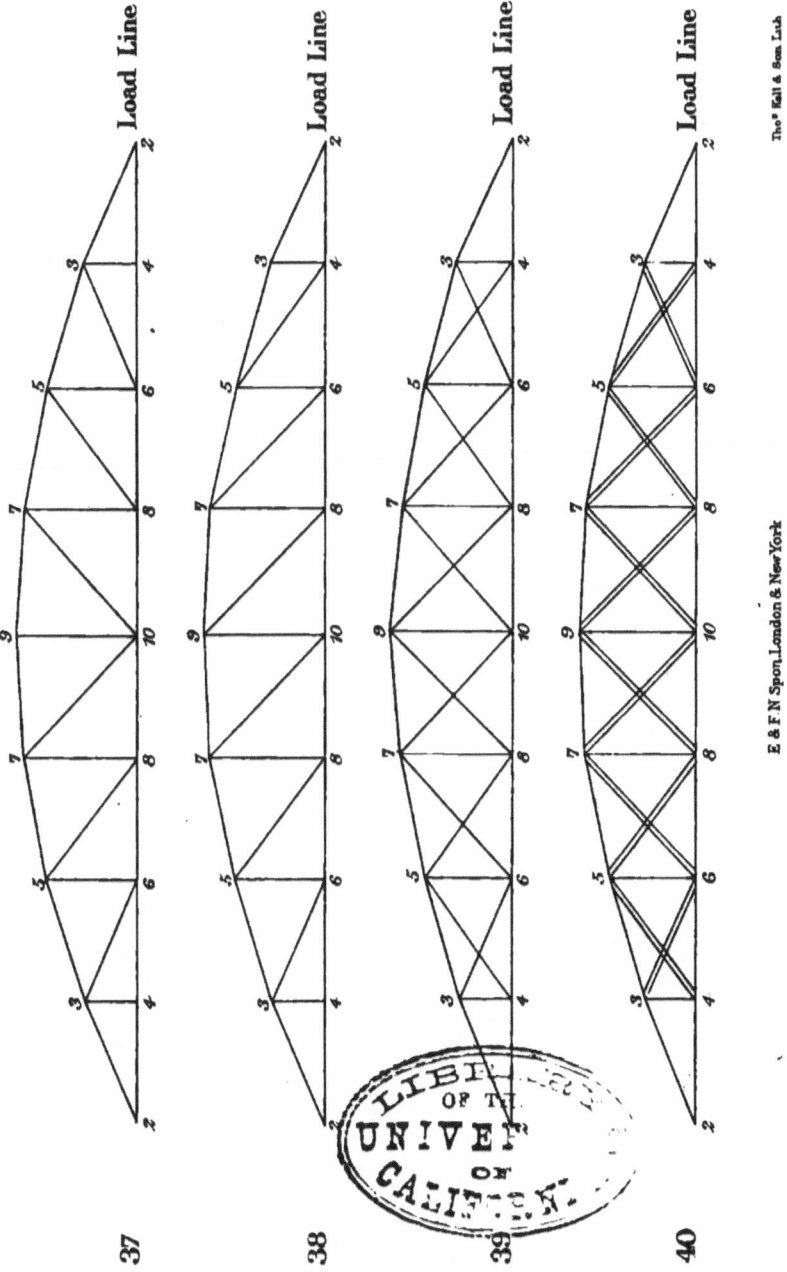

# TRUSS DIAGRAM No. 41.

## PARABOLIC BOWSTRING.

### CONDITIONS.

1. Depth at centre      ..   ..   $\frac{1}{8}$ of the span.
2. Number of panels  ..   ..   12.
3. Method of loading  ..   ..   On bottom flange.
4. Description of bracing  ..   Vertical and inclined two ways.

### EVENLY DISTRIBUTED DEAD LOAD.

*Stress Constants.*

Top flange:

| | | | | |
|---|---|---|---|---|
| S. 2·3 | + 13·20 | | S. 7·9 | + 12·26 |
| 3·5 | + 12·82 | | 9·11 | + 12·10 |
| 5·7 | + 12·50 | | 11·13 | + 12·01 |

Bottom flange:

| | | | | |
|---|---|---|---|---|
| S. 2·4 | − 12·00 | | S. 8·10 | − 12·00 |
| 4·6 | − 12·00 | | 10·12 | − 12·00 |
| 6·8 | − 12·00 | | 12·14 | − 12·00 |

Vertical bracing:

| | | | | |
|---|---|---|---|---|
| S. 3·4 | − 1·00 | | S. 9·10 | − 1·00 |
| 5·6 | − 1·00 | | 11·12 | − 1·00 |
| 7·8 | − 1·00 | | 13·14 | − 1·00 |

Inclined bracing:

| | | | | |
|---|---|---|---|---|
| S. 3·6 | 0·00 | | S. 9·12 | 0·00 |
| 5·8 | 0·00 | | 11·14 | 0·00 |
| 7·10 | 0·00 | | | |

### EVENLY DISTRIBUTED LIVE LOAD ADVANCING FROM EITHER ABUTMENT.

*Maximum Stress Constants.*

Top flange :

| | | | | | |
|---|---|---|---|---|---|
| S. 2·3 | + 13·20 | | S. 7·9 | + 12·26 |
| 3·5 | + 12·82 | | 9·11 | + 12·10 |
| 5·7 | + 12·50 | | 11·13 | + 12·01 |

Bottom flange :

| | | | | | |
|---|---|---|---|---|---|
| S. 2·4 | − 12·00 | | S. 8·10 | − 12·00 |
| 4·6 | − 12·00 | | 10·12 | − 12·00 |
| 6·8 | − 12·00 | | 12·14 | − 12·00 |

Vertical bracing :

| | | | | | |
|---|---|---|---|---|---|
| S. 3·4 | + | 0·000 | | S. 9·10 | + | 0·874 |
| 3·4 | − | 1·000 | | 9·10 | − | 1·874 |
| 5·6 | + | 0·371 | | 11·12 | + | 1·000 |
| 5·6 | − | 1·371 | | 11·12 | − | 2·000 |
| 7·8 | + | 0·666 | | 13·14 | + | 0·000 |
| 7·8 | − | 1·666 | | 13·14 | − | 1·000 |

Inclined bracing :

| | | | | | |
|---|---|---|---|---|---|
| S. 3·6 | + | 1·102 | | S. 7·10 | − | 1·505 |
| 3·6 | − | 1·102 | | 9·12 | + | 1·666 |
| 5·8 | + | 1·302 | | 9·12 | − | 1·666 |
| 5 8 | − | 1·302 | | 11·14 | + | 1·768 |
| 7·10 | + | 1·505 | | 11·14 | − | 1·768 |

## TRUSS DIAGRAM No. 42.

### PARABOLIC BOWSTRING.

#### CONDITIONS.

1. Depth at centre  .. .. $\frac{1}{6}$ of the span.
2. Number of panels  .. .. 12.
3. Method of loading  .. .. On bottom flange.
4. Description of bracing  .. Vertical and inclined one way.

### EVENLY DISTRIBUTED DEAD LOAD.

#### *Stress Constants.*

Top flange:

| | | | | |
|---|---|---|---|---|
| S. 2·3 | + 13·20 | | S. 7·9 | + 12·26 |
| 3·5 | + 12·82 | | 9·11 | + 12·10 |
| 5·7 | + 12·50 | | 11·13 | + 12·01 |

Bottom flange:

| | | | | |
|---|---|---|---|---|
| S. 2·4 | − 12·00 | | S. 8·10 | − 12·00 |
| 4·6 | − 12·00 | | 10·12 | − 12·00 |
| 6·8 | − 12·00 | | 12·14 | − 12·00 |

Vertical bracing:

| | | | | |
|---|---|---|---|---|
| S. 3·4 | − | 1·00 | S. 9·10 | − 1·00 |
| 5·6 | − | 1·00 | 11·12 | − 1·00 |
| 7·8 | − | 1·00 | 13·14 | − 1·00 |

Inclined bracing:

| | | | |
|---|---|---|---|
| S. 3·6 | 0·00 | S. 13·12 | 0·00 |
| 5·8 | 0·00 | 11·10 | 0·00 |
| 7·10 | 0·00 | 9·8 | 0·00 |
| 9·12 | 0·00 | 7·6 | 0·00 |
| 11·14 | 0·00 | 5·4 | 0·00 |

EVENLY DISTRIBUTED LIVE LOAD ADVANCING FROM
EITHER ABUTMENT.

*Maximum Stress Constants.*

Top flange:

| | | | | | |
|---|---|---|---|---|---|
| S. 2·3 | + 13·20 | | S. 7·9 | + 12·26 |
| 3·5 | + 12·82 | | 9·11 | + 12·10 |
| 5·7 | + 12·50 | | 11·13 | + 12·01 |

Bottom flange:

| | | | | | |
|---|---|---|---|---|---|
| S. 2·4 | − 12·00 | | S. 8·10 | − 12·00 |
| 4·6 | − 12·00 | | 10·12 | − 12·00 |
| 6·8 | − 12·00 | | 12·14 | − 12·00 |

Vertical bracing:

| | | | | | |
|---|---|---|---|---|---|
| S. 3·4 | + | 0·000 | S. 9·10 | + | 0·874 |
| 3·4 | − | 1·000 | 9·10 | − | 1·874 |
| 5·6 | + | 0·371 | 11·12 | + | 1·000 |
| 5·6 | − | 1·371 | 11·12 | − | 2·000 |
| 7·8 | + | 0·666 | 13·14 | + | 1·042 |
| 7·8 | − | 1·666 | 13·14 | − | 2·042 |

Inclined bracing:

| | | | | | |
|---|---|---|---|---|---|
| S. 3·6 | + | 1·102 | S. 13·12 | + | 1·803 |
| 3·6 | − | 1·102 | 13·12 | − | 1·803 |
| 5·8 | + | 1·302 | 11·10 | + | 1·768 |
| 5·8 | − | 1·302 | 11·10 | − | 1·768 |
| 7·10 | + | 1·505 | 9·8 | + | 1·666 |
| 7·10 | − | 1·505 | 9·8 | − | 1·666 |
| 9·12 | + | 1·666 | 7·6 | + | 1·505 |
| 9·12 | − | 1·666 | 7·6 | − | 1·505 |
| 11·14 | + | 1·768 | 5·4 | + | 1·302 |
| 11·14 | − | 1·768 | 5·4 | − | 1·302 |

# TRUSS DIAGRAM No. 43.

### PARABOLIC BOWSTRING.

#### CONDITIONS.

1. Depth at centre .. .. $\frac{1}{8}$ of the span.
2. Number of panels .. 12.
3. Method of loading .. On bottom flange.
4. Description of bracing.. Vertical and inclined cross bracing.

#### EVENLY DISTRIBUTED DEAD LOAD.

*Stress Constants.*

Top flange :

| | | |
|---|---|---|
| S. 2·3 | + 13·20 | S. 7·9 + 12·26 |
| 3·5 | + 12·82 | 9·11 + 12·10 |
| 5·7 | + 12·50 | 11·13 + 12·01 |

Bottom flange :

| | | |
|---|---|---|
| S. 2·4 | − 12·00 | S. 8·10 − 12·00 |
| 4·6 | − 12·00 | 10·12 − 12·00 |
| 6·8 | − 12·00 | 12·14 − 12·00 |

Vertical bracing :

| | | |
|---|---|---|
| S. 3·4 | − 1·00 | S. 9·10 − 1·00 |
| 5·6 | − 1·00 | 11·12 − 1·00 |
| 7·8 | − 1·00 | 13·14 − 1·00 |

Inclined bracing :

| | | |
|---|---|---|
| S. 3·6 | 0·00 | S. 4·5 0·00 |
| 5·8 | 0·00 | 6·7 0·00 |
| 7·10 | 0·00 | 8·9 0·00 |
| 9·12 | 0·00 | 10·11 0·00 |
| 11·14 | 0·00 | 12·13 0·00 |

EVENLY DISTRIBUTED LIVE LOAD ADVANCING FROM
EITHER ABUTMENT.

*Maximum Stress Constants.*

Top flange:

| | | |
|---|---|---|
| S. 2·3 | + 13·20 | S. 7·9   + 12·26 |
| 3·5 | + 12·82 | 9·11 + 12·10 |
| 5·7 | + 12·50 | 11·13 + 12·01 |

Bottom flange:

| | | |
|---|---|---|
| S. 2·4 | − 12·00 | S. 8·10 − 12·00 |
| 4·6 | − 12·00 | 10·12 − 12·00 |
| 6·8 | − 12·00 | 12·14 − 12·00 |

Vertical bracing:

| | | |
|---|---|---|
| S. 3·4 | + 0·000 | S. 9·10 + 0·874 |
| 3·4 | − 1·000 | 9·10 − 1·000 |
| 5·6 | + 0·371 | 11·12 + 1·000 |
| 5·6 | − 1·000 | 11·12 − 1·000 |
| 7·8 | +. 0·666 | 13·14 + 1·042 |
| 7·8 | − 1·000 | 13·14 − 1·000 |

Inclined bracing all ties with live load:

| | | |
|---|---|---|
| S. 3·6 | − 1·102 | S. 4·5 − 1·302 |
| 5·8 | − 1·302 | 6·7 − 1·505 |
| 7·10 | − 1·505 | 8·9 − 1·666 |
| 9·12 | − 1·666 | 10·11 − 1·768 |
| 11·14 | − 1·768 | 12·13 − 1·803 |

# TRUSS DIAGRAM No. 44.

### PARABOLIC BOWSTRING.

#### CONDITIONS.

1. Depth at centre　..　..　$\frac{1}{8}$ of the span.
2. Number of panels　..　..　12.
3. Method of loading　..　..　On bottom flange.
4. Description of bracing　..　Vertical and inclined cross bracing.

### EVENLY DISTRIBUTED DEAD LOAD.

#### *Stress Constants.*

Top flange:

| | | | | | |
|---|---|---|---|---|---|
| S. 2·3 | + 13·20 | | S. 7·9 | + 12·26 |
| 3·5 | + 12·82 | | 9·11 | + 12·10 |
| 5·7 | + 12·50 | | 11·13 | + 12·01 |

Bottom flange:

| | | | | | |
|---|---|---|---|---|---|
| S. 2·4 | − 12·00 | | S. 8·10 | − 12·00 |
| 4·6 | − 12·00 | | 10·12 | − 12·00 |
| 6·8 | − 12·00 | | 12·14 | − 12·00 |

Vertical bracing:

| | | | | | |
|---|---|---|---|---|---|
| S. 3·4 | − 1·00 | | S. 9·10 | − 1·00 |
| 5·6 | − 1·00 | | 11·12 | − 1·00 |
| 7·8 | − 1·00 | | 13·14 | − 1·00 |

Inclined bracing:

| | | | | | |
|---|---|---|---|---|---|
| S. 3·6 | 0·00 | | S. 4·5 | 0·00 |
| 5·8 | 0·00 | | 6·7 | 0·00 |
| 7·10 | 0·00 | | 8·9 | 0·00 |
| 9·12 | 0·00 | | 10·11 | 0·00 |
| 11·14 | 0·00 | | 12·13 | 0·00 |

H

EVENLY DISTRIBUTED LIVE LOAD ADVANCING FROM
EITHER ABUTMENT.

*Maximum Stress Constants.*

Top flange:

| | | | | |
|---|---|---|---|---|
| S. 2·3 | + 13·20 | S. 7·9 | + 12·26 |
| 3·5 | + 12·82 | 9·11 | + 12·10 |
| 5·7 | + 12·50 | 11·13 | + 12·01 |

Bottom flange:

| | | | |
|---|---|---|---|
| S. 2·4 | − 12·00 | 8·10 | − 12·00 |
| 4·6 | − 12·00 | 10·12 | − 12·00 |
| 6·8 | − 12·00 | 12·14 | − 12·00 |

Vertical bracing all ties with live load:

| | | | |
|---|---|---|---|
| S. 3·4 | − 1·000 | S. 9·10 | − 1·874 |
| 5·6 | − 1·371 | 11·12 | − 2·000 |
| 7·8 | − 1·666 | 13·14 | − 2·042 |

Inclined bracing all struts with live load:

| | | | |
|---|---|---|---|
| S. 3·6 | + 1·102 | S. 4·5 | + 1·302 |
| 5·8 | + 1·302 | 6·7 | + 1·505 |
| 7·10 | + 1·505 | 8·9 | + 1·666 |
| 9·12 | + 1·666 | 10·11 | + 1·768 |
| 11·14 | + 1·768 | 12·13 | + 1·803 |

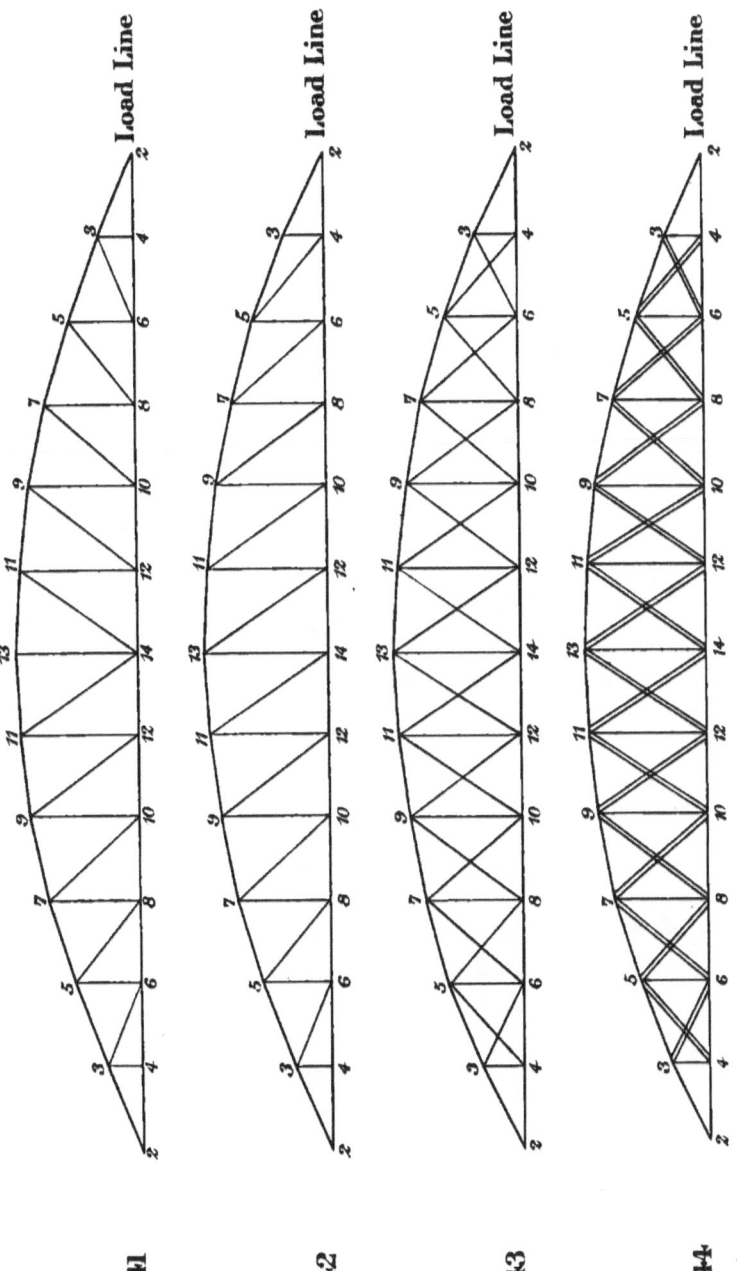

41

42

43

44

## TRUSS DIAGRAM No. 45.

### PARABOLIC BOWSTRING.

#### CONDITIONS.

1. Depth at centre .. .. $\frac{1}{8}$ of the span nearly.
2. Number of panels .. .. 13.
3. Method of loading .. .. On bottom flange.
4. Description of bracing .. Vertical, and inclined two ways.

### EVENLY DISTRIBUTED DEAD LOAD.

*Stress Constants.*

Top flange :

| | | | | |
|---|---|---|---|---|
| S. 2·3 | + 14·31 | S. 9·11 | + 13·16 |
| 3·5 | + 13·92 | 11·13 | + 13·04 |
| 5·7 | + 13·60 | 13·13 | + 13·08 |
| 7·9 | + 13·34 | | |

Bottom flange :

| | | | | |
|---|---|---|---|---|
| S. 2·4 | − 13·08 | S. 10·12 | − 13·08 |
| 4·6 | − 13·08 | 12·14 | − 13·08. |
| 6·8 | − 13·08 | 14·14 | − 13·08 |
| 8·10 | − 13·08 | | |

Vertical bracing :

| | | | | |
|---|---|---|---|---|
| S. 3·4 | − 1·00 | S. 9·10 | − 1·00 |
| 5·6 | − 1·00 | 11·12 | − 1·00 |
| 7·8 | − 1·00 | 13·14 | − 1·00 |

Inclined bracing :

| | | | | |
|---|---|---|---|---|
| S. 3·6 | 0·00 | S. 9·12 | 0·00 |
| 5·8 | 0·00 | 11·14 | 0·00 |
| 7·10 | 0·00 | 13·14 | 0·00 |

H 2

EVENLY DISTRIBUTED LIVE LOAD ADVANCING FROM
EITHER ABUTMENT.

*Maximum Stress Constants.*

Top flange :

| | | |
|---|---|---|
| S. 2·3 | + 14·31 | S. 9·11   + 13·16 |
| 3·5 | + 13·92 | 11·13   + 13·04 |
| 5·7 | + 13·60 | 13·13   + 13·08 |
| 7·9 | + 13·34 | |

Bottom flange :

| | | |
|---|---|---|
| S. 2·4 | − 13·08 | S. 10·12   − 13·08 |
| 4·6 | − 13·08 | 12·14   − 13·08 |
| 6·8 | − 13·08 | 14·14   − 13·08 |
| 8·10 | − 13·08 | |

Vertical bracing :

| | | |
|---|---|---|
| S. 3·4 | + 0·000 | S. 9·10   + 0·922 |
| 3·4 | − 1·000 | 9·10   − 1·922 |
| 5·6 | + 0·385 | 11·12   + 1·077 |
| 5·6 | − 1·385 | 11·12   − 2·077 |
| 7·8 | + 0·692 | 13·14   + 1·153 |
| 7·8 | − 1·692 | 13·14   − 2·153 |

Inclined bracing :

| | | |
|---|---|---|
| S. 3·6 | + 1·101 | S. 9·12   + 1·708 |
| 3·6 | − 1·101 | 9·12   − 1·708 |
| 5·8 | + 1·309 | 11·14   + 1·835 |
| 5·8 | − 1·309 | 11·14   − 1·835 |
| 7·10 | + 1·527 | 13·14   + 1·900 |
| 7·10 | − 1·527 | 13·14   − 1·900 |

*Note.*—The depth at the centre of the girder is not
quite ⅛th of the span, owing to the top flange, 13·13,
being straight instead of curved. This causes the
horizontal stress to be 13·08 instead of 13·00.

## TRUSS DIAGRAM No. 46.

PARABOLIC BOWSTRING.

### CONDITIONS.

1. Depth at centre　.. 　.. 　$\frac{1}{4}$ of the span nearly.
2. Number of panels 　.. 　.. 　13.
3. Method of loading 　.. 　.. 　On bottom flange.
4. Description of bracing 　.. 　Vertical, and inclined one way.

EVENLY DISTRIBUTED DEAD LOAD.

*Stress Constants.*

Top flange:

| | |
|---|---|
| S. 2·3　+ 14·31 | S. 9·11 　+ 13·16 |
| 3·5　+ 13·92 | 11·13 　+ 13·04 |
| 5·7　+ 13·60 | ·13·13 　+ 13·08 |
| 7·9　+ 13·34 | |

Bottom flange:

| | |
|---|---|
| S. 2·4　− 13·08 | S. 10·12 　− 13·08 |
| 4·6　− 13·08 | 12·14 　− 13·08 |
| 6·8　− 13·08 | 14·14 　− 13·08 |
| 8·10　− 13·08 | |

Vertical bracing:

| | |
|---|---|
| S. 3·4　−　1·00 | S. 9·10 　−　1·00 |
| 5·6　−　1·00 | 11·12 　−　1·00 |
| 7·8　−　1·00 | 13·14 　−　1·00 |

Inclined bracing:

| | |
|---|---|
| S. 3·6　0·00 | S. 13·12 　0·00 |
| 5·8　0·00 | 11·10 　0·00 |
| 7·10　0·00 | 9·8 　0·00 |
| 9·12　0·00 | 7·6 　0·00 |
| 11·14　0·00 | 5·4 　0·00 |
| 13·14　0·00 | |

## EVENLY DISTRIBUTED LIVE LOAD ADVANCING FROM EITHER ABUTMENT.

### *Maximum Stress Constants.*

Top flange:

| | | | | | |
|---|---|---|---|---|---|
| S. 2·3 | + | 14·31 | S. 9·11 | + | 13·16 |
| 3·5 | + | 13·92 | 11·13 | + | 13·04 |
| 5·7 | + | 13·60 | 13·13 | + | 13·08 |
| 7·9 | + | 13·34 | | | |

Bottom flange:

| | | | | | |
|---|---|---|---|---|---|
| S. 2·4 | − | 13·08 | S. 10·12 | − | 13·08 |
| 4·6 | − | 13·08 | 12·14 | − | 13·08 |
| 6·8 | − | 13·08 | 14·14 | − | 13·08 |
| 8·10 | − | 13·08 | | | |

Vertical bracing:

| | | | | | |
|---|---|---|---|---|---|
| S. 3·4 | + | 0·000 | S. 9·10 | + | 0·922 |
| 3·4 | − | 1·000 | 9·10 | − | 1·922 |
| 5·6 | + | 0·385 | 11·12 | + | 1·077 |
| 5·6 | − | 1·385 | 11·12 | − | 2·077 |
| 7·8 | + | 0·692 | 13·14 | + | 1·153 |
| 7·8 | − | 1·692 | 13·14 | − | 2·153 |

Inclined bracing:

| | | | | | |
|---|---|---|---|---|---|
| S. 3·6 | + | 1·101 | S. 9·12 | − | 1·708 |
| 3·6 | − | 1·101 | 11·14 | + | 1·835 |
| 5·8 | + | 1·309 | 11·14 | − | 1·835 |
| 5·8 | − | 1·309 | 13·14 | + | 1·900 |
| 7·10 | + | 1·527 | 13·14 | − | 1·900 |
| 7·10 | − | 1·527 | 13·12 | + | 1·900 |
| 9·12 | + | 1·708 | 13·12 | − | 1·900 |

Inclined bracing—*continued*.

| | | |
|---|---|---|
| S. 11·10 | + | 1·835 |
| 11·10 | − | 1·835 |
| 9·8 | + | 1·708 |
| 9·8 | − | 1·708 |

| | | |
|---|---|---|
| S. 7·6 | + | 1·527 |
| 7·6 | − | 1·527 |
| 5·4 | + | 1·309 |
| 5·4 | − | 1·309 |

*Note.*—The depth at the centre of the girder is not quite ⅛th of the span, owing to the top flange, 13·13, being straight instead of curved. This causes the horizontal stress to be 13·08 instead of 13·00.

---

## TRUSS DIAGRAM No. 47.

### PARABOLIC BOWSTRING.

#### CONDITIONS.

1. Depth at centre    ..    ..    ⅛ of the span nearly.
2. Number of panels   ..    ..    13.
3. Method of loading  ..    ..    On bottom flange.
4. Description of bracing    ..    Vertical and inclined cross bracing.

#### EVENLY DISTRIBUTED DEAD LOAD.

*Stress Constants.*

Top flange:

| | | |
|---|---|---|
| S. 2·3 | + | 14·31 |
| 3·5 | + | 13·92 |
| 5·7 | + | 13·60 |
| 7·9 | + | 13·34 |

| | | |
|---|---|---|
| S. 9·11 | + | 13·16 |
| 11·13 | + | 13·04 |
| 13·13 | + | 13·08 |

Bottom flange :

| S. 2·4 | — 13·08 | S. 10·12 | — 13·08 |
| 4·6 | — 13·08 | 12·14 | — 13·08 |
| 6·8 | — 13·08 | 14·14 | — 13·08 |
| 8·10 | — 13·08 | | |

Vertical bracing :

| S. 3·4 | — 1·00 | S. 9·10 | — 1·00 |
| 5·6 | — 1·00 | 11·12 | — 1·00 |
| 7·8 | — 1·00 | 13·14 | — 1·00 |

Inclined bracing :

| S. 3·6 | 0·00 | S. 4·5 | 0·00 |
| 5·8 | 0·00 | 6·7 | 0·00 |
| 7·10 | 0·00 | 8·9 | 0·00 |
| 9·12 | 0·00 | 10·11 | 0·00 |
| 11·14 | 0·00 | 12·13 | 0·00 |
| 13·14 | 0·00 | 14·13 | 0·00 |

## EVENLY DISTRIBUTED LIVE LOAD ADVANCING FROM EITHER ABUTMENT.

### *Maximum Stress Constants.*

Top flange :

| S. 2·3 | + 14·31 | S. 9·11 | + 13·16 |
| 3·5 | + 13·92 | 11·13 | + 13·04 |
| 5·7 | + 13·60 | 13·13 | + 13·08 |
| 7·9 | + 13·34 | | |

Bottom flange :

| S. 2·4 | — 13·08 | S. 10·12 | — 13·08 |
| 4·6 | — 13·08 | 12·14 | — 13·08 |
| 6·8 | — 13·08 | 14·14 | — 13·08 |
| 8·10 | — 13·08 | | |

Vertical bracing:

| | | | | | | |
|---|---|---|---|---|---|---|
| S. | 3·4 | + | 0·000 | S. | 9·10 + | 0·922 |
| | 3·4 | − | 1·000 | | 9·10 − | 1·000 |
| | 5·6 | + | 0·385 | | 11·12 + | 1·077 |
| | 5·6 | − | 1·000 | | 11·12 − | 1·000 |
| | 7·8 | + | 0·692 | | 13·14 + | 1·153 |
| | 7·8 | − | 1·000 | | 13·14 − | 1·000 |

Inclined bracing all ties with live load:

| | | | | | | |
|---|---|---|---|---|---|---|
| S. | 3·6 | − | 1·101 | S. | 4·5 − | 1·309 |
| | 5·8 | − | 1·309 | | 6·7 − | 1·527 |
| | 7·10 | − | 1·527 | | 8·9 − | 1·708 |
| | 9·12 | − | 1·708 | | 10·11 − | 1·835 |
| | 11·14 | − | 1·835 | | 12·13 − | 1·900 |
| | 13·14 | − | 1·900 | | 14·13 − | 1·900 |

*Note.*—The depth at the centre of the girder is not quite ⅛th of the span, owing to the top flange, 13·13, being straight instead of curved. This·causes the horizontal stress to be 13·08 instead of 13·00.

## TRUSS DIAGRAM No. 48.

### PARABOLIC BOWSTRING.

#### CONDITIONS.

1. Depth at centre    ..    ..    $\frac{1}{8}$ of the span nearly.
2. Number of panels    ..    ..    13.
3. Method of loading    ..    ..    On bottom flange.
4. Description of bracing    ..    Vertical and inclined cross bracing.

#### EVENLY DISTRIBUTED DEAD LOAD.

##### Stress Constants.

Top flange :

| | | | | | |
|---|---|---|---|---|---|
| S. 2·3 | + 14·31 | | S. 9·11 | + 13·16 |
| 3·5 | + 13·92 | | 11·13 | + 13·04 |
| 5·7 | + 13·60 | | 13·13 | + 13·08 |
| 7·9 | + 13·34 | | | |

Bottom flange :

| | | | | | |
|---|---|---|---|---|---|
| S. 2·4 | − 13·08 | | S. 10·12 | − 13·08 |
| 4·6 | − 13·08 | | 12·14 | − 13·08 |
| 6·8 | − 13·08 | | 14·14 | − 13·08 |
| 8·10 | − 13·08 | | | |

Vertical bracing :

| | | | | | |
|---|---|---|---|---|---|
| S. 3·4 | − 1·00 | | S. 9·10 | − 1·00 |
| 5·6 | − 1·00 | | 11·12 | − 1·00 |
| 7·8 | − 1·00 | | 13·14 | − 1·00 |

Inclined bracing :

| | | | | | |
|---|---|---|---|---|---|
| S. 3·6 | 0·00 | | S. 4·5 | 0·00 |
| 5·8 | 0·00 | | 6·7 | 0·00 |
| 7·10 | 0·00 | | 8·9 | 0·00 |
| 9·12 | 0·00 | | 10·11 | 0·00 |
| 11·14 | 0·00 | | 12·13 | 0·00 |
| 13·14 | 0·00 | | 14·13 | 0·00 |

EVENLY DISTRIBUTED LIVE LOAD ADVANCING FROM
EITHER ABUTMENT.

*Maximum Stress Constants.*

Top flange :

| | | |
|---|---|---|
| S. 2·3 | + 14·31 | S. 9·11 + 1$\cdot$|
| 3·5 | + 13·92 | 11·13 + 13·04 |
| 5·7 | + 13·60 | 13·13 + 13·08 |
| 7·9 | + 13·34 | |

Bottom flange :

| | | |
|---|---|---|
| S. 2·4 | − 13·08 | S. 10·12 − 13·08 |
| 4·6 | − 13·08 | 12·14 − 13·08 |
| 6·8 | − 13·08 | 14·14 − 13·08 |
| 8·10 | − 13·08 | |

Vertical bracing all ties with live load :

| | | |
|---|---|---|
| S. 3·4 | − 1·000 | S. 9·10 − 1·922 |
| 5·6 | − 1·385 | 11·12 − 2·077 |
| 7·8 | − 1·692 | 13·14 − 2·153 |

Inclined bracing all struts with live load :

| | | |
|---|---|---|
| S. 3·6 | + 1·101 | S. 4·5 + 1·309 |
| 5·8 | + 1·309 | 6·7 + 1·527 |
| 7·10 | + 1·527 | 8·9 + 1·708 |
| 9·12 | + 1·708 | 10·11 + 1·835 |
| 11·14 | + 1·835 | 12·13 + 1·900 |
| 13·14 | + 1·900 | 14·13 + 1·900 |

*Note.*—The depth at the centre of the girder is not
quite ⅛th of the span, owing to the top flange, 13·13,
being straight instead of curved. This causes the
horizontal stress to be 13·08 instead of 13·00.

## TRUSS DIAGRAM No. 49.

### PARABOLIC BOWSTRING.

#### CONDITIONS.

1. Depth at centre    ..    ..   $\frac{1}{8}$ of the span.
2. Number of panels    ..    ..   13.
3. Method of loading   ..    ..   On bottom flange.
4. Description of bracing    ..   Inclined alternate ways.

### EVENLY DISTRIBUTED DEAD LOAD.

*Stress Constants.*

Top flange:

| | |
|---|---|
| S. 2·3    + 13·84 | S. 9·11   + 13·32 |
| 3·5    + 14·46 | 11·13   + 13·15 |
| 5·7    + 13·92 | 13·15   + 13·09 |
| 7·9    + 13·57 | |

Bottom flange:

| | |
|---|---|
| S. 2·4    − 12·50 | S. 10·12   − 12·91 |
| 4·6    − 12·81 | 12·14   − 12·92 |
| 6·8    − 12·87 | 14·14   − 12·92 |
| 8·10   − 12·91 | |

Inclined bracing:

| | |
|---|---|
| S. 3·4    −   0·8819 | S. 9·10   −   0·5160 |
| 4·5    −   0·7764 | 10·11   −   0·5448 |
| 5·6    −   0·5616 | 11·12   −   0·5216 |
| 6·7    −   0·6140 | 12·13   −   0·5294 |
| 7·8    −   0·5275 | 13·14   −   0·5175 |
| 8·9    −   0·5685 | 14·15   −   0·5234 |

PLATE 12

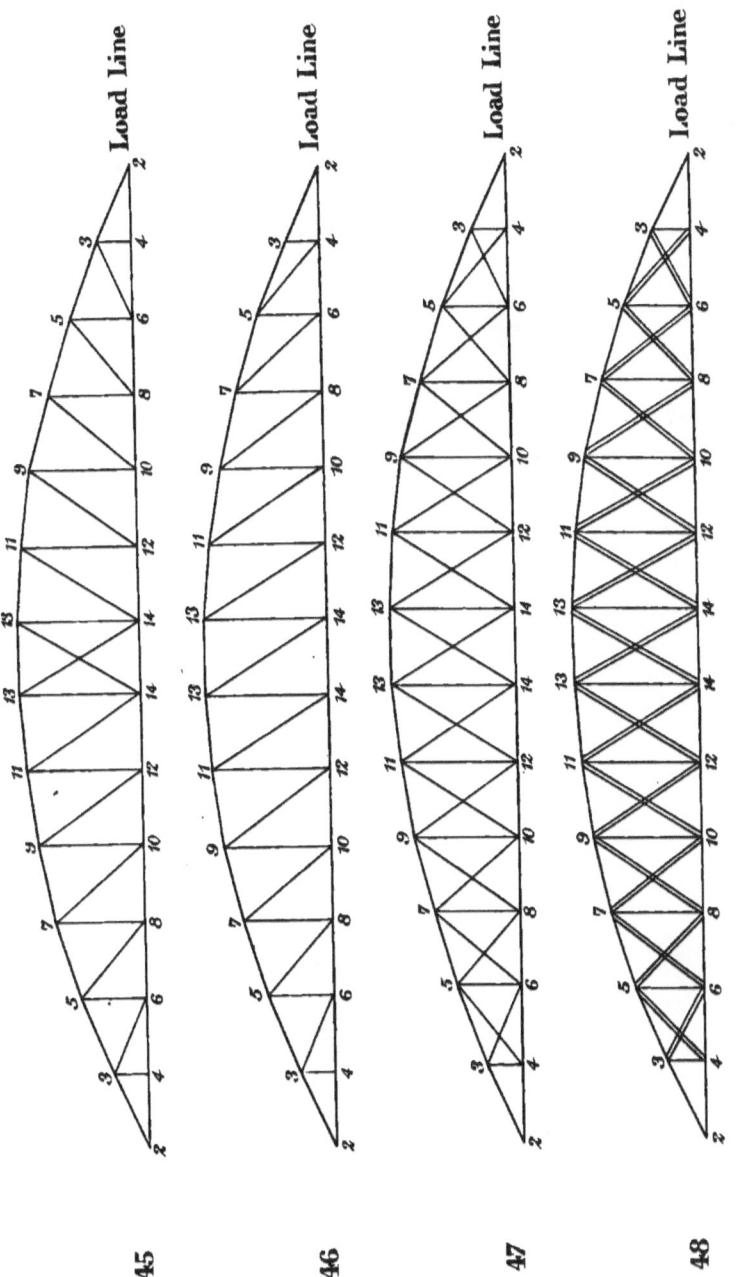

E & F N Spon, London & New York

Tho⁹ Kell & Son Lith

EVENLY DISTRIBUTED LIVE LOAD ADVANCING FROM
EITHER ABUTMENT.

*Maximum Stress Constants.*

Top flange:

| | | | | | |
|---|---|---|---|---|---|
| S. 2·3 | + 13·84 | | S. 9·11 | + 13·32 |
| 3·5 | + 14·46 | | 11·13 | + 13·15 |
| 5·7 | + 13·92 | | 13·15 | + 13·09 |
| 7·9 | + 13·57 | | | |

Bottom flange:

| | | | | | |
|---|---|---|---|---|---|
| S. 2·4 | − 12·50 | | S. 10·12 | − 12·91 |
| 4·6 | − 12·81 | | 12·14 | − 12·92 |
| 6·8 | − 12·87 | | 14·14 | − 12·92 |
| 8·10 | − 12·91 | | | |

Inclined bracing:

| | | | | | |
|---|---|---|---|---|---|
| S. 3·4 | + | 0·0000 | S. 9·10 | + | 1·1220 |
| 3·4 | − | 0·8819 | 9·10 | − | 1·6380 |
| 4·5 | + | 0·4026 | 10·11 | + | 1·2852 |
| 4·5 | − | 1·1790 | 10·11 | − | 1·8300 |
| 5·6 | + | 0·5340 | 11·12 | + | 1·3000 |
| 5·6 | − | 1·0956 | 11·12 | − | 1·8216 |
| 6·7 | + | 0·8140 | 12·13 | + | 1·4056 |
| 6·7 | − | 1·4280 | 12·13 | − | 1·9350 |
| 7·8 | + | 0·8640 | 13·14 | + | 1·4145 |
| 7·8 | − | 1·3915 | 13·14 | − | 1·9320 |
| 8·9 | + | 1·0935 | 14·15 | + | 1·4448 |
| 8·9 | − | 1·6620 | 14·15 | − | 1·9782 |

# TRUSS DIAGRAM No. 50.

### PARABOLIC BOWSTRING.

#### CONDITIONS.

1. Depth at centre    ..    ..   $\frac{1}{8}$ of the span.
2. Number of panels    ..    ..   18.
3. Method of loading    ..    ..   On bottom flange.
4. Description of bracing    ..   Vertical, and inclined two ways.

### EVENLY DISTRIBUTED DEAD LOAD.

#### *Stress Constants.*

Top flange :

| | | |
|---|---|---|
| S. 2·3 | + 19·90 | |
| 3·5 | + 19·50 | |
| 5·7 | + 19·15 | |
| 7·9 | + 18·82 | |
| 9·11 | + 18·55 | |

| | |
|---|---|
| S. 11·13 | + 18·33 |
| 13·15 | + 18·17 |
| 15·17 | + 18·06 |
| 17·19 | + 18·007 |

Bottom flange :

| | |
|---|---|
| S. 2·4 | − 18·00 |
| 4·6 | − 18·00 |
| 6·8 | − 18·00 |
| 8·10 | − 18·00 |
| 10·12 | − 18·00 |

| | |
|---|---|
| S. 12·14 | − 18·00 |
| 14·16 | − 18·00 |
| 16·18 | − 18·00 |
| 18·20 | − 18·00 |

Vertical bracing :

| | |
|---|---|
| S. 3·4 | − 1·00 |
| 5·6 | − 1·00 |
| 7·8 | − 1·00 |
| 9·10 | − 1·00 |
| 11·12 | − 1·00 |

| | |
|---|---|
| S. 13·14 | − 1·00 |
| 15·16 | − 1·00 |
| 17·18 | − 1·00 |
| 19·20 | − 1·00 |

Inclined bracing:

| | | | |
|---|---|---|---|
| S. 3·6 | 0·00 | S. 11·14 | 0·00 |
| 5·8 | 0·00 | 13·16 | 0·00 |
| 7·10 | 0·00 | 15·18 | 0·00 |
| 9·12 | 0·00 | 17·20 | 0·00 |

EVENLY DISTRIBUTED LIVE LOAD ADVANCING FROM
EITHER ABUTMENT.

*Maximum Stress Constants.*

Top flange:

| | | | |
|---|---|---|---|
| S. 2·3 + 19·90 | | S. 11·13 + 18·33 | |
| 3·5 + 19·50 | | 13·15 + 18·17 | |
| 5·7 + 19·15 | | 15·17 + 18·06 | |
| 7·9 + 18·82 | | 17·19 + 18·007 | |
| 9·11 + 18·55 | | | |

Bottom flange:

| | | | |
|---|---|---|---|
| S. 2·4 − 18·00 | | S. 12·14 − 18·00 | |
| 4·6 − 18·00 | | 14·16 − 18·00 | |
| 6·8 − 18·00 | | 16·18 − 18·00 | |
| 8·10 − 18·00 | | 18·20 − 18·00 | |
| 10·12 − 18·00 | | | |

Vertical bracing:

| | | | |
|---|---|---|---|
| S. 3·4 + 0·000 | | S. 11·12 − 2·332 | |
| 3·4 − 1·000 | | 13·14 + 1·525 | |
| 5·6 + 0·414 | | 13·14 − 2·525 | |
| 5·6 − 1·414 | | 15·16 + 1·668 | |
| 7·8 + 0·770 | | 15·16 − 2·668 | |
| 7·8 − 1·770 | | 17·18 + 1·750 | |
| 9·10 + 1·085 | | 17·18 − 2·750 | |
| 9·10 − 2·085 | | 19·20 + 0·000 | |
| 11·12 + 1·332 | | 19·20 − 1·000 | |

Inclined bracing:

| | | | | | |
|---|---|---|---|---|---|
| S. 3·6 | + | 1·106 | S. 11·14 | + | 2·064 |
| 3·6 | − | 1·106 | 11·14 | − | 2·064 |
| 5·8 | + | 1·338 | 13·16 | + | 2·237 |
| 5·8 | − | 1·338 | 13·16 | − | 2·237 |
| 7·10 | + | 1·601 | 15·18 | + | 2·360 |
| 7·10 | − | 1·601 | 15·18 | − | 2·360 |
| 9·12 | + | 1·852 | 17·20 | + | 2·439 |
| 9·12 | − | 1·852 | 17·20 | − | 2·439 |

---

## TRUSS DIAGRAM No. 51.

### PARABOLIC BOWSTRING.

#### CONDITIONS.

1. Depth at centre   ..   ..   $\frac{1}{4}$ of the span.
2. Number of panels   ..   ..   18.
3. Method of loading   ..   ..   On bottom flange.
4. Description of bracing   ..   Vertical, and inclined one way.

#### EVENLY DISTRIBUTED DEAD LOAD.

*Stress Constants.*

Top flange:

| | | | | | |
|---|---|---|---|---|---|
| S. 2·3 | + | 19·90 | S. 11·13 | + | 18·33 |
| 3·5 | + | 19·50 | 13·15 | + | 18·17 |
| 5·7 | + | 19·15 | 15·17 | + | 18·06 |
| 7·9 | + | 18·82 | 17·19 | + | 18·007 |
| 9·11 | + | 18·55 | | | |

Bottom flange:

| | | | | |
|---|---|---|---|---|
| S. 2·4 | − 18·00 | | S. 12·14 | − 18·00 |
| 4·6 | − 18·00 | | 14·16 | − 18·00 |
| 6·8 | − 18·00 | , | 16·18 | − 18·00 |
| 8·10 | − 18·00 | | 18·20 | − 18·00 |
| 10·12 | − 18·00 | | | |

Vertical bracing:

| | | | |
|---|---|---|---|
| S. 3·4 | − 1·00 | S. 13·14 | − 1·00 |
| 5·6 | − 1·00 | 15·16 | − 1·00 |
| 7·8 | − 1·00 | 17·18 | − 1·00 |
| 9·10 | − 1·00 | 19·20 | − 1·00 |
| 11·12 | − 1·00 | | |

Inclined bracing:

| | | | |
|---|---|---|---|
| S. 3·6 | 0·00 | S. 19·18 | 0·00 |
| 5·8 | 0·00 | 17·16 | 0·00 |
| 7·10 | 0·00 | 15·14 | 0·00 |
| 9·12 | 0·00 | 13·12 | 0·00 |
| 11·14 | 0·00 | 11·10 | 0·00 |
| 13·16 | 0·00 | 9·8 | 0·00 |
| 15·18 | 0·00 | 7·6 | 0·00 |
| 17·20 | 0·00 | 5·4 | 0·00 |

EVENLY DISTRIBUTED LIVE LOAD ADVANCING FROM
EITHER ABUTMENT.

*Maximum Stress Constants.*

Top flange:

| | | | |
|---|---|---|---|
| S. 2·3 | + 19·90 | S. 11·13 | + 18·33 |
| 3·5 | + 19·50 | 13·15 | + 18·17 |
| . 5·7 | + 19·15 | 15·17 | + 18·06 |
| 7·9 | + 18·82 | 17·19 | + 18·007 |
| 9·11 | + 18·55 | | |

Bottom flange:

| | | | | | |
|---|---|---|---|---|---|
| S. 2·4 | − | 18·00 | S. 12·14 | − | 18·00 |
| 4·6 | − | 18·00 | 14·16 | − | 18·00 |
| 6·8 | − | 18·00 | 16·18 | − | 18·00 |
| 8·10 | − | 18·00 | 18·20 | − | 18·00 |
| 10·12 | − | 18·00 | | | |

Vertical bracing:

| | | | | | |
|---|---|---|---|---|---|
| S. 3·4 | + | 0·000 | S. 11·12 | − | 2·332 |
| 3·4 | − | 1·000 | 13·14 | + | 1·525 |
| 5·6 | + | 0·414 | 13·14 | − | 2·525 |
| 5·6 | − | 1·414 | 15·16 | + | 1·668 |
| 7·8 | + | 0·770 | 15·16 | − | 2·668 |
| 7·8 | − | 1·770 | 17·18 | + | 1·750 |
| 9·10 | + | 1·085 | 17·18 | − | 2·750 |
| 9·10 | − | 2·085 | 19·20 | + | 1·778 |
| 11·12 | + | 1·332 | 19·20 | − | 2·778 |

Inclined bracing:

| | | | | | |
|---|---|---|---|---|---|
| S. 3·6 | + | 1·106 | S. 19·18 | + | 2·463 |
| 3·6 | − | 1·106 | 19·18 | − | 2·463 |
| 5·8 | + | 1·338 | 17·16 | + | 2·439 |
| 5·8 | − | 1·338 | 17·16 | − | 2·439 |
| 7·10 | + | 1·601 | 15·14 | + | 2·360 |
| 7·10 | − | 1·601 | 15·14 | − | 2·360 |
| 9·12 | + | 1·852 | 13·12 | + | 2·237 |
| 9·12 | − | 1·852 | 13·12 | − | 2·237 |
| 11·14 | + | 2·064 | 11·10 | + | 2·064 |
| 11·14 | − | 2·064 | 11·10 | − | 2·064 |
| 13·16 | + | 2·237 | 9·8 | + | 1·852 |
| 13·16 | − | 2·237 | 9·8 | − | 1·852 |
| 15·18 | + | 2·360 | 7·6 | + | 1·601 |
| 15·18 | − | 2·360 | 7·6 | − | 1·601 |
| 17·20 | + | 2·439 | 5·4 | + | 1·338 |
| 17·20 | − | 2·439 | 5·4 | − | 1·338 |

# TRUSS DIAGRAM No. 52.

### PARABOLIC BOWSTRING.

#### CONDITIONS.

1. Depth at centre    ..    ..    $\frac{1}{8}$ of the span.
2. Number of panels  ..    ..    18.
3. Method of loading  ..    ..    On bottom flange.
4. Description of bracing    ..    Vertical and inclined cross bracing.

### EVENLY DISTRIBUTED DEAD LOAD.

#### *Stress Constants.*

Top flange :

| | | | | | |
|---|---|---|---|---|---|
| S. 2·3 | + | 19·90 | S. 11·13 | + | 18·33 |
| 3·5 | + | 19·50 | 13·15 | + | 18·17 |
| 5·7 | + | 19·15 | 15·17 | + | 18·06 |
| 7·9 | + | 18·82 | 17·19 | + | 18·007 |
| 9·11 | + | 18·55 | | | |

Bottom flange :

| | | | | | |
|---|---|---|---|---|---|
| S. 2·4 | − | 18·00 | S. 12·14 | − | 18·00 |
| 4·6 | − | 18·00 | 14·16 | − | 18·00 |
| 6·8 | − | 18·00 | 16·18 | − | 18·00 |
| 8·10 | − | 18·00 | 18·20 | − | 18·00 |
| 10·12 | − | 18·00 | | | |

Vertical bracing :

| | | | | | |
|---|---|---|---|---|---|
| S. 3·4 | − | 1·00 | S. 13·14 | − | 1·00 |
| 5·6 | − | 1·00 | 15·16 | − | 1·00 |
| 7·8 | − | 1·00 | 17·18 | − | 1·00 |
| 9·10 | − | 1·00 | 19·20 | − | 1·00 |
| 11·12 | − | 1·00 | | | |

I 2

Inclined bracing:

| | | | | |
|---|---|---|---|---|
| S. 3·6 | 0·00 | S. 4·5 | 0·00 |
| 5·8 | 0·00 | 6·7 | 0·00 |
| 7·10 | 0·00 | 8·9 | 0·00 |
| 9·12 | 0·00 | 10·11 | 0·00 |
| 11·14 | 0·00 | 12·13 | 0·00 |
| 13·16 | 0·00 | 14·15 | 0·00 |
| 15·18 | 0·00 | 16·17 | 0·00 |
| 17·20 | 0·00 | 18·19 | 0·00 |

## EVENLY DISTRIBUTED LIVE LOAD ADVANCING FROM EITHER ABUTMENT.

### *Maximum Stress Constants.*

Top flange:

| | | | | |
|---|---|---|---|---|
| S. 2·3 | + 19·90 | S. 11·13 | + 18·33 |
| 3·5 | + 19·50 | 13·15 | + 18·17 |
| 5·7 | + 19·15 | 15·17 | + 18·06 |
| 7·9 | + 18·82 | 17·19 | + 18·007 |
| 9·11 | + 18·55 | | |

Bottom flange:

| | | | | |
|---|---|---|---|---|
| S. 2·4 | − 18·00 | S. 12·14 | − 18·00 |
| 4·6 | − 18·00 | 14·16 | − 18·00 |
| 6·8 | − 18·00 | 16·18 | − 18·00 |
| 8·10 | − 18·00 | 18·20 | − 18·00 |
| 10·12 | − 18·00 | | |

Vertical bracing:

| S. 3·4 | + | 0·000 | S. 11·12 | − | 1·000 |
|---|---|---|---|---|---|
| 3·4 | − | 1·000 | 13·14 | + | 1·525 |
| 5·6 | + | 0·414 | 13·14 | − | 1·000 |
| 5·6 | − | 1·000 | 15·16 | + | 1·668 |
| 7·8 | + | 0·770 | 15·16 | − | 1·000 |
| 7·8 | − | 1·000 | 17·18 | + | 1·750 |
| 9·10 | + | 1·085 | 17·18 | − | 1·000 |
| 9·10 | − | 1·000 | 19·20 | + | 1·778 |
| 11·12 | + | 1·332 | 19·20 | − | 1·000 |

Inclined bracing all ties with live load:

| S. 3·6 | − | 1·106 | S. 4·5 | − | 1·338 |
|---|---|---|---|---|---|
| 5·8 | − | 1·338 | 6·7 | − | 1·601 |
| 7·10 | − | 1·601 | 8·9 | − | 1·852 |
| 9·12 | − | 1·852 | 10·11 | − | 2·064 |
| 11·14 | − | 2·064 | 12·13 | − | 2·237 |
| 13·16 | − | 2·237 | 14·15 | − | 2·360 |
| 15·18 | − | 2·360 | 16·17 | − | 2·439 |
| 17·20 | − | 2·439 | 18·19 | − | 2·463 |

## TRUSS DIAGRAM No. 53.

### PARABOLIC BOWSTRING.

### CONDITIONS.

1. Depth at centre    ..    ..    $\frac{1}{4}$ of the span.
2. Number of panels    ..    ..    18.
3. Method of loading    ..    ..    On bottom flange.
4. Description of bracing    ..    Vertical and inclined cross bracing.

### EVENLY DISTRIBUTED DEAD LOAD.

#### *Stress Constants.*

Top flange :

| | | |
|---|---|---|
| S. 2·3 | + 19·90 | S. 11·13   + 18·33 |
| 3·5 | + 19·50 | 13·15   + 18·17 |
| 5·7 | + 19·15 | 15·17   + 18·06 |
| 7·9 | + 18·82 | 17·19   + 18·007 |
| 9·11 | + 18·55 | |

Bottom flange :

| | | |
|---|---|---|
| S. 2·4 | − 18·00 | S. 12·14   − 18·00 |
| 4·6 | − 18·00 | 14·16   − 18·00 |
| 6·8 | − 18·00 | 16·18   − 18·00 |
| 8·10 | − 18·00 | 18·20   − 18·00 |
| 10·12 | − 18·00 | |

Vertical bracing :

| | | |
|---|---|---|
| S. 3·4 | − 1·00 | S. 13·14   − 1·00 |
| 5·6 | − 1·00 | 15·16   − 1·00 |
| 7·8 | − 1·00 | 17·18   − 1·00 |
| 9·10 | − 1·00 | 19·20   − 1·00 |
| 11·12 | − 1·00 | |

# TRUSS DIAGRAMS

PLATE 13

49

50

51

52

Tho⁵ Kell & Son Lith

E & F N Spon, London & New York

Inclined bracing:

| S. 3·6 | 0·00 | S. 4·5 | 0·00 |
|---|---|---|---|
| 5·8 | 0·00 | 6·7 | 0·00 |
| 7·10 | 0·00 | 8·9 | 0·00 |
| 9·12 | 0·00 | 10·11 | 0·00 |
| 11·14 | 0·00 | 12·13 | 0·00 |
| 13·16 | 0·00 | 14·15 | 0·00 |
| 15·18 | 0·00 | 16·17 | 0·00 |
| 17·20 | 0·00 | 18·19 | 0·00 |

EVENLY DISTRIBUTED LIVE LOAD ADVANCING FROM EITHER ABUTMENT.

*Maximum Stress Constants.*

Top flange:

| S. 2·3 | + 19·90 | S. 11·13 | + 18·33 |
|---|---|---|---|
| 3·5 | + 19·50 | 13·15 | + 18·17 |
| 5·7 | + 19·15 | 15·17 | + 18·06 |
| 7·9 | + 18·82 | 17·19 | + 18·007 |
| 9·11 | + 18·55 | | |

Bottom flange:

| S. 2·4 | − 18·00 | S. 12·14 | − 18·00 |
|---|---|---|---|
| 4·6 | − 18·00 | 14·16 | − 18·00 |
| 6·8 | − 18·00 | 16·18 | − 18·00 |
| 8·10 | − 18·00 | 18·20 | − 18·00 |
| 10·12 | − 18·00 | | |

Vertical bracing all ties with live load:

| S. 3·4 | − 1·000 | S. 13·14 | − 2·525 |
|---|---|---|---|
| 5·6 | − 1·414 | 15·16 | − 2·668 |
| 7·8 | − 1·770 | 17·18 | − 2·750 |
| 9·10 | − 2·085 | 19·20 | − 2·778 |
| 11·12 | − 2·332 | | |

Inclined bracing all struts with live load:

| | | | | | |
|---|---|---|---|---|---|
| S. 3·6 | + | 1·106 | S. 4·5 | + | 1·338 |
| 5·8 | + | 1·338 | 6·7 | + | 1·601 |
| 7·10 | + | 1·601 | 8·9 | + | 1·852 |
| 9·12 | + | 1·852 | 10·11 | + | 2·064 |
| 11·14 | + | 2·064 | 12·13 | + | 2·237 |
| 13·16 | + | 2·237 | 14·15 | + | 2·360 |
| 15·18 | + | 2·360 | 16·17 | + | 2·439 |
| 17·20 | + | 2·439 | 18·19 | + | 2·463 |

---

## TRUSS DIAGRAM No. 54.

### MULTIPLE LINVILLE.

#### CONDITIONS.

1. Depth   ..   ..   ..   ..   ⅛ of the span.
2. Number of panels   ..   ..   16.
3. Method of loading   ..   ..   On top flange.
4. Description of bracing   ..   Vertical and inclined one way.

#### EVENLY DISTRIBUTED DEAD LOAD.

*Stress Constants.*

Top flange:

| | | | | | |
|---|---|---|---|---|---|
| S. 1·3 | + | 5·50 | S. 17·19 | + | 15·50 |
| 3·5 | + | 8·50 | 19·21 | + | 14·50 |
| 5·7 | + | 11·00 | 21·23 | + | 13·00 |
| 7·9 | + | 13·00 | 23·25 | + | 11·00 |
| 9·11 | + | 14·50 | 25·27 | + | 8·50 |
| 11·13 | + | 15·50 | 27·29 | + | 5·50 |
| 13·15 | + | 16·00 | 29·31 | + | 2·00 |
| 15·17 | + | 16·00 | 31·33 | + | 0·00 |

Bottom flange:

| | | | | | |
|---|---|---|---|---|---|
| S. 2·4 | − | 0·00 | S. 18·20 | − | 16·00 |
| 4·6 | − | 2·00 | 20·22 | − | 16·00 |
| 6·8 | − | 5·50 | 22·24 | − | 15·50 |
| 8·10 | − | 8·50 | 24·26 | − | 14·50 |
| 10·12 | − | 11·00 | 26·28 | − | 13·00 |
| 12·14 | − | 13·00 | 28·30 | − | 11·00 |
| 14·16 | − | 14·50 | 30·32 | − | 8·50 |
| 16·18 | − | 15·50 | 32·34 | − | 5·50 |

Vertical bracing:

| | | | | | |
|---|---|---|---|---|---|
| S. 1·2 | + | 8·00 | S. 19·20 | | 0·00 |
| 3·4 | + | 4·00 | 21·22 | − | 0·50 |
| 5·6 | + | 3·50 | 23·24 | − | 1·00 |
| 7·8 | + | 3·00 | 25·26 | − | 1·50 |
| 9·10 | + | 2·50 | 27·28 | − | 2·00 |
| 11·12 | + | 2·00 | 29·30 | − | 2·50 |
| 13·14 | + | 1·50 | 31·32 | − | 3·00 |
| 15·16 | + | 1·00 | 33·34 | + | 0·50 |
| 17·18 | + | 0·50 | | | |

Inclined bracing:

| | | | | | |
|---|---|---|---|---|---|
| S. 1·4 | − | 4·48 | S. 17·22 | + | 0·71 |
| 1·6 | − | 4·94 | 19·24 | + | 1·41 |
| 3·8 | − | 4·23 | 21·26 | + | 2·12 |
| 5·10 | − | 3·53 | 23·28 | + | 2·82 |
| 7·12 | − | 2·82 | 25·30 | + | 3·53 |
| 9·14 | − | 2·12 | 27·32 | + | 4·23 |
| 11·16 | − | 1·41 | 29·34 | + | 4·94 |
| 13·18 | − | 0·71 | 31·34 | + | 4·48 |
| 15·20 | | 0·00 | | | |

## EVENLY DISTRIBUTED LIVE LOAD ADVANCING FROM EITHER ABUTMENT.

### *Maximum Stress Constants.*

Top flange :

| | | | | | |
|---|---|---|---|---|---|
| S. 1·3 | + | 5·50 | S. 17·19 | + | 15·50 |
| 3·5 | + | 8·50 | 19·21 | + | 14·50 |
| 5·7 | + | 11·00 | 21·23 | + | 13·00 |
| 7·9 | + | 13·00 | 23·25 | + | 11·00 |
| 9·11 | + | 14·50 | 25·27 | + | 8·50 |
| 11·13 | + | 15·50 | 27·29 | + | 5·50 |
| 13·15 | + | 16·00 | 29·31 | + | 2·00 |
| 15·17 | + | 16·00 | 31·33 | + | 0·00 |

Bottom flange :

| | | | | | |
|---|---|---|---|---|---|
| S. 2·4 | − | 0·00 | S. 18·20 | − | 16·00 |
| 4·6 | − | 2·00 | 20·22 | − | 16·00 |
| 6·8 | − | 5·50 | 22·24 | − | 15·50 |
| 8·10 | − | 8·50 | 24·26 | − | 14·50 |
| 10·12 | − | 11·00 | 26·28 | − | 13·00 |
| 12·14 | − | 13·00 | 28·30 | − | 11·00 |
| 14·16 | − | 14·50 | 30·32 | − | 8·50 |
| 16·18 | − | 15·50 | 32·34 | − | 5·50 |

Vertical bracing :

| | | | | | |
|---|---|---|---|---|---|
| S. 1·2 | + | 8·000 | S. 9·10 | + | 2·625 |
| 1·2 | − | 0·000 | 9·10 | − | 0·125 |
| 3·4 | + | 4·000 | 11·12 | + | 2·250 |
| 3·4 | − | 0·000 | 11·12 | − | 0·250 |
| 5·6 | + | 3·500 | 13·14 | + | 1·875 |
| 5·6 | − | 0·000 | 13·14 | − | 0·375 |
| 7·8 | + | 3·063 | 15·16 | + | 1·563 |
| 7·8 | − | 0·063 | 15·16 | − | 0·563 |

Vertical bracing—*continued*:

| | | | | | |
|---|---|---|---|---|---|
| S. 17·18 | + | 1·250 | S. 25·26 | − | 1·875 |
| 17·18 | − | 0·750 | 27·28 | + | 0·250 |
| 19·20 | + | 1·000 | 27·28 | − | 2·250 |
| 19·20 | − | 1·000 | 29·30 | + | 0·125 |
| 21·22 | + | 0·750 | 29·30 | − | 2·625 |
| 21·22 | − | 1·250 | 31·32 | + | 0·062 |
| 23·24 | + | 0·563 | 31·32 | − | 3·062 |
| 23·24 | − | 1·563 | 33·34 | + | 0·500 |
| 25·26 | + | 0·375 | 33·34 | − | 0·000 |

Inclined bracing:

| | | | | | |
|---|---|---|---|---|---|
| S. 1·4 | + | 0·000 | S. 15·20 | − | 1·414 |
| 1·4 | − | 4·480 | 17·22 | + | 1·762 |
| 1·6 | + | 0·000 | 17·22 | − | 1·057 |
| 1·6 | − | 4·935 | 19·24 | + | 2·203 |
| 3·8 | + | 0·088 | 19·24 | − | 0·793 |
| 3·8 | − | 4·318 | 21·26 | + | 2·643 |
| 5·10 | + | 0·176 | 21·26 | − | 0·528 |
| 5·10 | − | 3·701 | 23·28 | + | 3·172 |
| 7·12 | + | 0·352 | 23·28 | − | 0·352 |
| 7·12 | − | 3·172 | 25·30 | + | 3·701 |
| 9·14 | + | 0·528 | 25·30 | − | 0·176 |
| 9·14 | − | 2·643 | 27·32 | + | 4·318 |
| 11·16 | + | 0·793 | 27·32 | − | 0·088 |
| 11·16 | − | 2·203 | 29·34 | + | 4·935 |
| 13·18 | + | 1·057 | 29·34 | − | 0·000 |
| 13·18 | − | 1·762 | 31·34 | + | 4·480 |
| 15·20 | + | 1·414 | 31·34 | − | 0·000 |

*Note.*—The stresses in the bracing when inclined opposite ways from the centre can easily be determined from these constants, also the stresses in counterbraces if these are added in some of the panels. The parts 2·4 would practically be made of the same strength as 4·6, and 33·34 require particularly to be considered for axle loads.

# TRUSS DIAGRAM No. 55.

## MULTIPLE LINVILLE.

### CONDITIONS.

1. Depth     ..   ..   ..   ..   $\frac{1}{10}$ of the span.
2. Number of panels   ..   ..   20.
3. Method of loading   ..   ..   On top flange.
4. Description of bracing   ..   Vertical and inclined one way.

### EVENLY DISTRIBUTED DEAD LOAD.

*Stress Constants.*

Top flange:

| | | | | | |
|---|---|---|---|---|---|
| S. 1·3 | + | 7·00 | S. 21·23 | + | 24·50 |
| 3·5 | + | 11·00 | 23·25 | + | 23·50 |
| 5·7 | + | 14·50 | 25·27 | + | 22·00 |
| 7·9 | + | 17·50 | 27·29 | + | 20·00 |
| 9·11 | + | 20·00 | 29·31 | + | 17·50 |
| 11·13 | + | 22·00 | 31·33 | + | 14·50 |
| 13·15 | + | 23·50 | 33·35 | + | 11·00 |
| 15·17 | + | 24·50 | 35·37 | + | 7·00 |
| 17·19 | + | 25·00 | 37·39 | + | 2·50 |
| 19·21 | + | 25·00 | 39·41 | + | 0·00 |

Bottom flange:

| | | | | | |
|---|---|---|---|---|---|
| S. 2·4 | — | 0·00 | S. 22·24 | — | 25·00 |
| 4·6 | — | 2·50 | 24·26 | — | 25·00 |
| 6·8 | — | 7·00 | 26·28 | — | 24·50 |
| 8·10 | — | 11·00 | 28·30 | — | 23·50 |
| 10·12 | — | 14·50 | 30·32 | — | 22·00 |
| 12·14 | — | 17·50 | 32·34 | — | 20·00 |
| 14·16 | — | 20·00 | 34·36 | — | 17·50 |
| 16·18 | — | 22·00 | 36·38 | — | 14·50 |
| 18·20 | — | 23·50 | 38·40 | — | 11·00 |
| 20·22 | — | 24·50 | 40·42 | — | 7·00 |

Vertical bracing:

| | | | | | |
|---|---|---|---|---|---|
| S. 1·2 | + | 10·00 | S. 23·24 | | 0·00 |
| 3·4 | + | 5·00 | 25·26 | − | 0·50 |
| 5·6 | + | 4·50 | 27·28 | − | 1·00 |
| 7·8 | + | 4·00 | 29·30 | − | 1·50 |
| 9·10 | + | 3·50 | 31·32 | − | 2·00 |
| 11·12 | + | 3·00 | 33·34 | − | 2·50 |
| 13·14 | + | 2·50 | 35·36 | − | 3·00 |
| 15·16 | + | 2·00 | 37·38 | − | 3·50 |
| 17·18 | + | 1·50 | 39·40 | − | 4·00 |
| 19·20 | + | 1·00 | 41·42 | + | 0·50 |
| 21·22 | + | 0·50 | | | |

Inclined bracing:

| | | | | | |
|---|---|---|---|---|---|
| S. 1·4 | − | 5·60 | S. 21·26 | + | 0·70 |
| 1·6 | − | 6·34 | 23·28 | + | 1·41 |
| 3·8 | − | 5·64 | 25·30 | + | 2·11 |
| 5·10 | − | 4·93 | 27·32 | + | 2·82 |
| 7·12 | − | 4·23 | 29·34 | + | 3·52 |
| 9·14 | − | 3·52 | 31·36 | + | 4·23 |
| 11·16 | − | 2·82 | 33·38 | + | 4·93 |
| 13·18 | − | 2·11 | 35·40 | + | 5·64 |
| 15·20 | − | 1·41 | 37·42 | + | 6·34 |
| 17·22 | − | 0·70 | 39·42 | + | 5·60 |
| 19·24 | | 0·00 | | | |

EVENLY DISTRIBUTED LIVE LOAD ADVANCING FROM EITHER ABUTMENT.

*Maximum Stress Constants.*

Top flange:

| | | | | | |
|---|---|---|---|---|---|
| S. 1·3 | + | 7·00 | S. 7·9 | + | 17·50 |
| 3·5 | + | 11·00 | 9·11 | + | 20·00 |
| 5·7 | + | 14·50 | 11·13 | + | 22·00 |

Top flange—*continued:*

| | | |
|---|---|---|
| S. 13·15 | + | 23·50 |
| 15·17 | + | 24·50 |
| 17·19 | + | 25·00 |
| 19·21 | + | 25·00 |
| 21·23 | + | 24·50 |
| 23·25 | + | 23·50 |
| 25·27 | + | 22·00 |

| | | |
|---|---|---|
| S. 27·29 | + | 20·00 |
| 29·31 | + | 17·50 |
| 31·33 | + | 14·50 |
| 33·35 | + | 11·00 |
| 35·37 | + | 7·00 |
| 37·39 | + | 2·50 |
| 39·41 | + | 0·00 |

Bottom flange:

| | | |
|---|---|---|
| S. 2·4 | − | 0·00 |
| 4·6 | − | 2·50 |
| 6·8 | − | 7·00 |
| 8·10 | − | 11·00 |
| 10·12 | − | 14·50 |
| 12·14 | − | 17·50 |
| 14·16 | − | 20·00 |
| 16·18 | − | 22·00 |
| 18·20 | − | 23·50 |
| 20·22 | − | 24·50 |

| | | |
|---|---|---|
| S. 22·24 | − | 25·00 |
| 24·26 | − | 25·00 |
| 26·28 | − | 24·50 |
| 28·30 | − | 23·50 |
| 30·32 | − | 22·00 |
| 32·34 | − | 20·00 |
| 34·36 | − | 17·50 |
| 36·38 | − | 14·50 |
| 38·40 | − | 11·00 |
| 40·42 | − | 7·00 |

Vertical bracing:

| | | |
|---|---|---|
| S. 1·2 | + | 10·00 |
| 1·2 | − | 0·00 |
| 3·4 | + | 5·00 |
| 3·4 | − | 0·00 |
| 5·6 | + | 4·50 |
| 5·6 | − | 0·00 |
| 7·8 | + | 4·05 |
| 7·8 | − | 0·05 |
| 9·10 | + | 3·60 |
| 9·10 | − | 0·10 |
| 11·12 | + | 3·20 |
| 11·12 | − | 0·20 |
| 13·14 | + | 2·80 |
| 13·14 | − | 0·30 |

| | | |
|---|---|---|
| S. 15·16 | + | 2·45 |
| 15·16 | − | 0·45 |
| 17·18 | + | 2·10 |
| 17·18 | − | 0·60 |
| 19·20 | + | 1·80 |
| 19·20 | − | 0·80 |
| 21·22 | + | 1·50 |
| 21·22 | − | 1·00 |
| 23·24 | + | 1·25 |
| 23·24 | − | 1·25 |
| 25·26 | + | 1·00 |
| 25·26 | − | 1·50 |
| 27·28 | + | 0·80 |
| 27·28 | − | 1·80 |

Vertical bracing—*continued*:

| | | | | | |
|---|---|---|---|---|---|
| S. 29·30 | + | 0·60 | S. 35·36 | − | 3·20 |
| 29·30 | − | 2·10 | 37·38 | + | 0·10 |
| 31·32 | + | 0·45 | 37·38 | − | 3·60 |
| 31·32 | − | 2·45 | 39·40 | + | 0·05 |
| 33·34 | + | 0·30 | 39·40 | − | 4·05 |
| 33·34 | − | 2·80 | 41·42 | + | 0·50 |
| 35·36 | + | 0·20 | 41·42 | − | 0·00 |

Inclined bracing:

| | | | | | |
|---|---|---|---|---|---|
| S. 1·4 | + | 0·000 | S. 19·24 | − | 1·762 |
| 1·4 | − | 5·600 | 21·26 | + | 2·121 |
| 1·6 | + | 0·000 | 21·26 | − | 1·414 |
| 1·6 | − | 6·345 | 23·28 | + | 2·538 |
| 3·8 | + | 0·070 | 23·28 | − | 1·128 |
| 3·8 | − | 5·710 | 25·30 | + | 2·961 |
| 5·10 | + | 0·141 | 25·30 | − | 0·846 |
| 5·10 | − | 5·076 | 27·32 | + | 3·454 |
| 7·12 | + | 0·282 | 27·32 | − | 0·634 |
| 7·12 | − | 4·512 | 29·34 | + | 3·948 |
| 9·14 | + | 0·423 | 29·34 | − | 0·423 |
| 9·14 | − | 3·948 | 31·36 | + | 4·512 |
| 11·16 | + | 0·634 | 31·36 | − | 0·282 |
| 11·16 | − | 3·454 | 33·38 | + | 5·076 |
| 13·18 | + | 0·846 | 33·38 | − | 0·141 |
| 13·18 | − | 2·961 | 35·40 | + | 5·710 |
| 15·20 | + | 1·128 | 35·40 | − | 0·070 |
| 15·20 | − | 2·538 | 37·42 | + | 6·345 |
| 17·22 | + | 1·414 | 37·42 | − | 0·000 |
| 17·22 | − | 2·121 | 39·42 | + | 5·600 |
| 19·24 | + | 1·762 | 39·42 | − | 0·000 |

*Note.*—The stresses in the bracing when inclined opposite ways from the centre can easily be determined from these constants, also the stresses in counterbraces if these are added in some of the panels. The parts 2·4 would practically be made of the same strength as 4·6, and 41·42 require particularly to be considered for axle loads.

---

## TRUSS DIAGRAM No. 56.

### PARABOLIC BOWSTRING.

#### CONDITIONS.

1. Depth at centre     ..    ..   ⅛ of the span.
2. Number of panels   ..    ..   8.
3. Method of loading  ..    ..   On bottom flange.
4. Description of bracing  ..   Vertical and inclined two ways.

### EVENLY DISTRIBUTED DEAD LOAD.

*Stress Constants.*

Top flange:

| | | |
|---|---|---|
| S. 2·3 + 6·94 | S. 5·7 + 6·18 |
| 3·5 + 6·50 | 7·9 + 6·02 |

Bottom flange:

| | |
|---|---|
| S. 2·4 − 6·00 | S. 6·8 − 6·00 |
| 4·6 − 6·00 | 8·10 − 6·00 |

Vertical bracing:

| | |
|---|---|
| S. 3·4 − 1·00 | S. 7·8 − 1·00 |
| 5·6 − 1·00 | 9·10 − 1·00 |

Inclined bracing:

| | | | | |
|---|---|---|---|---|
| S. 3·6 | .. | .. | .. | 0·00 |
| 5·8 | .. | .. | .. | 0·00 |
| 7·10 | .. | .. | .. | 0·00 |

EVENLY DISTRIBUTED LIVE LOAD ADVANCING FROM EITHER ABUTMENT.

*Maximum Stress Constants.*

Top flange:

| | | | | |
|---|---|---|---|---|
| S. 2·3 + 6·94 | | S. 5·7 + 6·18 | |
| 3·5 + 6·50 | | 7·9 + 6·02 | |

Bottom flange:

| | | |
|---|---|---|
| S. 2·4 − 6·00 | S. 6·8 − 6·00 |
| 4·6 − 6·00 | 8·10 − 6·00 |

Vertical bracing:

| | | |
|---|---|---|
| S. 3·4 + 0·000 | S. 7·8 + 0·500 |
| 3·4 − 1·000 | 7·8 − 1·500 |
| 5·6 + 0·312 | 9·10 + 0·000 |
| 5·6 − 1·312 | 9·10 − 1·000 |

Inclined bracing:

| | | |
|---|---|---|
| S. 3·6 + 0·868 | S. 5·8 − 1·060 |
| 3·6 − 0·868 | 7·10 + 1·200 |
| 5·8 + 1·060 | 7·10 − 1·200 |

K

## TRUSS DIAGRAM No. 57.

PARABOLIC BOWSTRING.

### CONDITIONS.

1. Depth at centre     ..   ..   $\frac{1}{6}$ of the span.
2. Number of panels    ..   ..   8.
3. Method of loading   ..   ..   On bottom flange.
4. Description of bracing   ..   Vertical and inclined one way.

### EVENLY DISTRIBUTED DEAD LOAD.

*Stress Constants.*

Top flange:

|  |  |  |  |
|---|---|---|---|
| S. 2·3 | + 6·94 | S. 5·7 | + 6·18 |
| 3·5 | + 6·50 | 7·9 | + 6·02 |

Bottom flange:

|  |  |  |  |
|---|---|---|---|
| S. 2·4 | − 6·00 | S. 6·8 | − 6·00 |
| 4·6 | − 6·00 | 8·10 | − 6·00 |

Vertical bracing:

|  |  |  |  |
|---|---|---|---|
| S. 3·4 | − 1·00 | S. 7·8 | − 1·00 |
| 5·6 | − 1·00 | 9·10 | − 1·00 |

Inclined bracing:

|  |  |  |  |
|---|---|---|---|
| S. 3·6 | 0·00 | S. 9·8 | 0·00 |
| 5·8 | 0·00 | 7·6 | 0·00 |
| 7·10 | 0·00 | 5·4 | 0·00 |

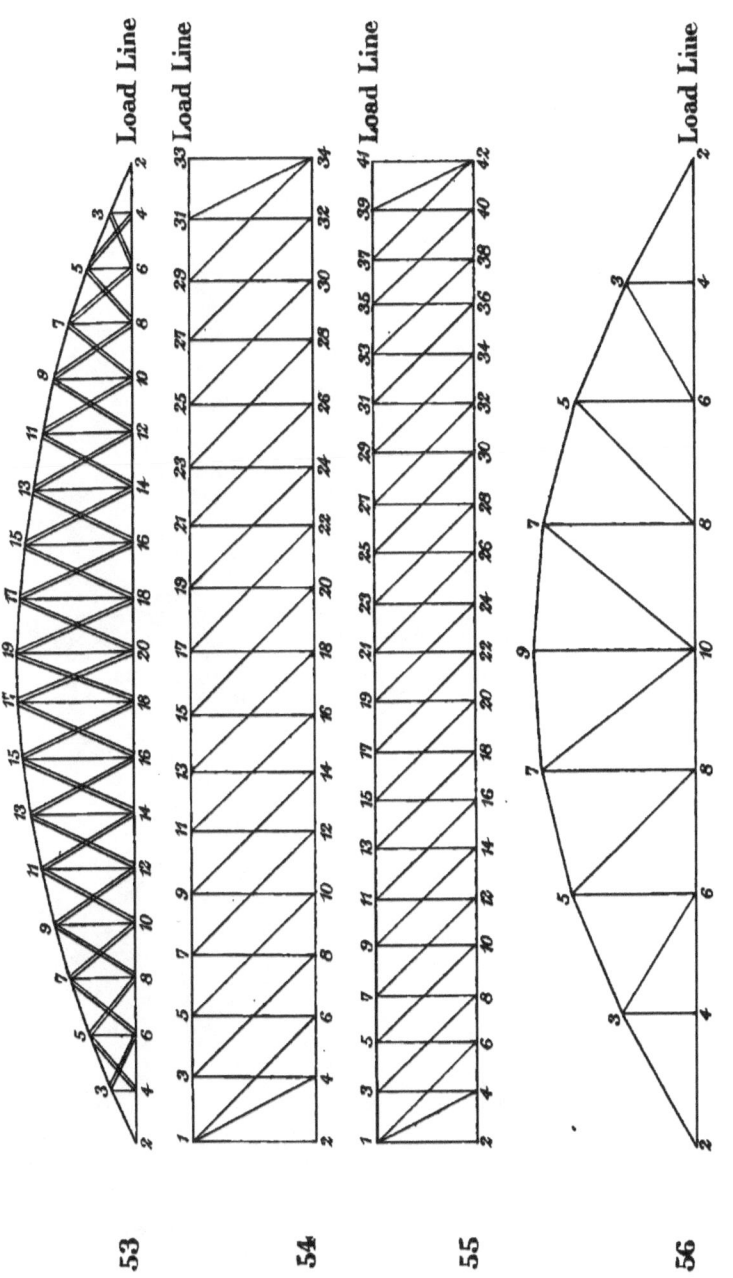

PLATE 14

Tho⁵ Kell & Son Lith

E & F N Spon. London & New York

Load Line

Load Line

Load Line

Load Line

53

54

55

56

EVENLY DISTRIBUTED LIVE LOAD ADVANCING FROM
EITHER ABUTMENT.

*Maximum Stress Constants.*

Top flange:

| | | | | | | |
|---|---|---|---|---|---|---|
| S. 2·3 | + | 6·94 | S. 5·7 | + | 6·18 |
| 3·5 | + | 6·50 | 7·9 | + | 6·02 |

Bottom flange:

| | | | | | | |
|---|---|---|---|---|---|---|
| S. 2·4 | − | 6·00 | S. 6·8 | − | 6·00 |
| 4·6 | − | 6·00 | 8·10 | − | 6·00 |

Vertical bracing:

| | | | | | | |
|---|---|---|---|---|---|---|
| S. 3·4 | + | 0·000 | S. 7·8 | + | 0·500 |
| 3·4 | − | 1·000 | 7·8 | − | 1·500 |
| 5·6 | + | 0·312 | 9·10 | + | 0·562 |
| 5·6 | − | 1·312 | 9·10 | − | 1·562 |

Inclined bracing:

| | | | | | | |
|---|---|---|---|---|---|---|
| S. 3·6 | + | 0·868 | S. 9·8 | + | 1·250 |
| 3·6 | − | 0·868 | 9·8 | − | 1·250 |
| 5·8 | + | 1·060 | 7·6 | + | 1·200 |
| 5·8 | − | 1·060 | 7·6 | − | 1·200 |
| 7·10 | + | 1·200 | 5·4 | + | 1·060 |
| 7·10 | − | 1·200 | 5·4 | − | 1·060 |

K 2

# TRUSS DIAGRAM No. 58.

### PARABOLIC BOWSTRING.

#### CONDITIONS.

1. Depth at centre    ..    ..    $\frac{1}{8}$ of the span.
2. Number of panels    ..    ..    8.
3. Method of loading    ..    ..    On bottom flange.
4. Description of bracing    ..    Vertical and inclined cross bracing.

### EVENLY DISTRIBUTED DEAD LOAD.

#### *Stress Constants.*

Top flange :

    S. 2·3   +   6·94      S. 5·7   +   6·18
        3·5   +   6·50         7·9   +   6·02

Bottom flange :

    S. 2·4   —   6·00      S. 6·8   —   6·00
        4·6   —   6·00         8·10 —   6·00

Vertical bracing :

    S. 3·4   —   1·00      S. 7·8   —   1·00
        5·6   —   1·00         9·10 —   1·00

Inclined bracing :

    S. 3·6      0·00      S. 4·5      0·00
        5·8      0·00         6·7      0·00
       7·10      0·00         8·9      0·00

EVENLY DISTRIBUTED LIVE LOAD ADVANCING FROM
EITHER ABUTMENT.

*Maximum Stress Constants.*

Top flange :

| S. 2·3 | + | 6·94 | S. 5·7 | + | 6·18 |
|---|---|---|---|---|---|
| 3·5 | + | 6·50 | 7·9 | + | 6·02 |

Bottom flange :

| S. 2·4 | − | 6·00 | S. 6·8 | − | 6·00 |
|---|---|---|---|---|---|
| 4·6 | − | 6·00 | 8·10 | − | 6·00 |

Vertical bracing :

| S. 3·4 | + | 0·000 | S. 7·8 | + | 0·500 |
|---|---|---|---|---|---|
| 3·4 | − | 1·000 | 7·8 | − | 1·000 |
| 5·6 | + | 0·312 | 9·10 | + | 0·562 |
| 5·6 | − | 1·000 | 9·10 | − | 1·000 |

Inclined bracing all ties with live load :

| S. 3·6 | − | 0·868 | S. 4·5 | − | 1·060 |
|---|---|---|---|---|---|
| 5·8 | − | 1·060 | 6·7 | − | 1·200 |
| 7·10 | − | 1·200 | 8·9 | − | 1·250 |

## STRESS DIAGRAM No. 59.

### PARABOLIC BOWSTRING.

#### CONDITIONS.

1. Depth at centre    ..    ..   $\frac{1}{8}$ of the span.
2. Number of panels   ..    ..   8.
3. Method of loading   ..    ..   On bottom flange.
4. Description of bracing    ..   Vertical and inclined cross bracing.

#### EVENLY DISTRIBUTED DEAD LOAD.

*Stress Constants.*

Top flange :

| | | |
|---|---|---|
| S. 2·3 | + | 6·94 |
| 3·5 | + | 6·50 |

| | | |
|---|---|---|
| S. 5·7 | + | 6·18 |
| 7·9 | + | 6·02 |

Bottom flange :

| | | |
|---|---|---|
| S. 2·4 | − | 6·00 |
| 4·6 | − | 6·00 |

| | | |
|---|---|---|
| S. 6·8 | − | 6·00 |
| 8·10 | − | 6·00 |

Vertical bracing :

| | | |
|---|---|---|
| S. 3·4 | − | 1·00 |
| 5·6 | − | 1·00 |

| | | |
|---|---|---|
| S. 7·8 | − | 1·00 |
| 9·10 | − | 1·00 |

Inclined bracing :

| | |
|---|---|
| S. 3·6 | 0·00 |
| 5·8 | 0·00 |
| 7·10 | 0·00 |

| | |
|---|---|
| S. 4·5 | 0·00 |
| 6·7 | 0·00 |
| 8·9 | 0·00 |

EVENLY DISTRIBUTED LIVE LOAD ADVANCING FROM
EITHER ABUTMENT.

*Maximum Stress Constants.*

Top flange:

| | | | | | |
|---|---|---|---|---|---|
| S. 2·3 | + | 6·94 | S. 5·7 | + | 6·18 |
| 3·5 | + | 6·50 | 7·9 | + | 6·02 |

Bottom flange:

| | | | | | |
|---|---|---|---|---|---|
| S. 2·4 | − | 6·00 | S. 6·8 | − | 6.00 |
| 4·6 | − | 6·00 | 8·10 | − | 6·00 |

Vertical bracing all ties with live load:

| | | | | | |
|---|---|---|---|---|---|
| S. 3·4 | − | 1·000 | S. 7·8 | − | 1·500 |
| 5·6 | − | 1·312 | 9·10 | − | 1·562 |

Inclined bracing all struts with live load:

| | | | | | |
|---|---|---|---|---|---|
| S. 3·6 | + | 0·868 | S. 4·5 | + | 1·060 |
| 5·8 | + | 1·060 | 6·7 | + | 1·200 |
| 7·10 | + | 1·200 | 8·9 | + | 1·250 |

## TRUSS DIAGRAM No. 60.

### PARABOLIC BRACED ARCH.

#### CONDITIONS.

1. Depth at centre .. .. $\frac{1}{80}$ of the span. Rise $\frac{1}{8}$ of the span.
2. Number of panels.: .. 20.
3. Method of loading .. On top flange.
4. Description of bracing.. Vertical and inclined.

#### EVENLY DISTRIBUTED DEAD LOAD.

*Stress Constants.*

Top flange :

| | | | | |
|---|---|---|---|---|
| S. 1·3 | 0·00 | S. 11·13 | 0·00 |
| 3·5 | 0·00 | 13·15 | 0·00 |
| 5·7 | 0·00 | 15·17 | 0·00 |
| 7·9 | 0·00 | 17·19 | 0·00 |
| 9·11 | 0·00 | 19·21 | 0·00 |

Bottom flange :

| | | | | |
|---|---|---|---|---|
| S. 2·4 | + 22·14 | S. 12·14 | + 20·48 |
| 4·6 | + 21·74 | 14·16 | + 20·31 |
| 6·8 | + 21·36 | 16·18 | + 20·16 |
| 8·10 | + 21·01 | 18·20 | + 20·07 |
| 10·12 | + 20·74 | 20·22 | + 20·01 |

Vertical bracing :

| | | | | |
|---|---|---|---|---|
| S. 1·2 | + 0·25 | S. 13·14 | + 0·50 |
| 3·4 | + 0·50 | 15·16 | + 0·50 |
| 5·6 | + 0·50 | 17·18 | + 0·50 |
| 7·8 | + 0·50 | 19·20 | + 0·50 |
| 9·10 | + 0·50 | 21·22 | + 0·25 |
| 11·12 | + 0·50 | | |

Inclined bracing:

| S. 1·4 | 0·00 | S. 11·14 | 0·00 |
|--------|------|----------|------|
| 3·6 | 0·00 | 13·16 | 0·00 |
| 5·8 | 0·00 | 15·18 | 0·00 |
| 7·10 | 0·00 | 17·20 | 0·00 |
| 9·12 | 0·00 | 19·22 | 0·00 |

*Note.*—The dead load is supposed to be divided between the flanges.

### EVENLY DISTRIBUTED LIVE LOAD ADVANCING FROM EITHER ABUTMENT.

*Maximum Stress Constants.*

Top flange:

| S. 1·3 | + | 1·30 | S. 11·13 | + | 10·89 |
|--------|---|------|----------|---|-------|
| 1·3 | − | 1·30 | 11·13 | − | 10·89 |
| 3·5 | + | 2·79 | 13·15 | + | 12·67 |
| 3·5 | − | 2·79 | 13·15 | − | 12·67 |
| 5·7 | + | 4·51 | 15·17 | + | 12·57 |
| 5·7 | − | 4·51 | 15·17 | − | 12·57 |
| 7·9 | + | 6·47 | 17·19 | + | 9·00 |
| 7·9 | − | 6·47 | 17·19 | − | 9·00 |
| 9·11 | + | 8·57 | 19·21 | + | 0·00 |
| 9·11 | − | 8·57 | 19·21 | − | 0·00 |

Bottom flange:

| S. 2·4 | + | 22·14 | S. 12·14 | + | 24·25 |
|--------|---|-------|----------|---|-------|
| 2·4 | − | 0·00 | 12·14 | − | 3·77 |
| 4·6 | + | 21·93 | 14·16 | + | 25·31 |
| 4·6 | − | 0·19 | 14·16 | − | 5·00 |
| 6·8 | + | 22·00 | 16·18 | + | 26·09 |
| 6·8 | − | 0·64 | 16·18 | − | 5·93 |
| 8·10 | + | 22·44 | 18·20 | + | 25·22 |
| 8·10 | − | 1·43 | 18·20 | − | 5·15 |
| 10·12 | + | 23·22 | 20·22 | + | 20·01 |
| 10·12 | − | 2·48 | 20·22 | − | 0·00 |

Vertical bracing:

| | | | | | | |
|---|---|---|---|---|---|---|
| S. 1·2 | + | 1·98 | S. 11·12 | − | 1·51 |
| 1·2 | − | 1·48 | 13·14 | + | 2·09 |
| 3·4 | + | 3·77 | 13·14 | − | 1·09 |
| 3·4 | − | 2·77 | 15·16 | + | 1·64 |
| 5·6 | + | 3·55 | 15·16 | − | 0·64 |
| 5·6 | − | 2·55 | 17·18 | + | 2·10 |
| 7·8 | + | 3·27 | 17·18 | − | 1·10 |
| 7·8 | − | 2·27 | 19·20 | + | 2·80 |
| 9·10 | + | 2·96 | 19·20 | − | 1·80 |
| 9·10 | − | 1·96 | 21·22 | + | 0·50 |
| 11·12 | + | 2·51 | 21·22 | − | 0·00 |

Inclined bracing:

| | | | | | | |
|---|---|---|---|---|---|---|
| S. 1·4 | + | 3·23 | S. 11·14 | + | 2·77 |
| 1·4 | − | 3·23 | 11·14 | − | 2·77 |
| 3·6 | + | 3·15 | 13·16 | + | 2·68 |
| 3·6 | − | 3·15 | 13·16 | − | 2·68 |
| 5·8 | + | 3·07 | 15·18 | + | 2·45 |
| 5·8 | − | 3·07 | 15·18 | − | 2·45 |
| 7·10 | + | 3·02 | 17·20 | + | 5·35 |
| 7·10 | − | 3·02 | 17·20 | − | 5·35 |
| 9·12 | + | 2·97 | 19·22 | + | 9·32 |
| 9·12 | − | 2·97 | 19·22 | − | 9·32 |

*Note.*—The parts 21·22 require particularly to be considered for Axle Loads.

END OF PART I.

PLATE 15

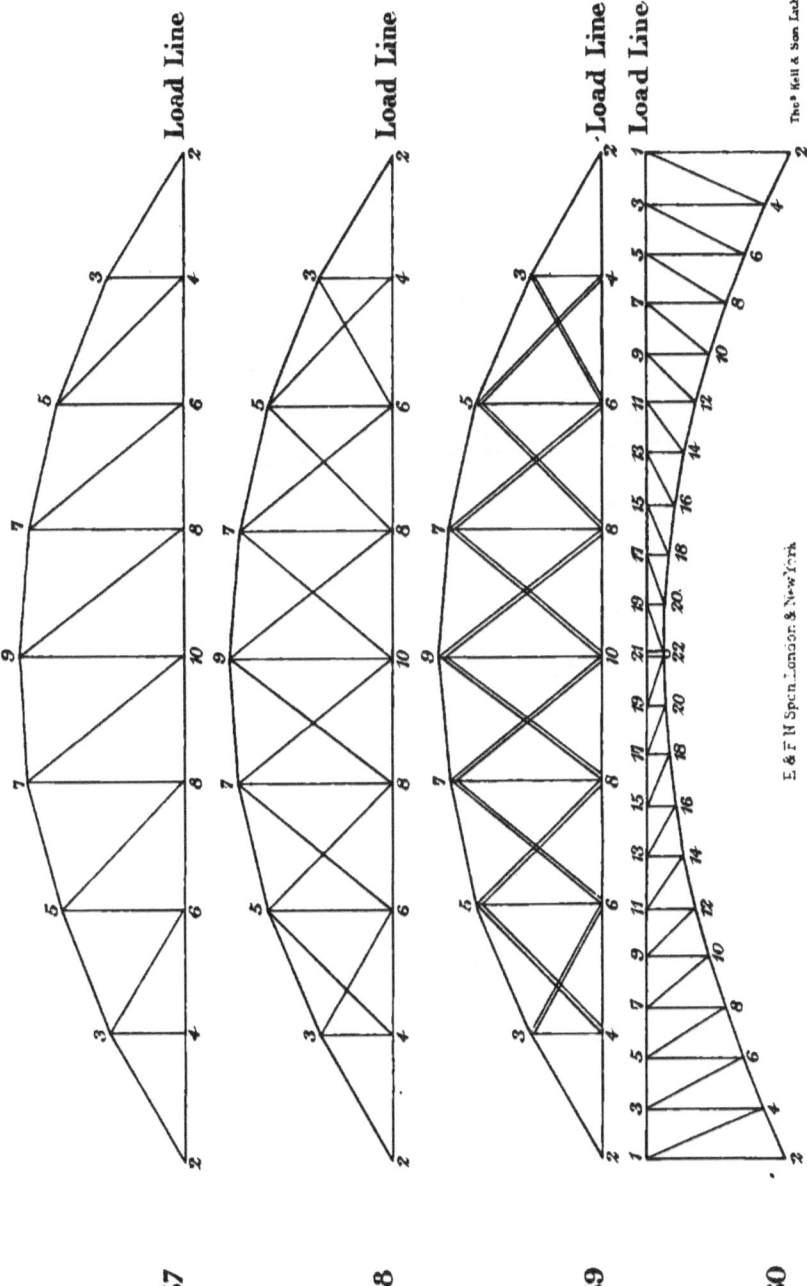

E & F N Spon London & New York

Thos Kell & Son Lith

# PART II.—ROOFS.

## INTRODUCTORY.

### 1. ABBREVIATIONS, &c.

S = Stress in.   + = Compression.   − = Tension.

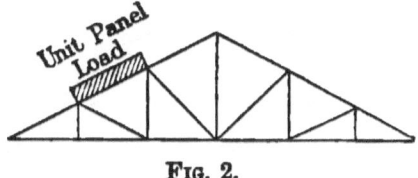

Fig. 2.

For Unit Panel Load see Fig. 2.

### 2. STRESS CONSTANTS FOR DEAD LOAD.

These are the stresses in each member of the roof truss when each panel is covered with a unit load. Taking Truss Diagram No. 72 as an example with a load of 1 ton, 1 kilogramme, or any other unit distributed over each of the eight panels on the principal rafters, the stress constants are the resulting stresses in terms of the load.

### 3. Maximum Stress Constants for Live Load.

These are the maximum stresses in each member of the roof truss which could be caused by a unit wind pressure per panel, acting normally to the principal rafters on one side only (either side indifferently), for Truss Diagrams Nos. 61 to 97, both inclusive, under the conditions of fixing shown in Figs. 3 and 4.

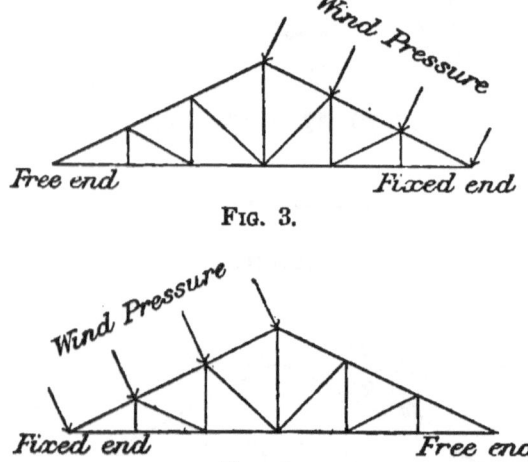

Fig. 3.

Fig. 4.

This arrangement gives the maximum stresses, and although, of course, there may be many cases where the method of fixing may be different, it is almost impossible to say how nearly they may approximate thereto by exigencies of construction, and it is best to be on the safe side.

For Truss Diagrams Nos. 98 to 100, both inclusive, the wind pressure has been supposed to act vertically on one side only (either side indifferently), as if a normal pressure had been taken it would have had, owing to the curved surface of the rafters, a different load value for each panel, which would have been very inconvenient.

Taking Truss Diagram No. 72 as an example with a load of 1 ton, 1 kilogramme, or any other unit per panel acting on all the panels on one side of the roof only (either side indifferently), the stress constants are the resulting maximum stresses in terms of the load.

It will be noticed that the only trusses subject to counter stresses in the bracing are Nos. 97 to 100.

### 4. REFERENCE NUMBERS.

The numbers on the Truss Diagrams serve to indicate each member of a roof truss for which the stress constant is given.

Taking Truss Diagram No. 72 as an example under the head "Live Load" (Wind Pressure), maximum stress constants will be found S. 6·8, and opposite the stress constant − 4·46.

This means that the stress in the member 6·8 of Truss Diagram No. 72 due to a Live Load (Wind Pressure) of unit panel intensity is tension 4·46.

### 5. POSITION OF LOAD.

The dead load is supposed to be concentrated wholly on the rafters. This is quite near enough in most cases for all practical purposes.

For very large and heavy roofs some allowance might be made to the tension members for the weight of the tie.

### 6. NORMAL WIND PRESSURE.

The following table gives the normal wind pressure per square foot for different slopes of roof equivalent to a horizontal wind pressure of 50 lbs. per square foot calculated by Hutton's formula :—

| Pitch of Roof. | | | | | | | | | | | |
|---|---|---|---|---|---|---|---|---|---|---|---|
| 10° | 15° | 20° | 21° 45′ ⅙ span | 25° | 26° 30′ ¼ span | 30° | 33° 30′ ⅓ span | 35° | 40° | 45° ½ span | 50° |
| 12·1 | 18 | 22·6 | 25·2 | 28·8 | 30·2 | 33 | 36·6 | 37·8 | 41·6 | 43 | 47·6 |

Normal Wind Pressure in lbs. per square foot.

## 7. FULLY WORKED OUT EXAMPLE.

As an example the stresses will be calculated in detail for a roof truss of the type shown in Truss Diagram No. 97 to cover a double line of railway, metre gauge, and two platforms, say 60 feet span, with trusses 8 feet apart, covered with 1-inch teak boarding and mangalore tiles, which makes a very light roof.

The dead load per panel will be length of panel, 6·48 feet × distance apart of trusses, 8 feet × weight of boarding, 3½ lbs., plus tiling, 8½ lbs., plus probable weight of truss, say 3 lbs.: total, 15 lbs. per square foot, which makes the panel load 778 lbs., say 0·35 of a ton.

The live load (wind pressure) will be area as above, say 52 square feet × 25 lbs. normal wind pressure: total, 1300 lbs., say 0·58 of a ton.

The stresses are as follows :—

*For Dead Load.*

Rafters:                                                                                             Tons.
S. 1·3 = stress constant + 10·72 × 0·35 ton panel load    + 3·75
   3·5                          + 17·20 × 0·35                              + 6·02
   5·7                          + 17·30 × 0·35                              + 6·05
   7·9                          + 14·37 × 0·35                              + 5·03
   9·11                        + 10·78 × 0·35                              + 3·77

Tie:                                   Tons.

S. 1·4 = stress constant − 10·00 × 0·35 ton panel load − 3·50
  4·6                − 10·59 × 0·35        − 3·70
  6·8                − 16·66 × 0·35        − 5·83
  8·10               − 16·15 × 0·35        − 5·65
 10·12              − 13·41 × 0·35        − 4·69

Bracing:

S. 3·4 = stress constant + 4·00 × 0·35 ton panel load + 1·40
  5·6                + 1·10 × 0·35        + 0·38
  7·8                − 1·54 × 0·35        − 0·54
  9·10               − 3·33 × 0·35        − 1·16
 11·12              − 7·00 × 0·35        − 2·45
  3·6                − 6·07 × 0·35        − 2·12
  5·8                − 0·16 × 0·35        − 0·05
  7·10               + 3·16 × 0·35        + 1·10
  9·12               + 4·33 × 0·35        + 1·51

*For Live Load (Wind Pressure).*

Rafters:

S. 1·3 = stress constant + 6·66 × 0·58 ton panel load + 3·86
  3·5               + 11·42 × 0·58       + 6·62
  5·7               + 11·06 × 0·58       + 6·41
  7·9               + 8·43 × 0·58       + 4·89
  9·11              + 5·80 × 0·58       + 3·36

Tie:

S. 1·4 = stress constant − 7·88 × 0·58 ton panel load − 4·57
  4·6               − 8·33 × 0·58       − 4·83
  6·8               − 12·28 × 0·58      − 7·12
  8·10              − 11·33 × 0·58      − 6·57
 10·12            − 8·40 × 0·58      − 4·87

Bracing:

S. 3·4 = stress constant + 3·10 × 0·58 ton panel load + 1·80
  3·4               − 0·00 × 0·58      − 0·00
  5·6               + 0·54 × 0·58      + 0·31
  5·6               − 0·00 × 0·58      − 0·00
  7·8               + 0·00 × 0·58      + 0·00
  7·8               − 1·44 × 0·58      − 0·83

Bracing—*continued.*          Tons.

| | | |
|---|---|---|
| 9·10 | + 0·00 × 0·58 | + 0·00 |
| 9·10 | − 2·70 × 0·58 | − 1·56 |
| 11·12 | + 0·00 × 0·58 | + 0·00 |
| 11·12 | − 3·77 × 0·58 | − 2·18 |
| 3·6 | + 0·00 × 0·58 | + 0·00 |
| 3·6 | − 4·06 × 0·58 | − 2·35 |
| 5·8 | + 0·74 × 0·58 | + 0·43 |
| 5·8 | − 0·88 × 0·58 | − 0·51 |
| 7·10 | + 3·13 × 0·58 | + 1·81 |
| 7·10 | − 0·00 × 0·58 | − 0·00 |
| 9·12 | + 3·97 × 0·58 | + 2·30 |
| 9·12 | − 0·00 × 0·58 | − 0·00 |

## *Maximum Stresses for Combined Dead and Live Loads.*

| Rafters: | Tons. | Tons. | Total tons. |
|---|---|---|---|
| S. 1·3 = | + 3·75 and | + 3·86 | + 7·61 |
| 3·5 | + 6·02 | + 6·62 | + 12·64 |
| 5·7 | + 6·05 | + 6·41 | + 12·46 |
| 7·9 | + 5·03 | + 4·89 | + 9·92 |
| 9·11 | + 3·77 | + 3·36 | + 7·13 |

| Tie: | | | |
|---|---|---|---|
| S. 1·4 = | − 3·50 and | − 4·57 | − 8·07 |
| 4·6 | − 3·70 | − 4·83 | − 8·53 |
| 6·8 | − 5·83 | − 7·12 | − 12·95 |
| 8·10 | − 5·65 | − 6·57 | − 12·22 |
| 10·12 | − 4·69 | − 4·87 | − 9·56 |

| Bracing: | | | |
|---|---|---|---|
| S. 3·4 = | + 1·40 and | + 1·80 | + 3·20 |
| 3·4 | + 1·40 | − 0·00 | − 0·00 |
| 5·6 | + 0·38 | + 0·31 | + 0·69 |
| 5·6 | + 0·38 | − 0·00 | − 0·00 |
| 7·8 | − 0·54 | + 0·00 | + 0·00 |
| 7·8 | − 0·54 | − 0·83 | − 1·37 |
| 9·10 | − 1·16 | + 0·00 | + 0·00 |

Bracing—*continued*:

| | Tons. | Tons. | Total tons. |
|---|---|---|---|
| S. 9·10 = | − 1·16 and | − 1·56 | − 2·72 |
| 11·12 | − 2·45 | + 0·00 | + 0·00 |
| 11·12 | − 2·45 | − 2·18 | − 4·63 |
| 3·6 | − 2·12 | + 0·00 | + 0·00 |
| 3·6 | − 2·12 | − 2·35 | − 4·47 |
| 5·8 | − 0·05 | + 0·43 | + 0·38 |
| 5·8 | − 0·05 | − 0·51 | − 0·56 |
| 7·10 | + 1·10 | + 1·81 | + 2·91 |
| 7·10 | + 1·10 | − 0·00 | − 0·00 |
| 9·12 | + 1·51 | + 2·30 | + 3·81 |
| 9·12 | + 1·51 | − 0·00 | − 0·00 |

It will be noticed that the only member of the Bracing which suffers counter stress is 5·8.

# STRESS CONSTANTS FOR DEAD AND LIVE LOADS OF UNIT PANEL INTENSITY.

## TRUSS DIAGRAM No. 61.

### CONDITIONS.

1. Rise of truss .. .. .. .. .. ..  ½ of the span.
2. Rise of tie rod .. .. .. .. ..  Nil.
3. Number of panels .. .. .. ..  4.
4. Description of truss · .. .. .. ..  Braced triangle.

### EVENLY DISTRIBUTED DEAD LOAD.

*Stress Constants.*

Rafters :

| | | | | |
|---|---|---|---|---|
| S. 2·3 | .. | .. | .. | + 2·12 |
| 3·5 | .. | .. | .. | + 1·41 |

Tie :

| | | | | |
|---|---|---|---|---|
| S. 2·4 | .. | .. | .. | − 1·50 |

Bracing :

| | | | | |
|---|---|---|---|---|
| S. 3·4 | .. | .. | .. | + 0·71 |
| 4·5 | .. | .. | .. | − 1·00 |

## LIVE LOAD (WIND PRESSURE).

### *Maximum Stress Constants.*

Rafters :

     S. 2·3      ..      ..      ..      +   1·00

         3·5      ..      ..      ..      +   1·00

Tie :

     S. 2·4      ..      ..      ..      −   1·41

Bracing :

     S. 3·4      ..      ..      ..      +   1·00

         4·5      ..      ..      ..      −   0·71

---

## TRUSS DIAGRAM No. 62.

### CONDITIONS.

1. Rise of truss ..   ..   ..   ..   ..   ..   ½ of the span.
2. Rise of tie rod   ..   ..   ..   ..   ..   ¼ ditto.
3. Number of panels   ..   ..   ..   ..   4.
4. Description of truss   ..   ..   ..   ..   Braced trapezium.

### EVENLY DISTRIBUTED DEAD LOAD.

### *Stress Constants.*

Rafters :

     S. 2·3      ..      ..      ..      +   4·23

         3·5      ..      ..      ..      +   2·82

Tie :

     S. 2·4      ..      ..      ..      −   3·40

TRUSS DIAGRAM NO. 62.

Bracing:

|        |     |     |     |   |      |
|--------|-----|-----|-----|---|------|
| S. 3·4 | ..  | ..  | .. . | + | 1·00 |
| 4·5    | ..  | ..  | ..  | − | 3·00 |

### LIVE LOAD (WIND PRESSURE).

#### *Maximum Stress Constants.*

Rafters:

|        |     |     |     |   |      |
|--------|-----|-----|-----|---|------|
| S. 2·3 | ..  | ..  | ..  | + | 2·50 |
| 3·5    | ..  | ..  | ..  | + | 2·00 |

Tie:

|        |     |     |     |   |      |
|--------|-----|-----|-----|---|------|
| S. 2·4 | ..  | ..  | ..  | − | 3·18 |

Bracing:

|        |     |     |     |   |      |
|--------|-----|-----|-----|---|------|
| S. 3·4 | ..  | ..  | ..  | + | 1·41 |
| 4·5    | ..  | ..  | ..  | − | 2·13 |

## TRUSS DIAGRAM No. 63.

### CONDITIONS.

1. Rise of truss ..   ..   ..   ..   ..   ..   $\frac{1}{3}$ of the span.
2. Rise of tie rod   ..   ..   ..   ..   ..   Nil.
3. Number of panels   ..   ..   ..   ..   4.
4. Description of truss   ..   ..   ..   ..   Braced triangle.

### EVENLY DISTRIBUTED DEAD LOAD.

#### *Stress Constants.*

Rafters:

    S. 2·3     ..     ..     ..     +   2·73

        3·5     ..     ..     ..     +   1·82

Tie:

    S. 2·4     ..     ..     ..     −   2·25

Bracing:

    S. 3·4     ..     ..     ..     +   0·91

        4·5     ..     ..     ..     −   1·00

### LIVE LOAD (WIND PRESSURE).

#### *Maximum Stress Constants.*

Rafters:

    S. 2·3     ..     ..     ..     +   1·17

        3·5     ..     ..     ..     +   1·08

Tie:

    S. 2·4     ..     ..     ..     −   1·82

Bracing:

    S. 3·4     ..     ..     ..     +   1·08

        4·5     ..     ..     ..     −   0·60

## TRUSS DIAGRAM No. 64.

### CONDITIONS.

1. Rise of truss .. .. .. .. .. .. $\frac{1}{4}$ of the span.
2. Rise of tie rod .. .. .. .. .. Nil.
3. Number of panels .. .. .. .. 4.
4. Description of truss .. .. .. .. Braced triangle.

### EVENLY DISTRIBUTED DEAD LOAD.

#### *Stress Constants.*

Rafters:

| | | | | |
|---|---|---|---|---|
| S. 2·3 | .. | .. | .. | + 3·36 |
| 3·5 | .. | .. | .. | + 2·24 |

Tie:

| | | | | |
|---|---|---|---|---|
| S. 2·4 | .. | .. | .. | − 3·00 |

Bracing:

| | | | | |
|---|---|---|---|---|
| S. 3·4 | .. | .. | .. | + 1·12 |
| 4·5 | .. | .. | .. | − 1·00 |

### LIVE LOAD (WIND PRESSURE).

#### *Maximum Stress Constants.*

Rafters:

| | | | | |
|---|---|---|---|---|
| S. 2·3 | .. | .. | .. | + 1·74 |
| 3·5 | .. | .. | .. | + 1·24 |

Tie:

| | | | | |
|---|---|---|---|---|
| S. 2·4 | .. | .. | .. | − 2·22 |

Bracing:

| | | | | |
|---|---|---|---|---|
| S. 3·4 | .. | .. | .. | + 1·24 |
| 4·5 | .. | .. | .. | − 0·56 |

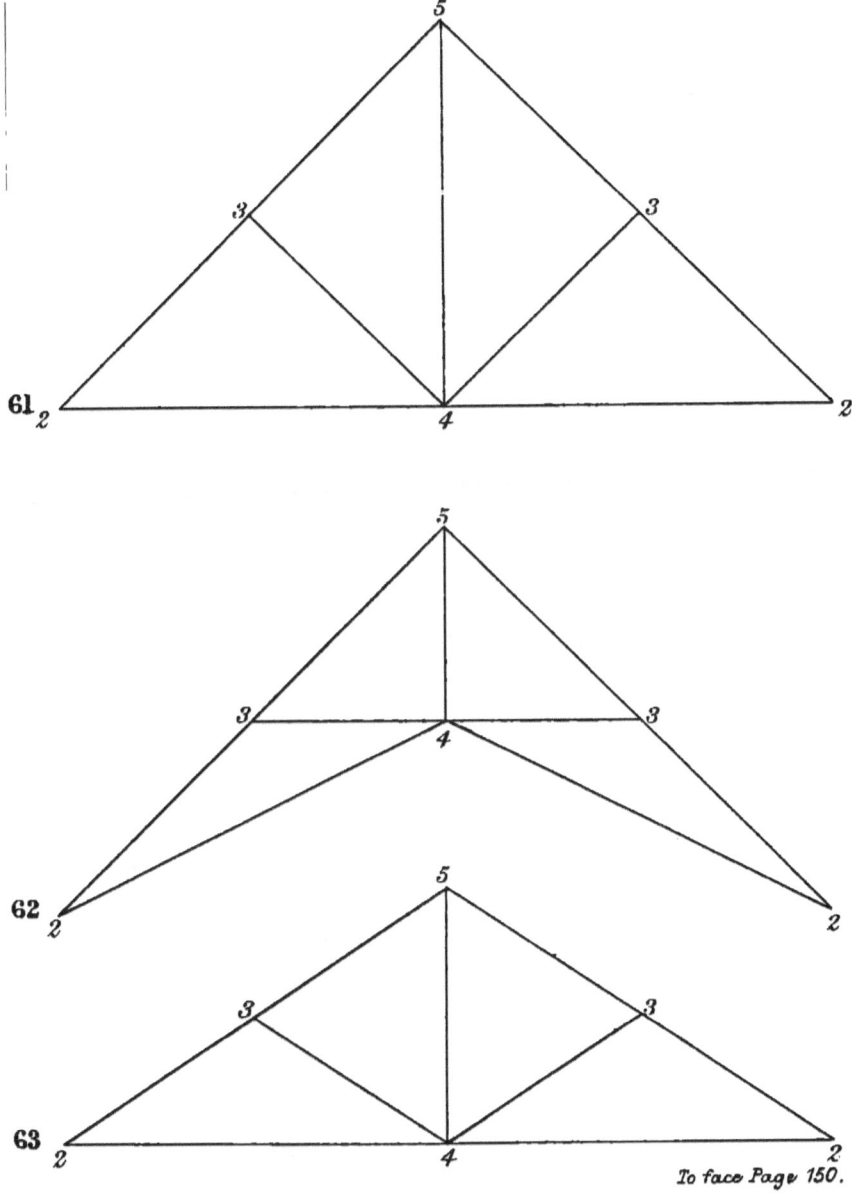

61

62

63

To face Page 150.

E & F N Spon, London & New York

Thoˢ Kell & Son Lith

## TRUSS DIAGRAM No. 65.

### CONDITIONS.

1. Rise of truss .. .. .. .. .. .. $\frac{1}{4}$ of the span.
2. Rise of tie rod .. .. .. .. .. $\frac{1}{50}$ of the span.
3. Number of panels .. .. .. .. 4.
4. Description of truss .. .. .. .. Braced trapezium.

### EVENLY DISTRIBUTED DEAD LOAD.

#### Stress Constants.

Rafters:

|  | S. 2·3 | .. | .. | .. | + | 4·23 |
|---|---|---|---|---|---|---|
|  | 3·5 | .. | .. | .. | + | 2·82 |

Tie:

|  | S. 2·4 | .. | .. | .. | − | 3·80 |
|---|---|---|---|---|---|---|

Bracing:

|  | S. 3·4 | .. | .. | .. | + | 1·30 |
|---|---|---|---|---|---|---|
|  | 4·5 | .. | .. | .. | − | 1·50 |

### LIVE LOAD (WIND PRESSURE).

#### Maximum Stress Constants.

Rafters:

|  | S. 2·3 | .. | .. | .. | + | 2·38 |
|---|---|---|---|---|---|---|
|  | 3·5 | .. | .. | .. | + | 1·56 |

Tie:

|  | S. 2·4 | .. | .. | .. | − | 2·85 |
|---|---|---|---|---|---|---|

Bracing:

|  | S. 3·4 | .. | .. | .. | + | 1·46 |
|---|---|---|---|---|---|---|
|  | 4·5 | .. | .. | .. | − | 0·84 |

# TRUSS DIAGRAM No. 66.

## CONDITIONS.

1. Rise of truss ..   ..   ..   ..   ..   ..   $\frac{1}{4}$ of the span.
2. Rise of tie rod   ..   ..   ..   ..   Nil.
3. Number of panels   ..   ..   ..   ..   4.
4. Description of truss   ..   ..   ..   Braced triangle.

## EVENLY DISTRIBUTED DEAD LOAD.

### *Stress Constants.*

Rafters:

    S. 2·3     ..     ..     ..     +   3·35
       3·5     ..     ..     ..     +   2·90

Tie:

    S. 2·4     ..     ..     ..     −   3·00
       4·6     ..     ..     ..     −   2·00

Bracing:

    S. 3·4     ..     ..     ••     +   0·90
       4·5     ..     ..     ..     −   1·00
       5·6 * (only supports part of tie rod).

## LIVE LOAD (WIND PRESSURE).

### *Maximum Stress Constants.*

Rafters:

    S. 2·3     ..     ..     ..     +   1·75
       3·5     ..     ..     ..     +   1·75

\* Not necessary to stability of truss.

Tie :

|  | S. 2·4 | .. | .. | .. | — | 2·22 |
|  | 4·6 | .. | .. | .. | — | 1·11 |

Bracing :

|  | S. 3·4 | .. | .. | .. | + | 1·00 |
|  | 4·5 | .. | .. | .. | — | 1·11 |
|  | 5·6 * | .. | .. | .. |  | 0·00 |

---

## TRUSS DIAGRAM No. 67.

### CONDITIONS.

1. Rise of truss ..   ..   ..   ..   ..   ..   $\frac{1}{4}$ of the span.
2. Rise of tie rod   ..   ..   ..   ..   ..   $\frac{1}{20}$ of the span.
3. Number of panels   ..   ..   ..   ..   4.
4. Description of truss   ..   ..   ..   ..   Braced polygon.

### EVENLY DISTRIBUTED DEAD LOAD.

#### *Stress Constants.*

Rafters :

|  | S. 2·3 | .. | .. | .. | + | 5·05 |
|  | 3·5 | .. | .. | .. | + | 4·60 |

Tie :

|  | S. 2·4 | .. | .. | .. | — | 4·60 |
|  | 4·6 | .. | .. | .. | — | 2·50 |

* Not necessary to stability of truss.

Bracing :

| | | | | | |
|---|---|---|---|---|---|
| S. 3·4 | .. | .. | .. | + | 0·90 |
| 4·5 | .. | .. | .. | − | 2·25 |

5·6 * (only supports part of tie rod).

### Live Load (Wind Pressure).

#### *Maximum Stress Constants.*

Rafters :

| | | | | | |
|---|---|---|---|---|---|
| S. 2·3 | .. | .. | .. | + | 3·11 |
| 3·5 | .. | .. | .. | + | 3·11 |

Tie :

| | | | | | |
|---|---|---|---|---|---|
| S. 2·4 | .. | .. | .. | − | 3·50 |
| 4·6 | .. | .. | .. | − | 1·40 |

Bracing :

| | | | | | |
|---|---|---|---|---|---|
| S. 3·4 | .. | .. | .. | + | 1·00 |
| 4·5 | .. | .. | .. | − | 2·20 |
| 5·6 * | .. | .. | .. | | 0·00 |

* Not necessary to stability of truss.

PLATE 17.

To face Page 154.

# TRUSS DIAGRAMS

64

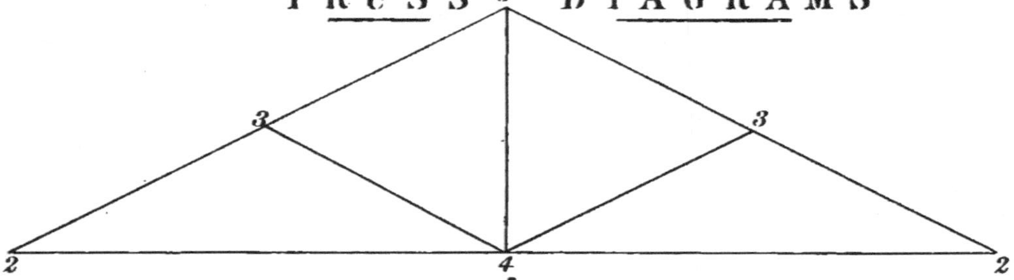

65

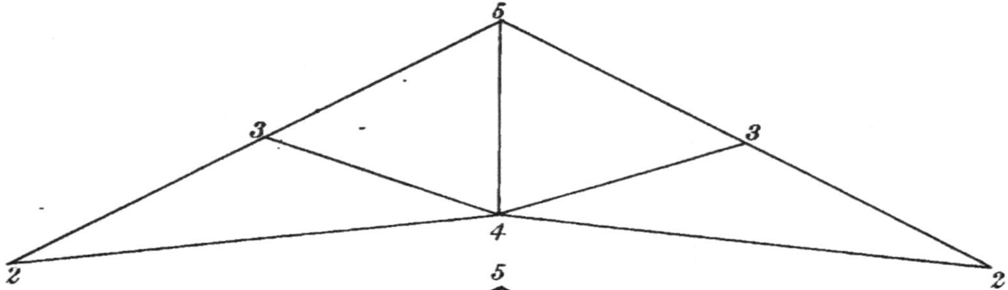

66

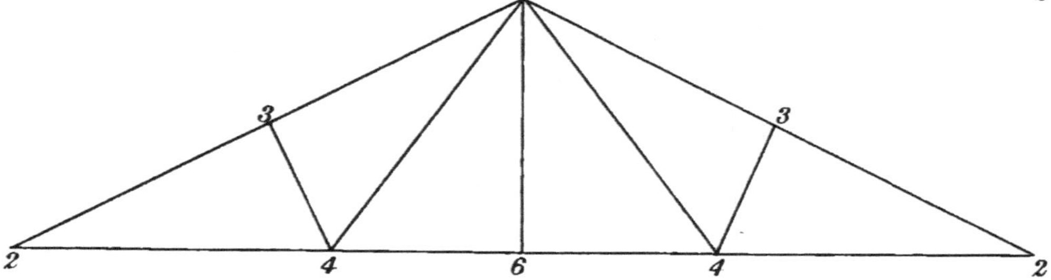

E & F N Spon London & New York

Kell & Son Ltd.

## TRUSS DIAGRAM No. 68.

### CONDITIONS.

1. Rise of truss .. .. .. .. .. .. ¼ of the span.
2. Rise of tie rod .. .. .. .. .. Nil.
3. Number of panels .. .. .. .. 6.
4. Description of truss .. .. .. .. Braced triang

### EVENLY DISTRIBUTED DEAD LOAD.

#### Stress Constants.

Rafters:

    S. 2·3 .. .. .. + 5·60

      3·5 .. .. .. + 4·57

      5·7 .. .. .. + 4·70

Tie:

    S. 2·4 .. .. .. − 5·00

      4·6 .. .. .. − 3·00

Bracing:

    S. 3·4 .. .. .. + 1·07

      4·5 .. .. .. + 1·07

      4·7 .. .. .. − 2·00

    6·7* (only supports part of tie rod).

### LIVE LOAD (WIND PRESSURE).

#### Maximum Stress Constants.

Rafters:

    S. 2·3 .. .. .. + 3·14

      3·5 .. .. .. + 2·46

      5·7 .. .. .. + 3·14

* Not necessary to stability of truss.

Tie :

| | | | | | |
|---|---|---|---|---|---|
| S. 2·4 | .. | .. | .. | — | 3·91 |
| 4·6 | .. | .. | .. | — | 1·68 |

Bracing :

| | | | | | |
|---|---|---|---|---|---|
| S. 3·4 | + | 1·20 | S. 4·7 | — | 2·25 |
| 4·5 | + | 1·20 | 6·7 * | | 0·00 |

---

# TRUSS DIAGRAM No. 69.

## CONDITIONS.

| | | |
|---|---|---|
| 1. Rise of truss .. .. .. .. .. .. | $\frac{1}{4}$ of the span. |
| 2. Rise of tie rod .. .. .. .. . | $\frac{1}{30}$ of the span. |
| 3. Number of panels .. .. .. .. | 6. |
| 4. Description of truss .. .. .. .. | Braced polygon. |

### EVENLY DISTRIBUTED DEAD LOAD.

#### *Stress Constants.*

Rafters :

| | | | | | |
|---|---|---|---|---|---|
| S. 2·3 | .. | .. | .. | + | 7·25 |
| 3·5 | .. | .. | .. | + | 6·00 |
| 5·7 | .. | .. | .. | + | 6·40 |

Tie :

| | | | | | |
|---|---|---|---|---|---|
| S. 2·4 | .. | . | .. | — | 6·55 |
| 4·6 | .. | .. | .. | — | 3·50 |

* Not necessary to stability of truss.

Bracing :

| | | | | | |
|---|---|---|---|---|---|
| S. 3·4 | .. | .. | .. | + | 1·22 |
| 4·5 | .. | .. | .. | + | 1·22 |
| 4·7 | .. | .. | .. | − | 3·25 |

6·7* (only supports part of tie rod).


## LIVE LOAD (WIND PRESSURE).

### *Maximum Stress Constants.*

Rafters :

| | | | | | |
|---|---|---|---|---|---|
| S. 2·3 | .. | .. | .. | + | 4·47 |
| 3·5 | .. | .. | .. | + | 3·54 |
| 5·7 | .. | .. | .. | + | 4·47 |

Tie :

| | | | | | |
|---|---|---|---|---|---|
| S. 2·4 | .. | .. | .. | − | 5·15 |
| 4·6 | .. | .. | .. | − | 1·93 |

Bracing :

| | | | | |
|---|---|---|---|---|
| S. 3·4 | + | 1·36 | S. 4·7 − | 3·30 |
| 4·5 | + | 1·36 | 6·7* | 0·00 |

\* Not necessary to stability of truss.

## TRUSS DIAGRAM No. 70.

### CONDITIONS.

1. Rise of truss .. .. .. .. .. ..  ¼ of the span.
2. Rise of tie rod .. .. .. .. .. Nil.
3. Number of panels .. .. .. .. 6.
4. Description of truss .. .. .. .. Braced triangle.

### EVENLY DISTRIBUTED DEAD LOAD.

*Stress Constants.*

Rafters :

| | | | | |
|---|---|---|---|---|
| S. 2·3 | .. | .. | .. | + 5·60 |
| 3·5 | .. | .. | .. | + 4·48 |
| 5·7 | .. | .. | .. | + 3·36 |

Tie :

| | | | | |
|---|---|---|---|---|
| S. 2·4 | .. | .. | .. | − 5·00 |
| 4·6 | .. | .. | .. | − 5·00 |
| 6·8 | .. | .. | .. | − 4·00 |

Bracing :

S. 3·4 * (only supports part of tie rod).

| | | | | |
|---|---|---|---|---|
| 5·6 | .. | .. | .. | − 0·50 |
| 7·8 | .. | .. | .. | − 2·00 |
| 3·6 | .. | .. | .. | + 1·12 |
| 5·8 | .. | .. | .. | + 1·40 |

* Not necessary to stability of truss.

PLATE 18.

To face Page 158.

# TRUSS DIAGRAMS

67

68

69

E & F N Spon, London & New York

Tho⁸ Kell & Son Lith

## LIVE LOAD (WIND PRESSURE).

### *Maximum Stress Constants.*

Rafters :

| | | | | | |
|---|---|---|---|---|---|
| S. 2·3 | .. | .. | .. | + | 3·14 |
| 3·5 | .. | .. | .. | + | 2·38 |
| 5·7 | .. | .. | .. | + | 1·86 |

Tie :

| | | | | | |
|---|---|---|---|---|---|
| S. 2·4 | .. | .. | .. | — | 3·93 |
| 4·6 | .. | .. | .. | — | 3·93 |
| 6·8 | .. | .. | .. | — | 2·79 |

Bracing :

| | | | | |
|---|---|---|---|---|
| S. 3·4 * | 0·00 | S. 3·6 | + | 1·26 |
| 5·6 — | 0·56 | 5·8 | + | 1·57 |
| 7·8 — | 1·12 | | | |

* Not necessary to stability of truss.

## TRUSS DIAGRAM No. 71.

### CONDITIONS.

1. Rise of truss .. .. .. .. .. .. $\frac{1}{4}$ of the span.
2. Rise of tie rod .. .. .. .. .. $\frac{1}{30}$ of the span.
3. Number of panels .. .. .. .. 6.
4. Description of truss .. .. .. .. Braced trapezium.

### EVENLY DISTRIBUTED DEAD LOAD.

#### *Stress Constants.*

Rafters:

| | | | | | |
|---|---|---|---|---|---|
| S. 2·3 | .. | .. | .. | + | 6·50 |
| 3·5 | .. | .. | .. | + | 5·20 |
| 5·7 | .. | .. | .. | + | 3·90 |

Tie:

| | | | | | |
|---|---|---|---|---|---|
| S. 2·4 | .. | .. | .. | − | 5·82 |
| 4·6 | .. | .. | .. | − | 5·82 |
| 6·8 | .. | .. | .. | − | 4·66 |

Bracing:

S. 3·4 * (only supports part of tie rod).

| | | | | | |
|---|---|---|---|---|---|
| 5·6 | .. | .. | .. | − | 0·50 |
| 7·8 | .. | .. | .. | − | 2·47 |
| 3·6 | .. | .. | .. | + | 1·23 |
| 5·8 | .. | .. | .. | + | 1·49 |

\* Not necessary to stability of truss.

## LIVE LOAD (WIND PRESSURE).

### *Maximum Stress Constants.*

Rafters :

| | | | | | |
|---|---|---|---|---|---|
| S. 2·3 | .. | .. | .. | + | 3·84 |
| 3·5 | .. | .. | .. | + | 2·88 |
| 5·7 | .. | .. | .. | + | 2·17 |

Tie :

| | | | | | |
|---|---|---|---|---|---|
| S. 2·4 | .. | .. | .. | − | 4·55 |
| 4·6 | .. | .. | .. | − | 4·55 |
| 6·8 | .. | .. | .. | − | 3·25 |

Bracing :

| | | | | | |
|---|---|---|---|---|---|
| S. 3·4* | | 0·00 | S. 3·6 | + | 1·40 |
| 5·6 | − | 0·56 | 5·8 | + | 1·65 |
| 7·8 | − | 1·38 | | | |

* Not necessary to stability of truss.

## TRUSS DIAGRAM No. 72.

### CONDITIONS.

1. Rise of truss ..    ..    ..    ..    ..    ..    $\frac{1}{4}$ of the span.
2. Rise of tie rod    ,.    ..    ..    ..    ..    Nil.
3. Number of panels    ..    ..    ..    ..    8.
4. Description of truss    ..    ..    ..    ..    Braced triangle.

### EVENLY DISTRIBUTED DEAD LOAD.

#### *Stress Constants.*

Rafters :

     S. 2·3   +   7·84      S. 5·7   +   5·60
        3·5   +   6·72         7·9   +   4·48

Tie :

     S. 2·4   −   7·00      S. 6·8   −   6·00
        4·6   −   7·00        8·10   −   5·00

Bracing :

     S. 3·4 * (only supports part of tie rod).
        5·6    ..      ..      ..      −   0·50
        7·8    ..      ..      . ..      −   1·00
        9·10    ..      ..      ..      −   3·00
        3·6    ..      ..      ..      +   1·12
        5·8    ..      ..      ..      +   1·43
        7·10    ..      ..      ..      +   1·80

\* Not necessary to stability of truss.

LIVE LOAD (WIND PRESSURE).

*Maximum Stress Constants.*

Rafters :

| | | | | | | | |
|---|---|---|---|---|---|---|---|
| S. | 2·3 | + | 4·50 | S. | 5·7 | + | 2·98 |
| | 3·5 | + | 3·74 | | 7·9 | + | 2·48 |

Tie :

| | | | | | | | |
|---|---|---|---|---|---|---|---|
| S. | 2·4 | − | 5·58 | S. | 6·8 | − | 4·46 |
| | 4·6 | − | 5·58 | | 8·10 | − | 3·34 |

Bracing :

| | | | | | | | |
|---|---|---|---|---|---|---|---|
| S. | 3·4 * | | 0·00 | S. | 3·6 | + | 1·25 |
| | 5·6 | − | 0·56 | | 5·8 | + | 1·57 |
| | 7·8 | − | 1·12 | | 7·10 | + | 2·01 |
| | 9·10 | − | 1·65 | | | | |

\* Not necessary to stability of truss.

## TRUSS DIAGRAM No. 73.

### CONDITIONS.

1. Rise of truss .. .. .. .. .. .. $\frac{1}{4}$ of the span.
2. Rise of tie rod .. .. .. .. .. $\frac{1}{30}$ of the span.
3. Number of panels .. .. .. .. 8.
4. Description of truss .. .. .. .. Braced trapezium.

### EVENLY DISTRIBUTED DEAD LOAD.

*Stress Constants.*

Rafters :

| | | | | | |
|---|---|---|---|---|---|
| S. 2·3 | + | 9·00 | S. 5·7 | + | 6·40 |
| 3·5 | + | 7·70 | 7·9 | + | 5·10 |

Tie :

| | | | | | |
|---|---|---|---|---|---|
| S. 2·4 | — | 8.05 | S. 6·8 | — | 6·90 |
| 4·6 | — | 8·05 | 8·10 | — | 5·75 |

Bracing :

S. 3·4 * (only supports part of tie rod).

| | | | | | |
|---|---|---|---|---|---|
| 5·6 | .. | .. | .. | — | 0·50 |
| 7·8 | .. | .. | .. | — | 1·00 |
| 9·10 | .. | .. | .. | — | 3·60 |
| 3·6 | .. | .. | .. | + | 1·23 |
| 5·8 | .. | .. | .. | + | 1·48 |
| 7·10 | .. | .. | .. | + | 1·84 |

\* Not necessary to stability of truss.

PLATE 19.

# TRUSS DIAGRAMS

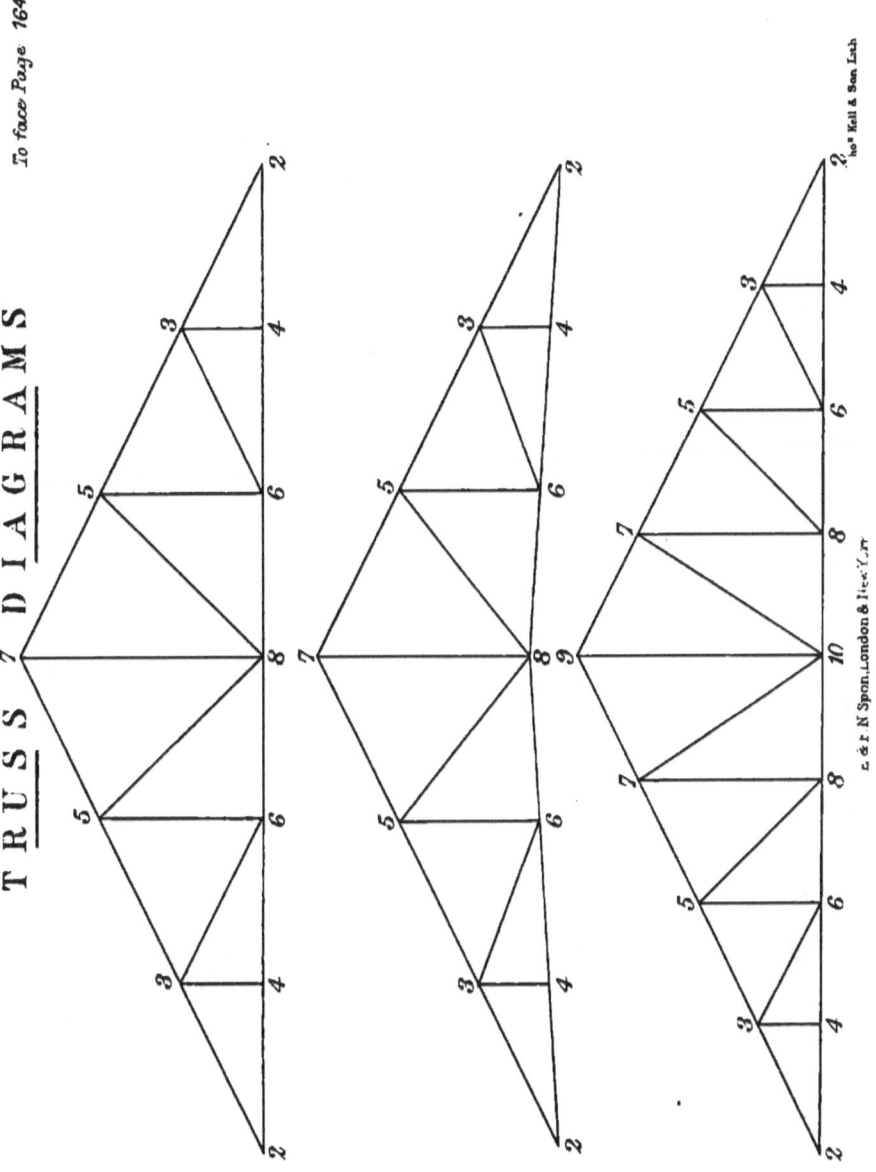

Tho⁵ Kell & Son Lith

L. & F N Spon, London & New York

## LIVE LOAD (WIND PRESSURE).

### *Maximum Stress Constants.*

Rafters :

| S. | 2·3 | + | 5·45 | | S. | 5·7 | + | 3·55 |
|---|---|---|---|---|---|---|---|---|
| | 3·5 | + | 4·50 | | | 7·9 | + | 2·88 |

Tie :

| S. | 2·4 | — | 6·45 | | S. | 6·8 | — | 5·15 |
|---|---|---|---|---|---|---|---|---|
| | 4·6 | — | 6·45 | | | 8·10 | — | 3·85 |

Bracing :

| S. | 3·4* | — | 0·00 | | S. | 3·6 | + | 1·39 |
|---|---|---|---|---|---|---|---|---|
| | 5·6 | — | 0·56 | | | 5·8 | + | 1·65 |
| | 7·8 | — | 1·12 | | | 7·10 | + | 2·05 |
| | 9·10 | — | 2·02 | | | | | |

\* Not necessary to stability of truss.

# TRUSS DIAGRAM No. 74.

## Conditions.

1. Rise of truss .. .. .. .. .. .. ¼ of the span.
2. Rise of tie rod .. .. .. .. .. Nil.
3. Number of panels .. .. .. .. 8.
4. Description of truss .. .. .. .. Braced triangle.

### Evenly distributed Dead Load.

#### Stress Constants.

Rafters:

| S. 2·3 | + | 7·80 | S. 5·7 | + | 6·90 |
| 3·5 | + | 7·35 | 7·9 | + | 6·45 |

Tie:

| S. 2·4 | .. | .. | .. | − | 7·00 |
| 4·6 | .. | .. | .. | − | 6·00 |
| 6·10 | .. | .. | .. | − | 4·00 |

Bracing:

| S. 3·4 | .. | .. | .. | + | 0·89 |
| 5·6 | .. | .. | .. | + | 1·78 |
| 7·8 | .. | .. | .. | + | 0·89 |
| 4·5 | .. | .. | .. | − | 1·00 |
| 5·8 | .. | .. | .. | − | 1·00 |
| 6·8 | .. | .. | .. | − | 2·00 |
| 8·9 | .. | .. | .. | − | 3·00 |

9·10 * (only supports part of tie rod).

\* Not necessary to stability of truss.

## LIVE LOAD (WIND PRESSURE).

### *Maximum Stress Constants.*

Rafters :

| | | | | | | |
|---|---|---|---|---|---|---|
| S. | 2·3 | + | 4·55 | S. 5·7 | + | 4·55 |
| | 3·5 | + | 4·55 | 7·9 | + | 4·55 |

Tie :

| | | | | | | |
|---|---|---|---|---|---|---|
| S. | 2·4 | .. | .. | .. | — | 5·64 |
| | 4·6 | .. | .. | .. | — | 4·51 |
| | 6·10 | .. | .. | .. | — | 2·25 |

Bracing :

| | | | | | | |
|---|---|---|---|---|---|---|
| S. | 3·4 | + | 1·00 | S. 5·8 | — | 1·12 |
| | 5·6 | + | 2·00 | 6·8 | — | 2·25 |
| | 7·8 | + | 1·00 | 8·9 | — | 3·38 |
| | 4·5 | — | 1·12 | 9·10 * | | 0·00 |

\* Not necessary to stability of truss.

## TRUSS DIAGRAM No. 75.

### CONDITIONS.

1. Rise of truss ..  ..  ..  ..  ..  .. $\frac{1}{4}$ of the span.
2. Rise of tie rod  ..  ..  ..  ..  .. $\frac{1}{30}$ of the span.
3. Number of panels  ..  ..  ..  .. 8.
4. Description of truss  ..  ..  ..  .. Braced polygon.

### EVENLY DISTRIBUTED DEAD LOAD.

#### *Stress Constants.*

Rafters :

|  | S. 2·3 | + 10·17 |  | S. 5·7 | + | 9·27 |
|---|---|---|---|---|---|---|
|  | 3·5 | + 9·72 |  | 7·9 | + | 8·82 |

Tie :

|  | S. 2·4 | .. | .. | .. | — | 9·15 |
|---|---|---|---|---|---|---|
|  | 4·6 | .. | .. | .. | — | 7·83 |
|  | 6·10 | .. | .. | .. | — | 4·65 |

Bracing :

|  | S. 3·4 | .. | .. | .. | + | 0·89 |
|---|---|---|---|---|---|---|
|  | 5·6 | .. | .. | .. | + | 1·78 |
|  | 7·8 | .. | .. | .. | + | 0·89 |
|  | 4·5 | .. | .. | .. | — | 1·32 |
|  | 5·8 | .. | .. | .. | — | 1·32 |
|  | 6·8 | .. | .. | .. | — | 3·42 |
|  | 8·9 | .. | .. | .. | — | 4·74 |

9·10 * (only supports part of tie rod).

\* Not necessary to stability of truss.

## LIVE LOAD (WIND PRESSURE).

### *Maximum Stress Constants.*

Rafters :

| | | | | | | |
|---|---|---|---|---|---|---|
| S. 2·3 | + | 6·36 | | S. 5·7 | + | 6·36 |
| 3·5 | + | 6·36 | | 7·9 | + | 6·36 |

Tie:

| | | | | | |
|---|---|---|---|---|---|
| S. 2·4 | .. | .. | .. | — | 7·30 |
| 4·6 | .. | .. | .. | — | 5·85 |
| 6·10 | .. | .. | .. | — | 2·62 |

Bracing :

| | | | | | | |
|---|---|---|---|---|---|---|
| S. 3·4 | + | 1·00 | | S. 5·8 | — | 1·45 |
| 5·6 | + | 2·00 | | 6·8 | — | 3·35 |
| 7·8 | + | 1·00 | | 8·9 | — | 4·80 |
| 4·5 | — | 1·45 | | 9·10* | | 0·00 |

* Not necessary to stability of truss.

## TRUSS DIAGRAM No. 76.

### CONDITIONS.

1. Rise of truss .. .. .. .. .. .. $\frac{1}{4}$ of the span.
2. Rise of tie rod .. .. .. .. .. Nil.
3. Number of panels .. .. .. .. 12.
4. Description of truss .. .. .. .. Braced triangle.

### EVENLY DISTRIBUTED DEAD LOAD.

*Stress Constants.*

Rafters:

| S. 2·3 | + 12·30 | S. 7·9 | + 8·94 |
| 3·5 | + 11·18 | 9·11 | + 7·82 |
| 5·7 | + 10·06 | 11·13 | + 6·70 |

Tie:

| S. 2·4 | − 11·00 | S. 8·10 | − 9·00 |
| 4·6 | − 11·00 | 10·12 | − 8·00 |
| 6·8 | − 10·00 | 12·14 | − 7·00 |

Bracing:

| S. 3·4* (only supports part of tie rod). | | | | |
| 5·6 | .. | .. | .. | − 0·50 |
| 7·8 | .. | .. | .. | − 1·00 |
| 9·10 | .. | .. | .. | − 1·50 |
| 11·12 | .. | .. | .. | − 2·00 |
| 13·14 | .. | .. | .. | − 5·00 |
| 3·6 | .. | .. | .. | + 1·12 |

\* Not necessary to stability of truss.

PLATE 20.

# TRUSS DIAGRAMS

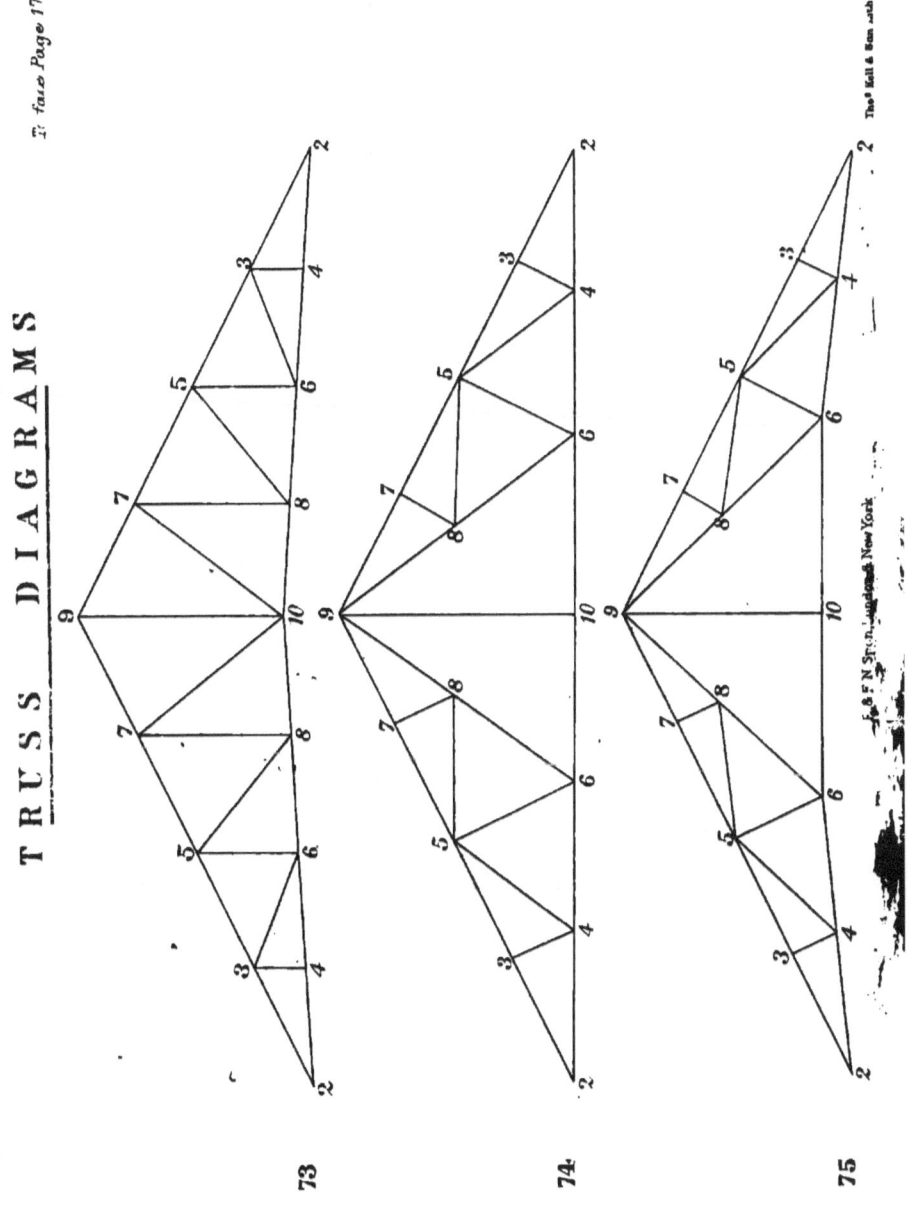

Bracing—*continued.*

| | | | | | |
|---|---|---|---|---|---|
| S. 5·8 | .. | .. | .. | + | 1·41 |
| 7·10 | .. | .. | .. | + | 1·80 |
| 9·12 | .. | .. | .. | + | 2·22 |
| 11·14 | .. | .. | .. | + | 2·68 |

## LIVE LOAD (WIND PRESSURE).

### *Maximum Stress Constants.*

Rafters :

| | | | | | |
|---|---|---|---|---|---|
| S. 2·3 | + | 7·26 | S. 7·9 | + | 4·98 |
| 3·5 | + | 6·50 | 9·11 | + | 4·22 |
| 5·7 | + | 5·74 | 11·13 | + | 3·72 |

Tie :

| | | | | | |
|---|---|---|---|---|---|
| S. 2·4 | — | 8·92 | S. 8·10 | — | 6·68 |
| 4·6 | — | 8·92 | 10·12 | — | 5·56 |
| 6·8 | — | 7·80 | 12·14 | — | 4·44 |

Bracing :

| | | | | | |
|---|---|---|---|---|---|
| S. 3·4 * | | 0·00 | S. 3·6 | + | 1·24 |
| 5·6 | — | 0·56 | 5·8 | + | 1·58 |
| 7·8 | — | 1·12 | 7·10 | + | 2·02 |
| 9·10 | — | 1·68 | 9·12 | + | 2·50 |
| 11·12 | — | 2·23 | 11·14 | + | 3·00 |
| 13·14 | — | 2·78 | | | |

\* Not necessary to stability of truss.

## TRUSS DIAGRAM No. 77.

### Conditions.

1. Rise of truss .. .. .. .. .. ..   $\frac{1}{4}$ of the span.
2. Rise of tie rod .. .. .. .. ..   $\frac{1}{40}$ of the span.
3. Number of panels .. .. .. ..   12.
4. Description of truss .. .. .. ..   Braced trapezium.

### Evenly distributed Dead Load.

*Stress Constants.*

Rafters :

| | | | |
|---|---|---|---|
| S. 2·3 | + 13·73 | S. 7·9 | + 9·98 |
| 3·5 | + 12·48 | 9·11 | + 8·73 |
| 5·7 | + 11·23 | 11·13 | + 7·48 |

Tie :

| | | | |
|---|---|---|---|
| S. 2·4 | − 12·30 | S. 8·10 | − 10·06 |
| 4·6 | − 12·30 | 10·12 | − 8·94 |
| 6·8 | − 11·18 | 12·14 | − 7·82 |

Bracing ·

| | | | | | |
|---|---|---|---|---|---|
| S. 3·4 * (only supports part of tie rod). | | | | | |
| 5·6 | .. | .. | .. | − | 0·50 |
| 7·8 | .. | .. | .. | − | 1·00 |
| 9·10 | .. | .. | .. | − | 1·50 |
| 11·12 | .. | .. | .. | − | 2·00 |
| 13·14 | .. | .. | .. | − | 5·00 |
| 3·6 | .. | .. | .. | + | 1·18 |

\* Not necessary to stability of truss.

Bracing—*continued.*

| | | | | | |
|---|---|---|---|---|---|
| S. 5·8 | .. | .. | .. | + | 1·45 |
| 7·10 | .. | .. | .. | + | 1·85 |
| 9·12 | .. | .. | .. | + | 2·24 |
| 11·14 | .. | .. | .. | + | 2·69 |

## LIVE LOAD (WIND PRESSURE).

### *Maximum Stress Constants.*

Rafters:

| | | | | | |
|---|---|---|---|---|---|
| S. 2·3 | + | 8·38 | S. 7·9 | + | 5·68 |
| 3·5 | + | 7·48 | 9·11 | + | 4·78 |
| 5·7 | + | 6·58 | 11·13 | + | 4·15 |

Tie:

| | | | | | |
|---|---|---|---|---|---|
| S. 2·4 | — | 9·98 | S. 8·10 | — | 7·46 |
| 4·6 | — | 9·98 | 10·12 | — | 6·20 |
| 6·8 | — | 8·72 | 12·14 | — | 4·94 |

Bracing:

| | | | | | |
|---|---|---|---|---|---|
| S. 3·4 * | | 0·00 | S. 3·6 | + | 1·35 |
| 5·6 | — | 0·56 | 5·8 | + | 1·63 |
| 7·8 | — | 1·12 | 7·10 | + | 2·04 |
| 9·10 | — | 1·68 | 9·12 | + | 2·50 |
| 11·12 | — | 2·23 | 11·14 | + | 3·00 |
| 13·14 | — | 3·16 | | | |

\* Not necessary to stability of truss.

## TRUSS DIAGRAM No. 78.

### CONDITIONS.

1. Rise of truss .. .. .. .. .. .. $\frac{1}{5}$ of the span.
2. Rise of tie rod .. .. .. .. .. Nil.
3. Number of panels .. .. ,. .. 4.
4. Description of truss .. .. .. .. Braced triangle.

### EVENLY DISTRIBUTED DEAD LOAD.

#### *Stress Constants.*

Rafters :

      S. 2·3 .. .. .. + 4·03
         3·5 .. .. .. + 2·69

Tie :

      S. 2·4 .. .. .. − 3·75

Bracing :

      S. 3·4 .. .. .. + 1·34
         5·4 .. .. .. − 1·00

### LIVE LOAD (WIND PRESSURE).

#### *Maximum Stress Constants.*

Rafters :

      S. 2·3 .. .. .. + 2.31
         3·5 .. .. .. + 1·46

Tie :

    S. 2·4        ..      ..      ..      −    2·70

Bracing :

    S. 3·4        ..      ..      ..      +    1·46
        4·5        ..      ..      ..      −    0·54

---

# TRUSS DIAGRAM No. 79.

## CONDITIONS.

1. Rise of truss ..   ..   ..   ..   ..   ..   $\frac{1}{5}$ of the span.
2. Rise of tie rod   ..   ..   ..   ..   ..   $\frac{1}{50}$ of the span.
3. Number of panels..   ..   ..   ..   ..   4.
4. Description of truss   ..   ..   ..   ..   Braced trapezium.

## EVENLY DISTRIBUTED DEAD LOAD.

### *Stress Constants*

Rafters :

    S. 2·3        ..      ..      ..      +    5·40
        3·5        ..      ..      ..      +    3·60

Tie :

    S. 2·4        ..      ..      ..      −    5·03

Bracing :

    S. 3·4        ..      ..      ..      +    1·70
        5·4        ..      ..      ..      −    1·67

## LIVE LOAD (WIND PRESSURE).

### *Maximum Stress Constants.*

Rafters:

    S. 2·3      ..    ..    ..    +   3·25

       3·5      ..    ..    ..    +   1·90

Tie:

    S. 2·4      ..    ..    ..    −   3·58

Bracing:

    S. 3·4      ..    ..    ..    +   1·84

       4·5      ..    ..    ..    −   0·90

---

## TRUSS DIAGRAM No. 80.

### CONDITIONS.

1. Rise of truss ..   ..   ..   ..   ..   ¼ of the span.
2. Rise of tie rod   ..   ..   ..   ..   Nil.
3. Number of panels   ..   ..   ..   4.
4. Description of truss   ..   ..   ..   Braced triangle.

### EVENLY DISTRIBUTED DEAD LOAD.

#### *Stress Constants.*

Rafters:

    S. 2·3      ..    ..    ..    +   4·03

       3·5      ..    ..    ..    +   3·66

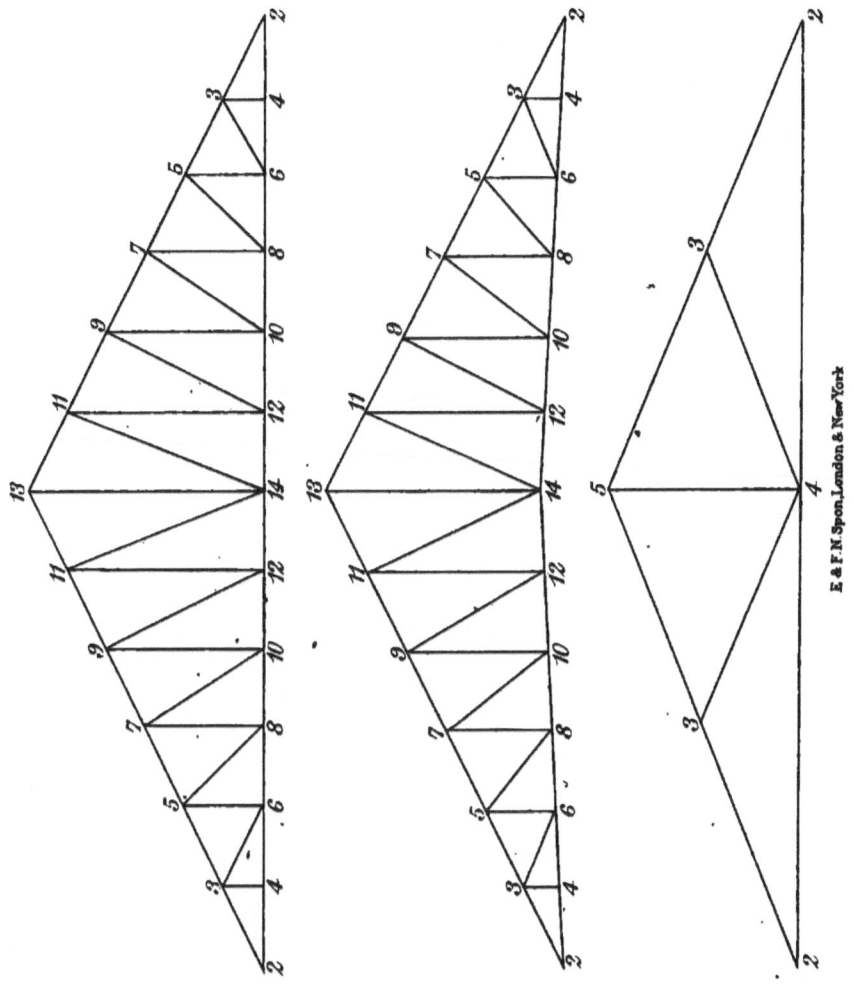

E & F. N. Spon, London & New York

Tie :

|  |  |  |  |  |  |
|---|---|---|---|---|---|
| S. 2·4 | .. | .. | .. | — | 3·75 |
| 4·6 | .. | .. | .. | — | 2·50 |

Bracing :

|  |  |  |  |  |  |
|---|---|---|---|---|---|
| S. 3·4 | .·. | .. | .. | + | 0·93 |
| 5·4 | .. | .. | .. | — | 1·25 |
| 5·6 * (only supports part of tie rod). | | | | | |

### Live Load (Wind Pressure).

#### *Maximum Stress Constants.*

Rafters :

|  |  |  |  |  |  |
|---|---|---|---|---|---|
| S. 2·3 | .. | .. | .. | + | 2·30 |
| 3·5 | .. | .. | .. | + | 2·30 |

Tie :

|  |  |  |  |  |  |
|---|---|---|---|---|---|
| S. 2·4 | .. | .. | .. | — | 2·70 |
| 4·6 | .. | .. | .. | — | 1·35 |

Bracing :

|  |  |  |  |  |  |
|---|---|---|---|---|---|
| S. 3·4 | .. | .. | .. | + | 1·00 |
| 4·5 | .. | .. | .. | — | 1·35 |
| 5·6* | .. | .. | .. |  | 0·00 |

* Not necessary to stability of truss.

N

# TRUSS DIAGRAM No. 81.

## CONDITIONS.

| | |
|---|---|
| 1. Rise of truss .. .. .. .. .. .. | $\frac{1}{5}$ of the span. |
| 2. Rise of tie rod .. .. .. .. .. | $\frac{1}{30}$ of the span. |
| 3. Number of panels .. .. .. .. | 4. |
| 4. Description of truss .. .. .. .. | Braced polygon. |

### EVENLY DISTRIBUTED DEAD LOAD.

#### *Stress Constants.*

Rafters :

| | | | | |
|---|---|---|---|---|
| S. 2·3 | .. | .. | .. | + 5·70 |
| 3·5 | .. | .. | .. | + 5·33 |

Tie :

| | | | | |
|---|---|---|---|---|
| S. 2·4 | .. | .. | .. | − 5·33 |
| 4·6 | .. | .. | .. | − 2·98 |

Bracing :

| | | | | |
|---|---|---|---|---|
| S. 3·4 | .. | .. | .. | + 0·93 |
| 5·4 | .. | .. | .. | − 2·47 |
| 5·6 * (only supports part of tie rod). | | | | |

### LIVE LOAD (WIND PRESSURE).

#### *Maximum Stress Constants.*

Rafters :

| | | | | |
|---|---|---|---|---|
| S. 2·3 | .. | .. | .. | + 3·70 |
| 3·5 | .. | .. | .. | + 3·70 |

* Not necessary to stability of truss.

Tie :

| | | | | | | |
|---|---|---|---|---|---|---|
| S. 2·4 | .. | .. | .. | — | 4·04 |
| 4·6 | .. | .. | .. | — | 1·65 |

Bracing :

| | | | | | | |
|---|---|---|---|---|---|---|
| S. 3·4 | .. | .. | .. | + | 1·00 |
| 4·5 | .. | .. | .. | — | 2·45 |
| 5·6 * | .. | .. | .. | | 0·00 |

---

## TRUSS DIAGRAM No. 82.

### CONDITIONS.

| | |
|---|---|
| 1. Rise of truss  .. .. .. .. .. .. | ⅛ of the span. |
| 2. Rise of tie rod .. .. .. .. .. .. | Nil. |
| 3. Number of panels .. .. .. .. .. | 6. |
| 4. Description of truss.. .. .. .. .. | Braced triangle. |

### EVENLY DISTRIBUTED DEAD LOAD.

#### *Stress Constants.*

Rafters :

| | | | | | | |
|---|---|---|---|---|---|---|
| S. 2·3 | .. | .. | .. | + | 6·78 |
| 3·5 | .. | .. | .. | + | 5·64 |
| 5·7 | .. | .. | .. | + | 6·04 |

Tie :

| | | | | | | |
|---|---|---|---|---|---|---|
| S. 2·4 | .. | .. | .. | — | 6·30 |
| 4·6 | .. | .. | .. | — | 3·80 |

* Not necessary to stability of truss.

N 2

Bracing :

| | | | | | |
|---|---|---|---|---|---|
| S. 3·4 | .. | .. | .. | + | 1·20 |
| 5·4 | .. | .. | .. | + | 1·20 |
| 7·4 | .. | .. | .. | − | 2·52 |

6·7* (only supports part of tie rod).

## LIVE LOAD (WIND PRESSURE).

### *Maximum Stress Constants.*

Rafters :

| | | | | | |
|---|---|---|---|---|---|
| S. 2·3 | .. | .. | .. | + | 4·07 |
| 3·5 | .. | .. | .. | + | 3·24 |
| 5·7 | .. | .. | .. | + | 4·07 |

Tie :

| | | | | | |
|---|---|---|---|---|---|
| S. 2·4 | .. | .. | .. | − | 4·72 |
| 4·6 | .. | .. | .. | − | 2·02 |

Bracing :

| | | | | |
|---|---|---|---|---|
| S. 3·4 | + 1·31 | S. 4·7 | − | 2·70 |
| 4·5 | + 1·31 | 6·7* | | 0·00 |

* Not necessary to stability of truss.

PLATE 22 .

STRESS DIAGRAMS

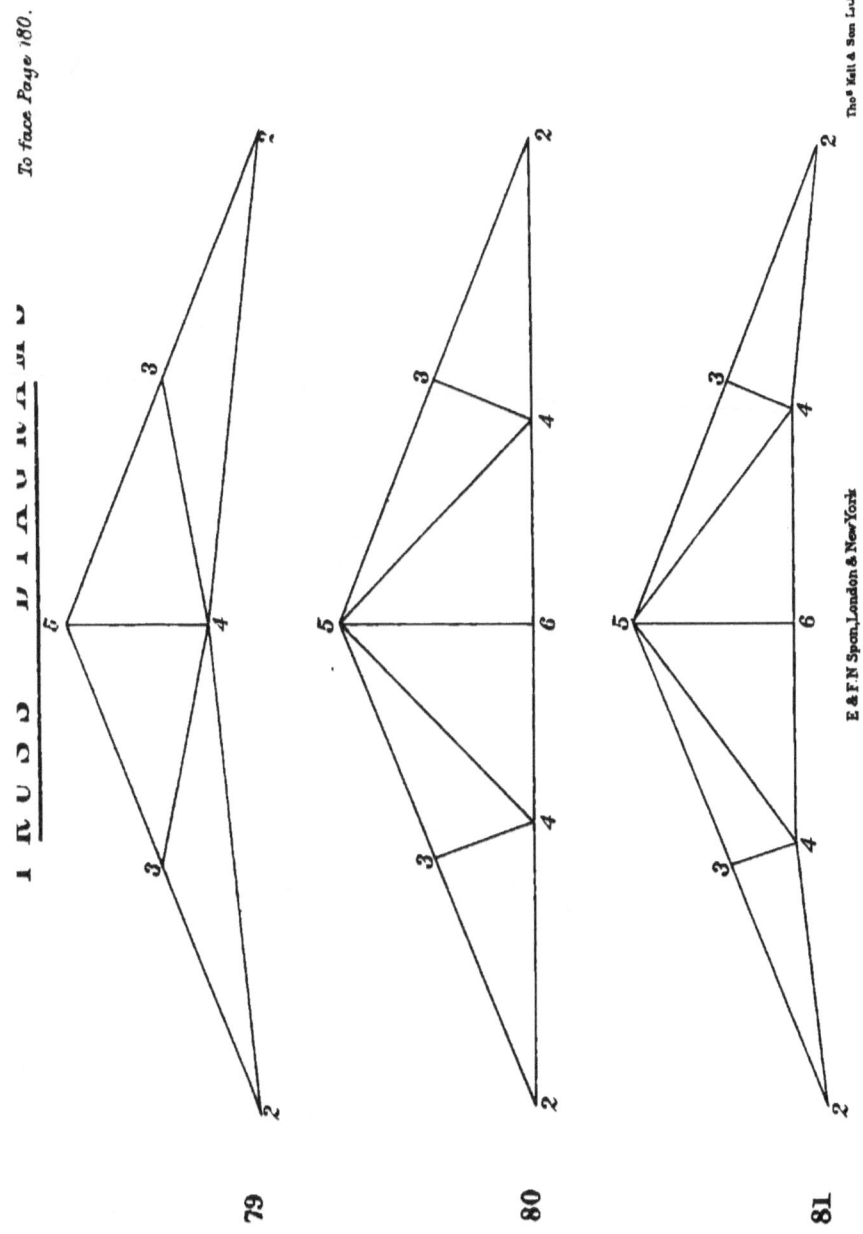

79

80

81

E & F N Spon, London & New York

Thos Kell & Son Lith

## TRUSS DIAGRAM No. 83.

### CONDITIONS.

1. Rise of truss .. .. .. .. .. ..  $\frac{1}{5}$ of the span.
2. Rise of tie rod .. .. .. .. ..  $\frac{1}{30}$ of the span.
3. Number of panels .. .. .. ..  6.
4. Description of truss .. .. .. ..  Braced polygon.

### EVENLY DISTRIBUTED DEAD LOAD.

#### *Stress Constants.*

Rafters:

| | | | | |
|---|---|---|---|---|
| S. 2·3 | .. | .. | .. | + 9·60 |
| 3·5 | .. | .. | .. | + 8·10 |
| 5·7 | .. | .. | .. | + 8·85 |

Tie:

| | | | | |
|---|---|---|---|---|
| S. 2·4 | .. | .. | .. | − 8·95 |
| 4·6 | .. | .. | .. | − 4·50 |

Bracing:

| | | | | |
|---|---|---|---|---|
| S. 3·4 | .. | .. | .. | + 1·48 |
| 5·4 | .. | .. | .. | + 1·48 |
| 7·4 | .. | .. | .. | − 4·70 |

6·7 * (only supports part of tie rod).

* Not necessary to stability of truss.

## LIVE LOAD (WIND PRESSURE).

### *Maximum Stress Constants.*

Rafters :

| | | | | | |
|---|---|---|---|---|---|
| S. 2·3 | .. | .. | .. | + | 6·13 |
| 3·5 | .. | .. | .. | + | 4·93 |
| 5·7 | .. | .. | .. | + | 6·13 |

Tie :

| | | | | | |
|---|---|---|---|---|---|
| S. 2·4 | .. | .. | .. | − | 6·71 |
| 4·6 | .. | .. | .. | − | 2·38 |

Bracing :

| | | | | |
|---|---|---|---|---|
| S. 3·4 | + 1·55 | S. 4·7 | − | 4·33 |
| 4·5 | + 1·55 | 6·7 * | | 0·00 |

---

## TRUSS DIAGRAM No. 84.

### CONDITIONS.

| | | |
|---|---|---|
| 1. Rise of truss .. .. .. .. | { | Long Slope 1 in 2½. |
| | | Short Slope 1 in 0·625. |
| 2. Rise of tie rod .. .. .. .. .. .. | | Nil. |
| 3. Number of panels .. .. .. .. .. | | 5. |
| 4. Description of truss .. .. .. .. | | Braced triangle. |

### EVENLY DISTRIBUTED DEAD LOAD.

### *Stress Constants.*

Rafters :

| | | | | |
|---|---|---|---|---|
| S. 2·3 | + 5·40 | S. 7·9 | + | 2·70 |
| 3·5 | + 5·40 | 9·12 | + | 2·35 |
| 5·7 | + 4·05 | | | |

\* Not necessary to stability of truss.

Tie:

| S. 2·4 | — | 5·00 | S. 8·10 | — | 1·25 |
|---|---|---|---|---|---|
| 4·6 | — | 3·75 | 10·12 | — | 1·25 |
| 6·8 | — | 2·50 | | | |

Bracing:

| S. 3·4 | .. | .. | .. | + | 1·00 |
|---|---|---|---|---|---|
| 5·6 | .. | .. | .. | + | 1·50 |
| 7·8 | .. | .. | .. | + | 2·00 |
| 9.10* (only supports part of tie rod). | | | | | |
| 4·5 | .. | .. | .. | — | 1·60 |
| 6·7 | .. | .. | .. | — | 1·95 |
| 8·9 | .. | .. | .. | — | 2·35 |

### LIVE LOAD (WIND PRESSURE).

#### *Maximum Stress Constants.*

Rafters:

| S. 2·3 | + | 4·12 | S. 7·9 | + | 2·43 |
|---|---|---|---|---|---|
| 3·5 | + | 4·52 | 9·12 | + | 2·04 |
| 5·7 | + | 3·48 | | | |

Tie:

| S. 2·4 | — | 5·12 | S. 8·10 | — | 1·09 |
|---|---|---|---|---|---|
| 4·6 | — | 3·80 | 10·12 | — | 1·09 |
| 6·8 | — | 2·46 | | | |

Bracing:

| S. 3·4 | + | 1·08 | S. 4·5 | — | 1·72 |
|---|---|---|---|---|---|
| 5·6 | + | 1·62 | 6·7 | — | 2·10 |
| 7·8 | + | 2·16 | 8·9 | — | 2·56 |
| 9·10* | | 0·00 | | | |

* Not necessary to stability of truss.

## TRUSS DIAGRAM No. 85.

### CONDITIONS.

1. Rise of truss ..    ..   ..   ..   ..   ..   ¼ of the span.
2. Rise of tie rod    ..   ..   ..   ..   ..   Nil.
3. Number of panels    ..   ..   ..   ..   6.
4. Description of truss   ..   ..   ..   ..   Braced triangle.

### EVENLY DISTRIBUTED DEAD LOAD.

#### Stress Constants.

Rafters :

| | | | | |
|---|---|---|---|---|
| S. 2·3 | .. | .. | .. | + 6·75 |
| 3·5 | .. | .. | .. | + 5·40 |
| 5·7 | .. | .. | .. | + 4·05 |

Tie :

| | | | | |
|---|---|---|---|---|
| S. 2·4 | .. | .. | .. | − 6·25 |
| 4·6 | .. | .. | .. | − 6·25 |
| 6·8 | .. | .. | .. | − 3·75 |

Bracing :

S. 3·4* (only supports part of tie rod).

| | | | | |
|---|---|---|---|---|
| 5·6 | .. | .. | .. | − 0·50 |
| 7·8 | .. | .. | .. | − 2·00 |
| 3·6 | .. | .. | .. | + 1·34 |
| 5·8 | .. | .. | .. | + 1·62 |

Not necessary to stability of truss.

PLATE 23.

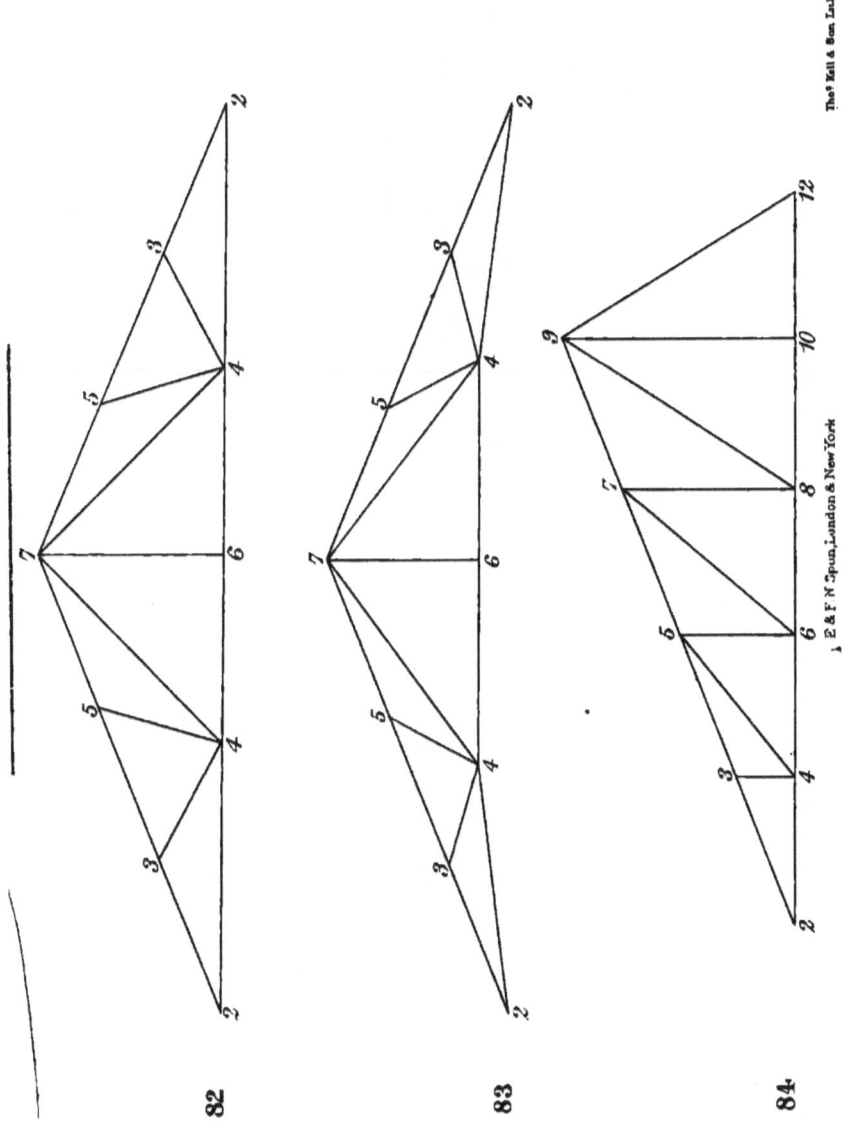

Tho? Kell & Son Lin.

A E & F N Spun, London & New York

LIVE LOAD (WIND PRESSURE).

*Maximum Stress Constants.*

Rafters :

|  |  |  |  |  |  |
|---|---|---|---|---|---|
| S. 2·3 | .. | .. | .. | + | 4·04 |
| 3·5 | .. | .. | .. | + | 2·99 |
| ·5·7 | .. | .. | .. | + | 2·15 |

Tie :

|  |  |  |  |  |  |
|---|---|---|---|---|---|
| S. 2·4 | .. | .. | .. | − | 4·68 |
| 4·6 | .. | .. | .. | − | 4·68 |
| 6·8 | .. | .. | .. | − | 3·33 |

Bracing :

| | | | |
|---|---|---|---|
| S. 3·4* | 0·00 | S. 3·6 + | 1·45 |
| 5·6 − 0·54 | | 5·8 + | 1·73 |
| 7·8 − 1·07 | | | |

\* Not necessary to stability of truss.

# TRUSS DIAGRAM No. 86.

## Conditions.

1. Rise of truss ..    ..    ..    ..    ..    ..    $\frac{1}{5}$ of the span.
2. Rise of tie rod    ..    ..    ..    ..    ..    $\frac{1}{80}$ of the span.
3. Number of panels    ..    ..    ..    ..    6.
4. Description of truss    ..    ..    ..    ..    Braced trapezium.

## Evenly distributed Dead Load.

### *Stress Constants.*

Rafters :

| | | | | | |
|---|---|---|---|---|---|
| S. 2·3 | .. | .. | .. | + | 8·08 |
| 3·5 | .. | .. | .. | + | 6·47 |
| 5·7 | .. | .. | .. | + | 4·86 |

Tie :

| | | | | | |
|---|---|---|---|---|---|
| S. 2·4 | .. | .. | .. | — | 7·52 |
| 4·6 | .. | .. | .. | — | 7·52 |
| 6·8 | .. | .. | .. | — | 6·02 |

Bracing :

S. 3·4 * (only supports part of tie rod).

| | | | | | |
|---|---|---|---|---|---|
| 5·6 | .. | .. | .. | — | 0·50 |
| 7·8 | .. | .. | .. | — | 2·60 |
| 3·6 | .. | .. | .. | + | 1·55 |
| 5·8 | .. | .. | .. | + | 1·77 |

\* Not necessary to stability of truss.

## Live Load (Wind Pressure).

### *Maximum Stress Constants.*

Rafters :

|       |       |    |    |    |        |
|-------|-------|----|----|----|--------|
| S. 2·3 | .. | .. | .. | + | 5·08 |
| 3·5 | .. | .. | .. | + | 3·74 |
| 5·7 | .. | .. | .. | + | 2·60 |

Tie :

|       |       |    |    |    |        |
|-------|-------|----|----|----|--------|
| S. 2·4 | .. | .. | .. | − | 5·67 |
| 4·6 | .. | .. | .. | − | 5·67 |
| 6·8 | .. | .. | .. | − | 4·04 |

Bracing :

| S. 3·4 * | 0·00 | S. 3·6 | + 1·67 |
|----------|------|--------|--------|
| 5·6 − | 0·54 | 5·8 | + 1·89 |
| 7·8 − | 1·41 |        |        |

* Not necessary to stability of truss.

## TRUSS DIAGRAM No. 87.

### CONDITIONS.

1. Rise of truss ..     ..    ..    ..    ..    ..    $\frac{1}{8}$ of the span.
2. Rise of tie rod    ..    ..    ..    ..    ..    Nil.
3. Number of panels     ..    ..    '..    ..    8.
4. Description of truss    ..    ..    ..    ..    Braced triangle.

### EVENLY DISTRIBUTED DEAD LOAD.

#### *Stress Constants.*

Rafters :

     S. 2·3    +    9·40       S. 5·7    +    6·70
        3·5    +    8·05          7·9    +    5·35

Tie :

     S. 2·4    −    8·75       S. 6·8    −    7·48
        4·6    −    8·75        8·10  −    6·22

Bracing :

     S. 3·4 * (only supports part of tie rod).
        5·6     ..      ..      ..       −    0·50
        7·8     ..      ..      ..       −    1·00
        9·10    ..      ..      ..       −    3·00
        3·6     ..      ..      ..       +    1·34
        5·8     ..      ..      ..       +    1·60
        7·10    .,      ..      ..       +    1·95

       * Not necessary to stability of truss.

## LIVE LOAD (WIND PRESSURE).

### *Maximum Stress Constants.*

Rafters :

| | | | | | | |
|---|---|---|---|---|---|---|
| S. 2·3 | + | 5·83 | | S. 5·7 | + | 3·73 |
| 3·5 | + | 4·78 | | 7·9 | + | 2·88 |

Tie :

| | | | | | | |
|---|---|---|---|---|---|---|
| S. 2·4 | − | 6·70 | | S. 6·8 | − | 5·35 |
| 4·6 | − | 6·70 | | 8·10 | − | 4·00 |

Bracing :

| | | | | | | |
|---|---|---|---|---|---|---|
| S. 3·4 * | 0·00 | | S. 3·6 | + | 1·45 |
| 5·6 | − | 0·54 | | 5·8 | + | 1·72 |
| 7·8 | − | 1·80 | | 7·10 | + | 2·10 |
| 9·10 | − | 1·62 | | | | |

\* Not necessary to stability of truss.

## TRUSS DIAGRAM No. 88.

### CONDITIONS.

1. Rise of truss .. .. .. .. .. .. $\frac{1}{8}$ of the span.
2. Rise of tie rod .. .. .. .. .. $\frac{1}{30}$ of the span.
3. Number of panels .. .. .. .. 8.
4. Description of truss] .. .. .. .. Braced trapezium.

### EVENLY DISTRIBUTED DEAD LOAD.

*Stress.Constants.*

Rafters :

| | | | | | |
|---|---|---|---|---|---|
| S. 2·3 | + | 11·30 | S. 5·7 | + | 8·06 |
| 3·5 | + | 9·68 | 7·9 | + | 6·44 |

Tie :

| | | | | | |
|---|---|---|---|---|---|
| S. 2·4 | − | 10·50 | S. 6·8 | − | 9·00 |
| 4·6 | − | 10·50 | 8·10 | − | 7·50 |

Bracing :

S. 3·4 * (only supports part of tie rod).

| | | | | | |
|---|---|---|---|---|---|
| 5·6 | .. | .. | .. | − | 0·50 |
| 7·8 | .. | .. | .. | − | 1·00 |
| 9·10 | .. | .. | .. | − | 3·80 |
| 3·6 | .. | .. | .. | + | 1·55 |
| 5·8 | .. | .. | .. | + | 1·75 |
| 7·10 | .. | .. | .. | + | 2·05 |

\* Not necessary to stability of truss.

PLATE 24.

# TRUSS DIAGRAMS

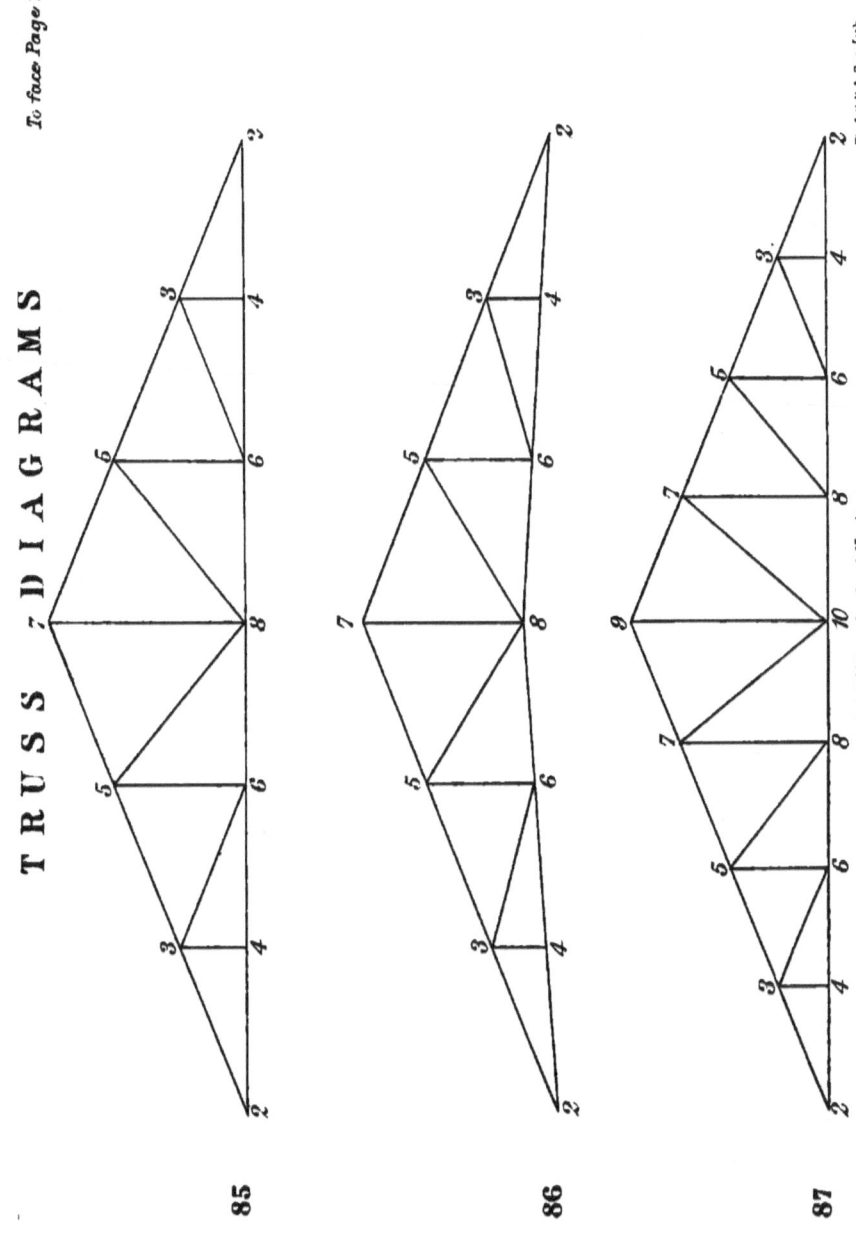

85

86

87

E & F N Spon, London & New York

Tho.ˢ Kell & Son Lith

LIVE LOAD (WIND PRESSURE).

*Maximum Stress Constants.*

Rafters:

| | | |
|---|---|---|
| S. 2·3 | + | 7·24 |
| 3·5 | + | 5·90 |

| | | |
|---|---|---|
| S. 5·7 | + | 4·56 |
| 7·9 | + | 3·44 |

Tie:

| | | |
|---|---|---|
| S. 2·4 | − | 8·06 |
| 4·6 | − | 8·06 |

| | | |
|---|---|---|
| S. 6·8 | − | 6·44 |
| 8·10 | − | 4·82 |

Bracing:

| | | |
|---|---|---|
| S. 3·4 * | | 0·00 |
| 5·6 | − | 0·54 |
| 7·8 | − | 1·08 |
| 9·10 | − | 2·02 |

| | | |
|---|---|---|
| S. 3·6 | + | 1·68 |
| 5·8 | + | 1·88 |
| 7·10 | + | 2·22 |

\* Not necessary to stability of truss.

## TRUSS DIAGRAM No. 89.

### CONDITIONS.

1. Rise of truss .. .. .. .. .. .. $\frac{1}{6}$ of the span.
2. Rise of tie rod .. .. .. .. .. Nil.
3. Number of panels .. .. .. .. 8.
4. Description of truss .. .. .. .. Braced triangle.

### EVENLY DISTRIBUTED DEAD LOAD.

#### *Stress Constants.*

Rafters :

| | | | | | | | |
|---|---|---|---|---|---|---|---|
| S. 2·3 | + | 9·40 | | S. 5·7 | + | 8·66 |
| 3·5 | + | 9·03 | | 7·9 | + | 8·29 |

Tie :

| | | | | | | |
|---|---|---|---|---|---|---|
| S. 2.4 | .. | .. | .. | — | 8·73 |
| 4·6 | .. | .. | .. | — | 7·48 |
| 6·10 | .. | .. | .. | — | 5·00 |

Bracing :

| | | | | | | |
|---|---|---|---|---|---|---|
| S. 3·4 | .. | .. | .. | + | 0·93 |
| 5·6 | .. | .. | .. | + | 1·86 |
| 7·8 | .. | .. | .. | + | 0·93 |
| 4·5 | .. | .. | .. | — | 1·24 |
| 5·8 | .. | .. | .. | — | 1·24 |
| 6·8 | .. | .. | .. | — | 2·48 |
| 8·9 | .. | .. | .. | — | 3·72 |

9·10* (only supports part of tie rod).

* Not necessary to stability of truss.

## LIVE LOAD (WIND PRESSURE).

### *Maximum Stress Constants.*

Rafters :

| | | |
|---|---|---|
| S. 2·3 | + | 5·90 |
| 3·5 | + | 5·90 |

| | | |
|---|---|---|
| S. 5·7 | + | 5·90 |
| 7·9 | + | 5·90 |

Tie :

| | | | | | |
|---|---|---|---|---|---|
| S. 2·4 | .. | .. | .. | — | 6·80 |
| 4·6 | .. | .. | .. | — | 5·45 |
| 6·10 | .. | .. | .. | — | 2·70 |

Bracing :

| | | |
|---|---|---|
| S. 3·4 | + | 1·00 |
| 5·6 | + | 2·00 |
| 7·8 | + | 1·00 |
| 4·5 | — | 1·35 |

| | | |
|---|---|---|
| S. 5·8 | — | 1·35 |
| 6·8 | — | 2·70 |
| 8·9 | — | 4·05 |
| 9·10 * | | 0·00 |

\* Not necessary to stability of truss.

## TRUSS DIAGRAM No. 90.

### Conditions.

1. Rise of truss .. .. .. .. .. .. $\frac{1}{4}$ of the span.
2. Rise of tie rod .. .. .. .. .. $\frac{1}{40}$ of the span.
3. Number of panels .. .. .. .. 8.
4. Description of truss .. .. .. .. Braced polygon.

### Evenly distributed Dead Load.

*Stress Constants.*

Rafters :

S. 2·3  + 12·24        S. 5·7  + 11·50
   3·5  + 11·87           7·9  + 11·13

Tie :

S. 2·4    ..    ..    ..    − 11·42
   4·6    ..    ..    ..    −  9·80
   6·10   ..    ..    ..    −  5·74

Bracing :

S. 3·4    ..    ..    ..    +  0·93
   5·6    ..    ..    ..    +  1·86
   7·8    ..    ..    ..    +  0·93
   4·5    ..    ..    ..    −  1·60
   5·8    ..    ..    ..    −  1·60
   6·8    ..    ..    ..    −  4·26
   8·9    ..    ..    ..    −  5·86
   9·10 * (only supports part of tie rod).

* Not necessary to stability of truss.

## LIVE LOAD (WIND PRESSURE).

### *Maximum Stress Constants.*

Rafters :

| | | | | | |
|---|---|---|---|---|---|
| S. 2·3 | + | 7·88 | S. 5·7 | + | 7·88 |
| 3·5 | + | 7·88 | 7·9 | + | 7·88 |

Tie :

| | | | | | |
|---|---|---|---|---|---|
| S. 2·4 | .. | .. | .. | — | 8·66 |
| 4·6 | .. | .. | .. | — | 6·92 |
| 6·10 | .. | .. | .. | — | 3·04 |

Bracing :

| | | | | | |
|---|---|---|---|---|---|
| S. 3·4 | + | 1·00 | S. 5·8 | — | 1·75 |
| 5·6 | + | 2·00 | 6·8 | — | 3·98 |
| 7·8 | + | 1·00 | 8·9 | — | 5·72 |
| 4·5 | — | 1·75 | 9·10* | | 0·00 |

\* Not necessary to stability of truss.

## TRUSS DIAGRAM No. 91.

### CONDITIONS.

1. Rise of truss .. .. .. .. .. .. $\frac{1}{8}$ of the span.
2. Rise of tie rod .. .. .. .. .. Nil.
3. Number of panels .. .. .. .. 12.
4. Description of truss .. .. .. .. Braced triangle.

### EVENLY DISTRIBUTED DEAD LOAD.

#### *Stress Constants.*

Rafters :

| | |
|---|---|
| S. 2·3 + 14·85 | S. 7·9 + 10·80 |
| 3·5 + 13·50 | 9·11 + 9·45 |
| 5·7 + 12·15 | 11·13 + 8·10 |

Tie :

| | |
|---|---|
| S. 2·4 − 13·80 | S. 8·10 − 11·30 |
| 4·6 − 13·80 | 10·12 − 10·05 |
| 6·8 − 12·55 | 12·14 − 8·80 |

Bracing :

S. 3·4* (only supports part of tie rod).
5·6 .. .. .. − 0·50
7·8 .. .. .. − 1·00
9·10 .. .. .. − 1·50
11·12 .. .. .. − 2·00
13·14 .. .. .. − 5·00

\* Not necessary to stability of truss.

PLATE 25.

To face Page 196.

# TRUSS DIAGRAMS

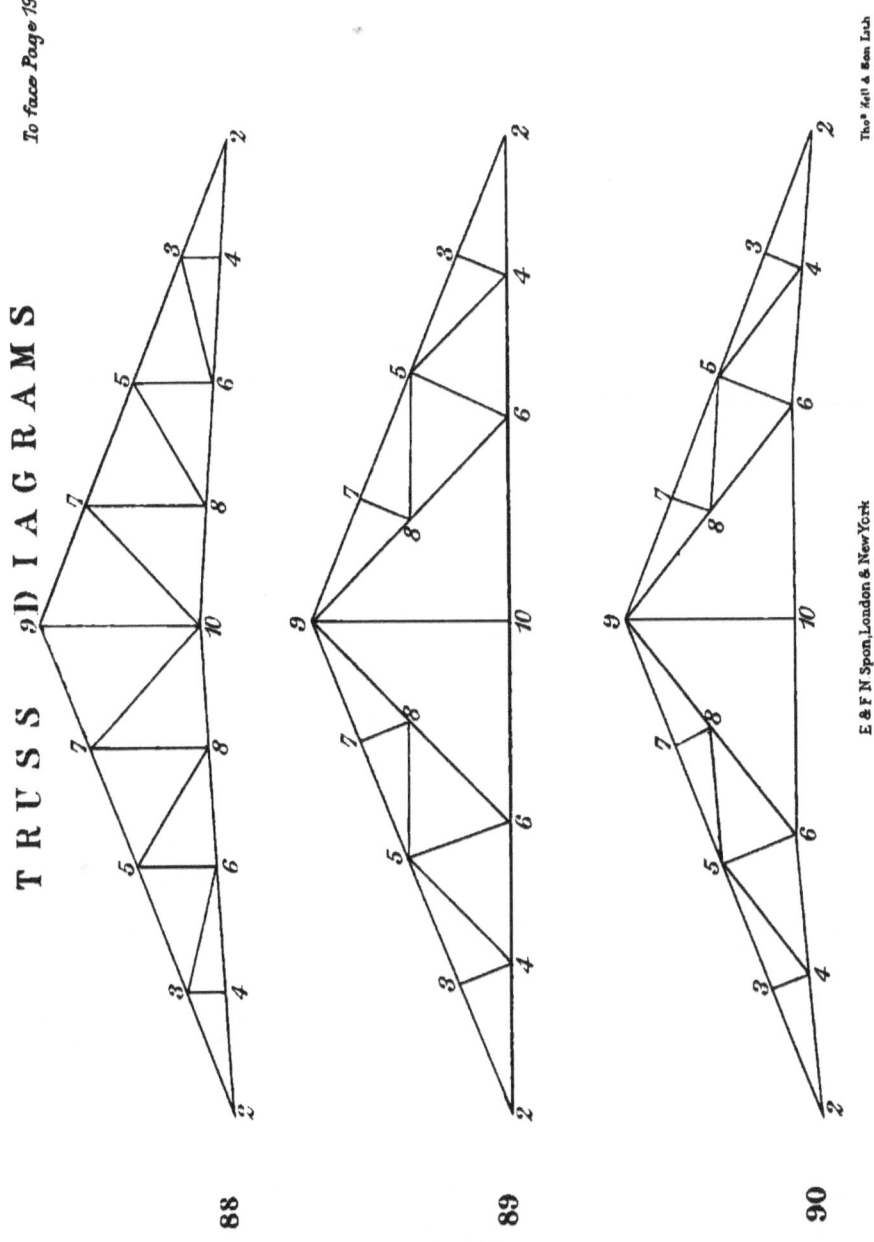

88

89

90

Bracing—*continued.*

| | | | | | |
|---|---|---|---|---|---|
| S. 3·6 | .. | .. | .. | + | 1·35 |
| 5·8 | .. | .. | .. | + | 1·52 |
| 7·10 | .. | .. | .. | + | 1·90 |
| 9·12 | .. | .. | .. | + | 2·34 |
| 11·14 | .. | .. | .. | + | 2·80 |

## LIVE LOAD (WIND PRESSURE).

### *Maximum Stress Constants.*

Rafters :

| | | | | | |
|---|---|---|---|---|---|
| S. 2·3 | + | 9·52 | S. 7·9 | + | 6·34 |
| 3·5 | + | 8·46 | 9·11 | + | 5·28 |
| 5·7 | + | 7·40 | 11·13 | + | 4·40 |

Tie :

| | | | | | |
|---|---|---|---|---|---|
| S. 2·4 | − | 10·86 | S. 8·10 | − | 8·14 |
| 4·6 | − | 10·86 | 10·12 | − | 6·78 |
| 6·8 | − | 9·50 | 12·14 | − | 5·42 |

Bracing :

| | | | | | |
|---|---|---|---|---|---|
| S. 3·4* | | 0·00 | S. 3·6 | + | 1·46 |
| 5·6 | − | 0·54 | 5·8 | + | 1·74 |
| 7·8 | − | 1·08 | 7·10 | + | 2·10 |
| 9·10 | − | 1·62 | 9·12 | + | 2·56 |
| 11·12 | − | 2·16 | 11·14 | + | 3·00 |
| 13·14 | − | 2·70 | | | |

* Not necessary to stability of truss.

## TRUSS DIAGRAM No. 92.

### CONDITIONS.

1. Rise of truss  ..  ..  ..  ..  ..  ..  $\frac{1}{8}$ of the span.
2. Rise of tie rod  ..  ..  ..  ..  ..  $\frac{1}{40}$ of the span.
3. Number of panels  ..  ..  ..  ..  12.
4. Description of truss  ..  ..  ..  ..  Braced trapezium.

### EVENLY DISTRIBUTED DEAD LOAD.

#### *Stress Constants.*

Rafters :

| S. 2·3 | + 16·90 | S. 7·9 | + 12·28 |
|---|---|---|---|
| 3·5 | + 15·36 | 9·11 | + 10·74 |
| 5·7 | + 13·82 | 11·13 | + 9·20 |

Tie :

| S. 2·4 | − 15·74 | S. 8·10 | − 12·84 |
|---|---|---|---|
| 4·6 | − 15·74 | 10·12 | − 11·39 |
| 6·8 | − 14·29 | 12·14 | − 9·94 |

Bracing :

| S. 3·4 * (only supports part of tie rod) | | | | |
|---|---|---|---|---|
| 5·6 | .. | .. | .. | − 0·50 |
| 7·8 | .. | .. | .. | − 1·00 |
| 9·10 | .. | .. | .. | − 1·50 |
| 11·12 | .. | .. | .. | − 2·00 |
| 13·14 | .. | .. | .. | − 5·80 |

\* Not necessary to stability of truss.

Bracing—*continued.*

| | | | | | |
|---|---|---|---|---|---|
| S. 3·6 | .. | .. | .. | + | 1·50 |
| 5·8 | .. | .. | .. | + | 1·70 |
| 7·10 | .. | .. | .. | + | 2·04 |
| 9·12 | .. | .. | .. | + | 2·38 |
| 11·14 | .. | .. | .. | + | 2·82 |

## LIVE LOAD (WIND PRESSURE).

### *Maximum Stress Constants.*

Rafters:

| | | | | |
|---|---|---|---|---|
| S. 2·3 | + 11·10 | S. 7·9 | + | 7·29 |
| 3·5 | + 9·83 | 9·11 | + | 6·02 |
| 5·7 | + 8·56 | 11·13 | + | 4·97 |

Tie:

| | | | | |
|---|---|---|---|---|
| S. 2·4 | − 12·36 | S. 8·10 | − | 9·26 |
| 4·6 | − 12·36 | 10·12 | − | 7·71 |
| 6·8 | − 10·81 | 12·14 | − | 6·16 |

Bracing:

| | | | | |
|---|---|---|---|---|
| S. 3·4 * | 0·00 | S. 3·6 | + | 1·60 |
| 5·6 | − 0·54 | 5·8 | + | 1·86 |
| 7·8 | − 1·08 | 7·10 | + | 2·17 |
| 9·10 | − 1·62 | 9·12 | + | 2·60 |
| 11·12 | − 2·16 | 11·14 | + | 3·04 |
| 13·14 | − 3·15 | | | |

\* Not necessary to stability of truss.

## TRUSS DIAGRAM No. 93.

### CONDITIONS.

1. Rise of truss .. .. .. .. .. ..    $\frac{1}{8}$ of the span.
2. Rise of tie rod .. .. .. .. ..    Nil.
3. Number of panels .. .. .. ..    8.
4. Description of truss .. .. .. ..    Braced triangle.

### EVENLY DISTRIBUTED DEAD LOAD.

#### *Stress Constants.*

Rafters :

S. 2·3   + 11·05      S. 5·7   + 10·43
3·5   + 10·74      7·9   + 10·12

Tie :

S. 2·4 .. .. .. − 10·50
4·6 .. .. .. − 9·00
6·10 .. .. .. − 6·00

Bracing :

S. 3·4 .. .. .. + 0·95
5·6 .. .. .. + 1·90
7·8 .. .. .. + 0·95
4·5 .. .. .. − 1·50
5·8 .. .. .. − 1·50
6·8 .. .. .. − 3·00
8·9 .. .. .. − 4·50
9·10 * (only supports part of tie rod).

* Not necessary to stability of truss.

LIVE LOAD (WIND PRESSURE).

*Maximum Stress Constants.*

Rafters :

| | | | | | | |
|---|---|---|---|---|---|---|
| S. | 2·3 | + | 7·18 | S. 5·7 | + | 7·18 |
| | 3·5 | + | 7·18 | 7·9 | + | 7·18 |

Tie :

| | | | | | | |
|---|---|---|---|---|---|---|
| S. | 2·4 | .. | .. | .. | − | 7·92 |
| | 4·6 | .. | .. | .. | − | 6·34 |
| | 6·10 | .. | .. | .. | − | 3·17 |

Bracing :

| | | | | | | |
|---|---|---|---|---|---|---|
| S. | 3·4 | + | 1·00 | S. 5·8 | − | 1·56 |
| | 5·6 | + | 2·00 | 6·8 | − | 3·16 |
| | 7·8 | + | 1·00 | 8·9 | − | 4·74 |
| | 4·5 | − | 1·56 | 9·10 * | | 0·00 |

\* Not necessary to stability of truss.

## TRUSS DIAGRAM No. 94.

### CONDITIONS.

1. Rise of truss ..   ..   ..   ..   ..   ..   $\frac{1}{8}$ of the span.
2. Rise of tie rod   ..   ..   ..   ..   ..   $\frac{1}{70}$ of the span.
3. Number of panels   ..   ..   ..   ..   8.
4. Description of truss   ..   ..   ..   ..   Braced polygon.

### EVENLY DISTRIBUTED DEAD LOAD.

#### Stress Constants.

Rafters :

| | | | |
|---|---|---|---|
| S. 2·3 | + 15·33 | S. 5·7 | + 14·71 |
| 3·5 | + 15·02 | 7·9 | + 14·40 |

Tie :

| | | | | |
|---|---|---|---|---|
| S. 2·4 | .. | .. | .. | − 14·60 |
| 4·6 | .. | .. | .. | − 12·55 |
| 6·10 | .. | .. | .. | − 7·15 |

Bracing :

| | | | | |
|---|---|---|---|---|
| S. 3·4 | .. | .. | .. | + 0·95 |
| 5·6 | .. | .. | .. | + 1·90 |
| 7·8 | .. | .. | .. | + 0·95 |
| 4·5 | .. | .. | .. | − 2·05 |
| 5·8 | .. | .. | .. | − 2·05 |
| 6·8 | .. | .. | .. | − 5·60 |
| 8·9 | .. | .. | .. | − 7·65 |

9·10 * (only supports part of tie rod).

\* Not necessary to stability of truss.

PLATE 26.

# TRUSS DIAGRAMS

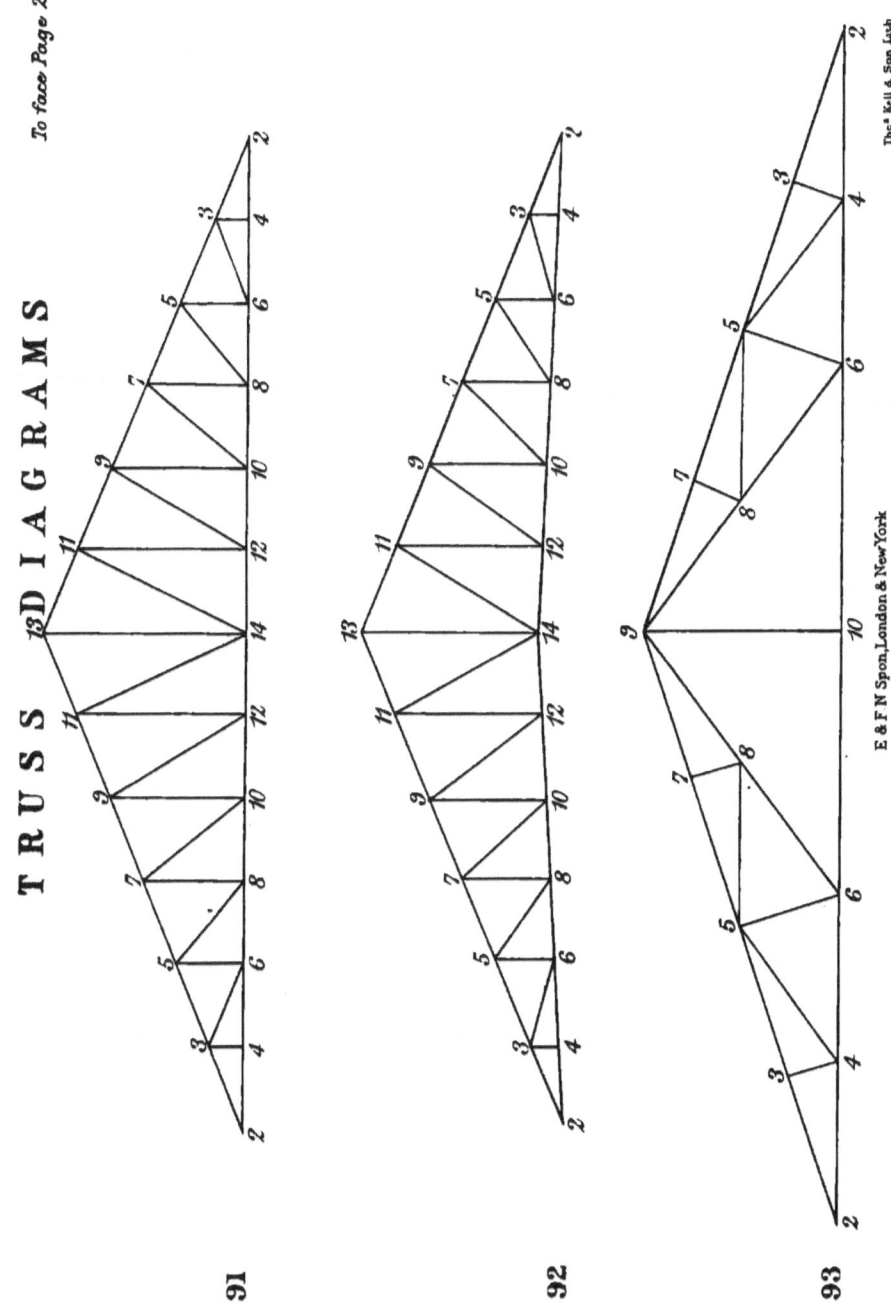

91

92

93

E & F N Spon, London & New York

Tho.ͤ Kell & Son Lith.

## LIVE LOAD (WIND PRESSURE).

### *Maximum Stress Constants.*

Rafters :

| | | | | | | |
|---|---|---|---|---|---|---|
| S. 2·3 | + 10·54 | | S. 5·7 | + 10·54 |
| 3·5 | + 10·54 | | 7·9 | + 10·54 |

Tie :

| | | | | | |
|---|---|---|---|---|---|
| S. 2·4 | .. | .. | .. | − 11·15 |
| 4·6 | .. | .. | .. | − 8·93 |
| 6·10 | .. | .. | .. | − 3·75 |

Bracing :

| | | | | | |
|---|---|---|---|---|---|
| S. 3·4 | + 1·00 | | S. 5·8 | − 2·22 |
| 5·6 | + 2·00 | | 6·8 | − 5·30 |
| 7·8 | + 1·00 | | 8·9 | − 7·52 |
| 4·5 | − 2·22 | | 9·10* | 0·00 |

\* Not necessary to stability of truss.

## TRUSS DIAGRAM No. 95.

### Conditions.

1. Rise of truss .. .. .. .. .. .. $\frac{1}{8}$ of the span.
2. Rise of tie rod .. .. .. .. .. Nil.
3. Number of panels .. .. .. .. 12.
4. Description of truss .. .. .. .. Braced triangle.

### Evenly distributed Dead Load.

#### *Stress Constants.*

Rafters:

| S. 2·3 | + 17·49 | S. 7·9 | + 12·72 |
|--------|---------|--------|---------|
| 3·5    | + 15·90 | 9·11   | + 11·13 |
| 5·7    | + 14·31 | 11·13  | +  9·54 |

Tie:

| S. 2·4 | − 16·50 | S. 8·10 | − 13·50 |
|--------|---------|---------|---------|
| 4·6    | − 16·50 | 10·12   | − 12·00 |
| 6·8    | − 15·00 | 12·14   | − 10·50 |

Bracing:

S. 3·4* (only supports part of tie rod).

| 5·6   | .. | .. | .. | − | 0·50 |
|-------|----|----|----|---|------|
| 7·8   | .. | .. | .. | − | 1·00 |
| 9·10  | .. | .. | .. | − | 1·50 |
| 11·12 | .. | .. | .. | − | 2·00 |
| 13·14 | .. | .. | .. | − | 5·00 |
| 3·6   | .. | .. | .. | + | 1·59 |
| 5·8   | .. | .. | .. | + | 1·80 |

* Not necessary to stability of truss.

Bracing—*continued.*

| | | | | |
|---|---|---|---|---|
| S. 7·10 | .. | .. | .. | + 2·12 |
| 9·12 | .. | .. | .. | + 2·52 |
| 11·14 | .. | .. | .. | + 2·92 |

## LIVE LOAD (WIND PRESSURE).

### *Maximum Stress Constants.*

Rafters.

| | | | |
|---|---|---|---|
| S. 2·3 + 11·52 | | S. 7·9 + 7·50 |
| 3·5 + 10·18 | | 9·11 + 6·16 |
| 5·7 + 8·84 | | 11·13 + 4·98 |

Tie:

| | |
|---|---|
| S. 2·4 − 12·66 | S. 8·10 − 9·48 |
| 4·6 − 12·66 | 10·12 − 7·89 |
| 6·8 − 11·07 | 12·14 − 6·30 |

Bracing:

| | |
|---|---|
| S. 3·4* 0·00 | S. 3·6 + 1·67 |
| 5·6 − 0·52 | 5·8 + 1·90 |
| 7·8 − 1·05 | 7·10 + 2·24 |
| 9·10 − 1·58 | 9·12 + 2·64 |
| 11·12 − 2·10 | 11·14 + 3·08 |
| 13·14 − 2·63 | |

* Not necessary to stability of truss.

.

## TRUSS DIAGRAM No. 96.

### CONDITIONS.

1. Rise of truss .. .. .. .. .. .. $\frac{1}{6}$ of the span.
2. Rise of tie rod .. .. .. .. .. $\frac{1}{40}$ of the span.
3. Number of panels .. .. .. .. 12.
4. Description of truss .. .. .. .. Braced trapezium.

### EVENLY DISTRIBUTED DEAD LOAD.

#### *Stress Constants.*

Rafters :

| | | |
|---|---|---|
| S. 2·3 + 20·55 | S. 7·9 + 14·94 |
| 3·5 + 18·68 | 9·11 + 13·07 |
| 5·7 + 16·81 | 11·13 + 11·20 |

Tie :

| | |
|---|---|
| S. 2·4 − 19·52 | S. 8·10 − 15·96 |
| 4·6 − 19·52 | 10·12 − 14·18 |
| 6·8 − 17·74 | 12·14 − 12·40 |

Bracing :

S. 3·4 * (only supports part of tie rod).

| | | | | |
|---|---|---|---|---|
| 5·6 | .. | .. | .. | − 0·50 |
| 7·8 | .. | .. | .. | − 1·00 |
| 9·10 | .. | .. | .. | − 1·50 |
| 11·12 | .. | .. | .. | − 2·00 |
| 13·14 | .. | .. | .. | − 6·08 |
| 3·6 | .. | .. | .. | + 1·84 |
| 5·8 | .. | .. | .. | + 2·00 |

\* Not necessary to stability of truss.

Bracing—*continued.*

| | | | | |
|---|---|---|---|---|
| S. 7·10 | .. | .. | .. | + 2·24 |
| 9·12 | .. | .. | .. | + 2·60 |
| 11·14 | .. | .. | .. | + .2·98 |

### Live Load (Wind Pressure).

#### *Maximum Stress Constants.*

Rafters :

| | | | | |
|---|---|---|---|---|
| S. 2·3 | + 13·70 | S. 7·9 | + | 8·86 |
| 3·5 | + 12·09 | 9·11 | + | 7·24 |
| 5·7 | + 10·47 | 11·13 | + | 5·84 |

Tie :

| | | | | |
|---|---|---|---|---|
| S. 2·4 | − 14·78 | S. 8·10 | − | 11·08 |
| 4·6 | − 14·78 | 10·12 | − | 9·23 |
| 6·8 | − 12·93 | 12·14 | − | 7·38 |

Bracing :

| | | | | |
|---|---|---|---|---|
| S. 3·4* | 0·00 | S. 3·6 | + | 1·88 |
| 5·6 | − 0·52 | 5·8 | + | 2·12 |
| 7·8 | − 1·05 | 7·10 | + | 2·37 |
| 9·10 | − 1·58 | 9·12 | + | 2·76 |
| 11·12 | − 2·10 | 11·14 | + | 3·14 |
| 13·14 | − 3·20 | | | |

\* Not necessary to stability of truss.

## TRUSS DIAGRAM No. 97.

### CONDITIONS.

1. Rise of truss .. .. .. .. $\begin{cases} \frac{1}{4} \text{ of the span.} \\ \text{Depth at ends } \frac{1}{30} \text{ of the span.} \end{cases}$
2. Rise of tie .. .. .. .. .. .. $\frac{1}{4}$ of the span.
3. Number of panels .. .. .. .. 10.
4. Description of truss .. .. $\begin{cases} \text{Top members inclined 1 in } 2\frac{1}{4}. \\ \text{Bottom ditto parabolic.} \end{cases}$

### EVENLY DISTRIBUTED DEAD LOAD.

#### *Stress Constants.*

Rafters :

| | | |
|---|---|---|
| S. 1·3   + 10·72 | S. 7·9   + 14·37 |
| 3·5   + 17·20 | 9·11 + 10·78 |
| 5·7   + 17·30 | |

Tie :

| | |
|---|---|
| S. 2·4 *   0·00 | S. 8·10   − 16·15 |
| 4·6   − 10·59 | 10·12   − 13·41 |
| 6·8   − 16·66 | |

Bracing :

| | |
|---|---|
| S. 1·2 *   0·00 | S. 1·4   − 10·00 |
| 3·4   + 4·00 | 3·6   − 6·07 |
| 5·6   + 1·10 | 5·8   − 0·16 |
| 7·8   − 1·54 | 7·10   + 3·16 |
| 9·10   − 3·33 | 9·12   + 4·33 |
| 11·12   − 7·00 | |

*Note.*—This truss should be supported at the points 1 − 1.

    * Not necessary to stability of truss.

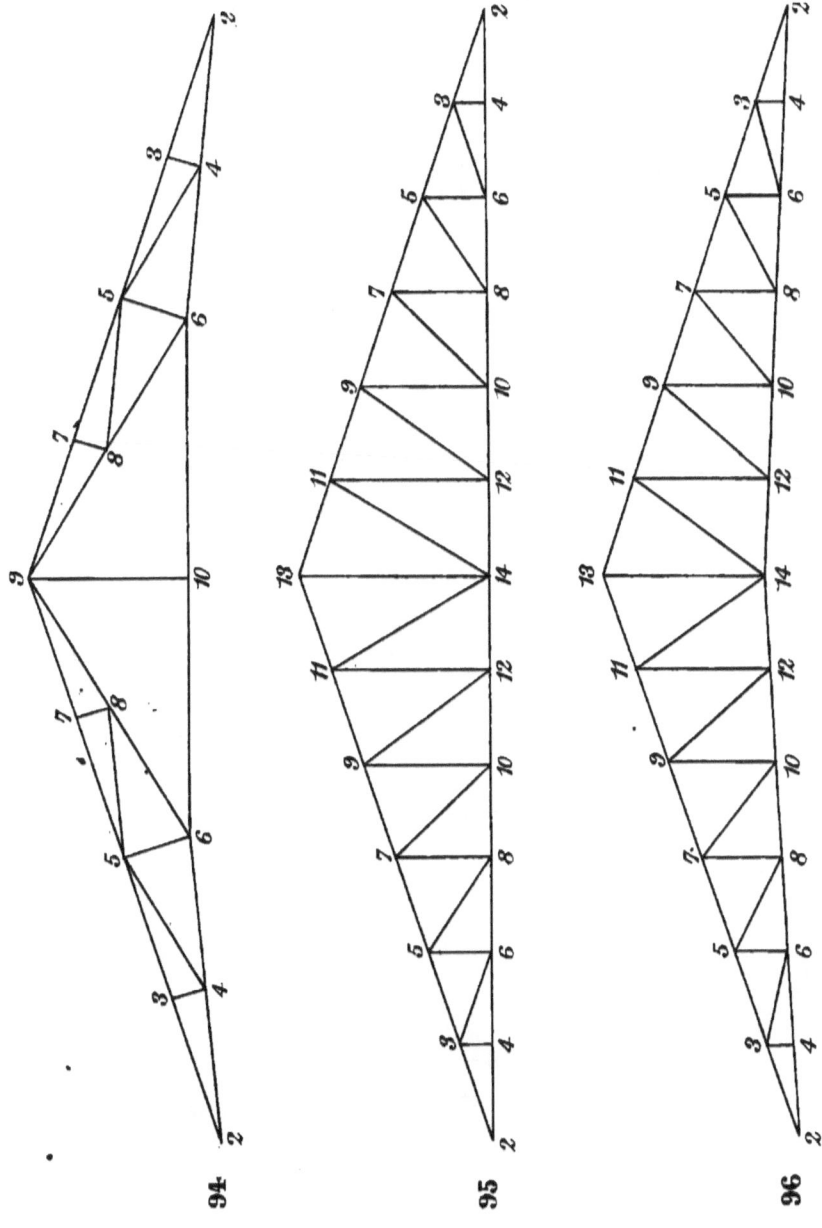

94

95

96

## LIVE LOAD (WIND PRESSURE).

### *Maximum Stress Constants.*

Rafters :

| | | | | | |
|---|---|---|---|---|---|
| S. 1·3 | + | 6·66 | S. 7·9 | + | 8·43 |
| 3·5 | + | 11·42 | 9·11 | + | 5·80 |
| 5·7 | + | 11·06 | | | |

Tie :

| | | | | | |
|---|---|---|---|---|---|
| S. 1·4 | − | 7·88 | S. 8·10 | − | 11·33 |
| 4·6 | − | 8·33 | 10·12 | − | 8·40 |
| 6·8 | − | 12·28 | | | |

Bracing :

| | | | | | |
|---|---|---|---|---|---|
| S. 3·4 | + | 3·10 | S. 11·12 | − | 3·77 |
| 3·4 | − | 0·00 | 3·6 | + | 0·00 |
| 5·6 | + | 0·54 | 3·6 | − | 4·06 |
| 5·6 | − | 0·00 | 5·8 | + | 0·74 |
| 7·8 | + | 0·00 | 5·8 | − | 0·88 |
| 7·8 | − | 1·44 | 7·10 | + | 3·13 |
| 9·10 | + | 0·00 | 7·10 | − | 0·00 |
| 9·10 | − | 2·70 | 9·12 | + | 3·97 |
| 11·12 | + | 0·00 | 9·12 | − | 0·00 |

*Note.*—This truss should be supported at the points 1 − 1.

# TRUSS DIAGRAM No. 98.

### CONDITIONS.

1. Rise of truss .. .. .. .. .. .. $\frac{1}{8}$ of the span.
2. Rise of tie .. .. .. .. .. .. $\frac{1}{4}$ of the span.
3. Number of panels .. .. .. .. 8.
4. Description of truss .. .. .. .. { Braced crescent (circular).

### EVENLY DISTRIBUTED DEAD LOAD.

*Stress Constants.*

Rafters :

| | | | | | |
|---|---|---|---|---|---|
| S. 2·3 | + 13·70 | | S. 5·7 | + 12·60 |
| 3·5 | + 12·70 | | 7·9 | + 12·60 |

Tie :

| | | | | | |
|---|---|---|---|---|---|
| S. 2·4 | − 11·80 | | S. 6·8 | − 12·60 |
| 4·6 | − 12·30 | | 8·10 | − 12·70 |

Bracing :

| | | | | | |
|---|---|---|---|---|---|
| S. 3·4 | − 1·75 | | S. 5·4 | − 1·70 |
| 5·6 | + 0·60 | | 7·6 | + 0·20 |
| 7·8 | − 1·65 | | 9·8 | − 1·40 |
| 9·10 | + 0·45 | | | |

### LIVE LOAD (WIND PRESSURE).

*Maximum Stress Constants.*

Rafters :

| | | | | | |
|---|---|---|---|---|---|
| S. 2·3 | + 9·34 | | S. 5·7 | + 8·28 |
| 3·5 | + 8·48 | | 7·9 | + 7·42 |

Tie:

| | | | |
|---|---|---|---|
| S. 2·4 | − 7·98 | S. 6·8 | − 7·48 |
| 4·6 | − 8·18 | 8·10 | − 6·37 |

Bracing:

| | | | |
|---|---|---|---|
| S. 3·4 | + 0·00 | S. 9·10 | − 0·72 |
| 3·4 | − 1·08 | 4·5 | + 0·98 |
| 5·6 | + 0·00 | 4·5 | − 0·00 |
| 5·6 | − 0·98 | 6·7 | + 0·98 |
| 7·8 | + 0·00 | 6·7 | − 0·72 |
| 7·8 | − 1·42 | 8·9 | + 1·70 |
| 9·10 | + 0·00 | 8·9 | − 1·22 |

---

# TRUSS DIAGRAM No. 99.

## CONDITIONS.

1. Rise of truss .. .. .. .. .. .. $\frac{1}{6}$ of the span.
2. Rise of tie .. .. .. .. .. .. $\frac{1}{8}$ of the span.
3. Number of panels .. .. .. .. 8.
4. Description of truss .. .. .. .. { Braced crescent (circular).

### EVENLY DISTRIBUTED DEAD LOAD.

#### Stress Constants.

Rafters:

| | | | |
|---|---|---|---|
| S. 2·3 | + 12·30 | S. 5·7 | + 13·10 |
| 3·5 | + 13·50 | 7·9 | + 12·90 |

Tie :

|  |  |  |  |
|---|---|---|---|
| S. 2·4 | − 10·40 | S. 6·8 | − 12·20 |
| 4·6 | − 11·70 | 8·8 | − 12·20 |

Bracing :

|  |  |  |  |
|---|---|---|---|
| S. 3·4 | − 2·40 | S. 6·7 | − 0·91 |
| 4·5 | − 1·05 | 7·8 | − 1·04 |
| 5·6 | − 1·36 | 8·9 | − 1·00 |

### LIVE LOAD (WIND PRESSURE).

#### *Maximum Stress Constants.*

Rafters :

|  |  |  |  |
|---|---|---|---|
| S. 2·3 | + 8·62 | S. 5·7 | + 8·42 |
| 3·5 | + 9·22 | 7·9 | + 7·22 |

Tie :

|  |  |  |  |
|---|---|---|---|
| S. 2·4 | − 7·30 | S. 6·8 | − 7·36 |
| 4·6 | − 8·08 | 8·8 | − 6·21 |

Bracing :

|  |  |  |  |
|---|---|---|---|
| S. 3·4 | + 0·00 | S. 6·7 | + 0·20 |
| 3·4 | − 1·52 | 6·7 | − 1·28 |
| 4·5 | + 0·00 | 7·8 | + 0·16 |
| 4·5 | − 0·70 | 7·8 | − 1·45 |
| 5·6 | + 0·00 | 8·9 | + 0·60 |
| 5·6 | − 1·10 | 8·9 | − 1·34 |

## TRUSS DIAGRAM No. 100.

### CONDITIONS.

1. Rise of truss .. .. .. .. .. .. $\frac{5}{36}$ of the span.
2. Rise of tie .. .. .. .. .. .. $\frac{1}{15}$ of the span.
3. Number of panels .. .. .. .. 13.
4. Description of truss .. .. .. .. { Braced crescent (parabolic).

### EVENLY DISTRIBUTED DEAD LOAD.

#### Stress Constants.

Rafters:

| | |   | | |
|---|---|---|---|---|
| S. | 2·3 | + 17·29 | S. 15·17 | + 14·18 |
| | 3·5 | + 16·37 | 17·19 | + 14·47 |
| | 5·7 | + 15·58 | 19·21 | + 14·94 |
| | 7·9 | + 14·94 | 21·23 | + 15·58 |
| | 9·11 | + 14·47 | 23·25 | + 16·37 |
| | 11·13 | + 14·18 | 25·28 | + 17·29 |
| | 13·15 | + 14·08 | | |

Tie:

| | |   | | |
|---|---|---|---|---|
| S. | 2·4 | − 14·63 | S. 16·18 | − 14·10 |
| | 4·6 | − 14·47 | 18·20 | − 14·15 |
| | 6·8 | − 14·35 | 20·22 | − 14·22 |
| | 8·10 | − 14·22 | 22·24 | − 14·35 |
| | 10·12 | − 14·15 | 24·26 | − 14·47 |
| | 12·14 | − 14·10 | 26·28 | − 14·63 |
| | 14·16 | − 14·08 | | |

Bracing :

| S. | 3·4 | — | 0·66 | S. | 3·6 | 0·00 |
|----|------|---|------|----|------|------|
| | 5·6 | — | 0·66 | | 5·8 | 0·00 |
| | 7·8 | — | 0·66 | | 7·10 | 0·00 |
| | 9·10 | — | 0·66 | | 9·12 | 0·00 |
| | 11·12 | — | 0·66 | | 11·14 | 0·00 |
| | 13·14 | — | 0·66 | | 13·16 | 0·00 |
| | 15·16 | — | 0·66 | | 15·18 | 0·00 |
| | 17·18 | — | 0·66 | | 17·20 | 0·00 |
| | 19·20 | — | 0·66 | | 19·22 | 0·00 |
| | 21·22 | — | 0·66 | | 21·24 | 0·00 |
| | 23·24 | — | 0·66 | | 23·26 | 0·00 |
| | 25·26 | — | 0·66 | | | |

## LIVE LOAD (WIND PRESSURE).

### Maximum Stress Constants.

Rafters :

| S. | 2·3 | + | 12·90 | S. | 15·17 | + | 8·50 |
|----|------|---|-------|----|-------|---|------|
| | 3·5 | + | 11·60 | | 17·19 | + | 9·38 |
| | 5·7 | + | 10·56 | | 19·21 | + | 10·26 |
| | 7·9 | + | 9·50 | | 21·23 | + | 11·10 |
| | 9·11 | + | 8·63 | | 23·25 | + | 12·20 |
| | 11·13 | + | 7·59 | | 25·28 | + | 12·90 |
| | 13·15 | + | 7·57 | | | | |

Tie :

| S. | 2·4 | — | 11·00 | S. | 16·18 | — | 7·59 |
|----|------|---|-------|----|-------|---|------|
| | 4·6 | — | 10·86 | | 18·20 | — | 8·47 |
| | 6·8 | — | 10·15 | | 20·22 | — | 9·24 |
| | 8·10 | — | 9·62 | | 22·24 | — | 9·86 |
| | 10·12 | — | 9·04 | | 24·26 | — | 10·34 |
| | 12·14 | — | 8·40 | | 26·28 | — | 11·00 |
| | 14·16 | — | 7·57 | | | | |

Bracing :

| | | | | | | |
|---|---|---|---|---|---|---|
| S. 3·4 | − | 0·58 | S. 25·26 | + | 0·00 |
| 3·4 | + | 0·00 | 3·6 | + | 0·62 |
| 5·6 | − | 0·70 | 3·6 | − | 0·23 |
| 5·6 | + | 0·00 | 5·8 | + | 0·52 |
| 7·8 | − | 0·92 | 5·8 | − | 0·48 |
| 7·8 | + | 0·08 | 7·10 | + | 0·77 |
| 9·10 | − | 0·78 | 7·10 | − | 0·68 |
| 9·10 | + | 0·40 | 9·12 | + | 0·92 |
| 11·12 | − | 1·28 | 9·12 | − | 1·04 |
| 11·12 | + | 0·45 | 11·14 | + | 1·53 |
| 13·14 | − | 1·57 | 11·14 | − | 1·25 |
| 13·14 | + | 0·82 | 13·16 | + | 1·94 |
| 15·16 | − | 1·85 | 13·16 | − | 1·94 |
| 15·16 | + | 1·37 | 15·18 | + | 1·37 |
| 17·18 | − | 1·38 | 15·18 | − | 1·67 |
| 17·18 | + | 0·98 | 17·20 | + | 1·03 |
| 19·20 | − | 1·10 | 17·20 | − | 1·28 |
| 19·20 | + | 0·48 | 19·22 | + | 0·85 |
| 21·22 | − | 0·85 | 19·22 | − | 0·94 |
| 21·22 | + | 0·20 | 21·24 | + | 0·67 |
| 23·24 | − | 0·64 | 21·24 | − | 0·60 |
| 23·24 | + | 0·00 | 23·26 | + | 0·40 |
| 25·26 | − | 0·46 | 23·26 | − | 0·68 |

END OF PART II.

LONDON: PRINTED BY WILLIAM CLOWES AND SONS, LIMITED, STAMFORD STREET AND CHARING CROSS.

# TRUSS DIAGRAMS

E & F N Spon, London & New York

Thos Kell & Son, Lith.